Also by Jennifer L. Schiff

<u>Sanibel Island Mysteries</u>

A Shell of a Problem

Something Fishy

In the Market for Murder

Bye Bye Birdy

Shell Shocked

Trouble in Paradise

A Perilous Proposal

For Whom the Shell Tolls

The Crisis Before Christmas

Framed in Naples

<u>Novels</u>

Tinder Fella

Something's Cooking in Chianti

Finding Gemma Lovegood

Jennifer Lonoff Schiff

Shovel
& Pail
Press

FINDING GEMMA LOVEGOOD by Jennifer Lonoff Schiff

https://www.shovelandpailpress.com/

Cover design by Vesna Tisma

Formatting by Polgarus Studio

ISBN: 979-8-218-41154-1
Library of Congress Control Number: 2024909441

*Sometimes the person you are searching for
is yourself.*

—Gemma Lovegood, *Belle of the Ball*

CHAPTER 1

Hope gently knocked on Ashley's door. Her boss wanted to speak with her before she went on maternity leave. They had already discussed all of the projects Hope, as assistant editor, would be taking over during Ashley's absence—at least three times. (The joke among the editors at Herstory, the publishing company where Hope and Ashley worked, was that the A in Type A stood for Ashley.) But apparently, Ashley wanted to go over the list one more time.

Hope waited for Ashley to tell her to come in but received no reply. She knocked again and then opened the door a crack. Ashley was on the phone. And she did not look happy.

"I understand," said Ashley. "But we've already extended the deadline twice. And if there isn't a new Gemma Lovegood, her publisher, as well as her millions of fans, will be greatly disappointed."

Hope stood by the door, not wanting to interrupt her boss. Though she worried that Ashley was about to pop a blood vessel or, worse, go into labor. She was already several days past her due date, and Ashley's doctor had told her that stress wasn't good for the baby and to take it easy. But Ashley didn't do easy. And there was no way she was going on maternity leave until every loose end—or book—was taken care of.

Hope had assured her boss that she had everything well in hand. Well, except for Gemma Lovegood.

Gemma Lovegood—supposedly her real name, though Hope thought it had to be made up—was one of the company's top authors, her books selling in the millions. And she was missing, as was her latest manuscript.

Ashley had signed Gemma without actually meeting or talking to her. In fact, no one at Herstory had ever met or spoken with Gemma, just with her agent, Oscar Tennant.

Ashley had been introduced to Gemma via a friend, who had sent her Gemma's manuscript. It was a wry Victorian romance titled *Belle of the Ball*, and Ashley had immediately signed Ms. Lovegood, who lived in a village called Cupid's Bow (so appropriate for a romance author) in Southwest England.

Belle of the Ball was a smashing success, and Ashley immediately signed Gemma to a two-book deal. Less than a year later, Gemma's second book, *Balls Aren't Just for Men*, debuted. And it was an even bigger success than the first book, staying on the *New York Times* bestseller list for weeks.

So it was understandable that Ashley and Herstory had high hopes for Gemma's third book. However, despite extending the deadline twice, the manuscript had yet to arrive. And if Herstory didn't receive the manuscript soon, they would have to push back the publication date yet again, which Ashley was loath to do.

The plan had been to launch the book before Christmas. And if there was anything Ashley hated, it was having to change a plan.

Making matters worse, neither Ashley nor Hope had been able to reach Gemma. All communication had to go through her agent, whom Ashley referred to as Oscar the Grouch, and he had been making excuses for months.

Now Ashley was on the phone with him, trying yet again to find out what the holdup was with Gemma's latest book.

"I understand," said Ashley. "But we have a contract, Mr. Tennant. And I need that book."

Suddenly, Ashley clutched her stomach, letting go of the phone.

Hope froze. Then she rushed over to her boss.

"Are you all right?" she asked her. Though Ashley didn't look the least bit all right.

Ashley cried out and grabbed the corner of the desk.

"I'm calling an ambulance," said Hope, whipping out her phone and punching 9-1-1 into the keypad.

A short time later, the paramedics arrived. They took Ashley's vitals and placed her on a gurney.

"Should I come with you?" Hope asked her boss as the paramedics wheeled Ashley to the elevator.

"No. Derek's going to meet me at the hospital. And I need you to go to England."

"England?" said Hope.

"To get that manuscript."

The elevator door opened, and the paramedics wheeled Ashley inside.

"I don't understand," said Hope.

"I'll fill you in later, after…" The elevator door closed, cutting her off.

Hope stood staring at her reflection. Ashley wanted her to go to England? Was she serious? Hope couldn't help feeling excited at the thought. She hadn't been to England since her junior year of college, nearly ten years ago, when she had attended the University of London for a year. It had been one of the best years of her life.

Hope had planned on going back to England several times, but between graduate school and then work and other things, she hadn't made it. Now here was her chance.

However, she reined in her excitement. Was Ashley going to be okay? And what about the baby? The paramedics had told Ashley everything was going to be fine. But maybe they had just said that to soothe her. Well, Hope would call Derek, Ashley's husband, later to see how Ashley and the baby were doing. In the meantime, she would take care of business. That was what Ashley would want. However, it would be hard to concentrate on work not knowing how Ashley and the baby were.

Hope headed back to her office and stopped. Instead, she headed to Ashley's office. Ashley had been speaking to Oscar when she'd gone into labor, and Hope couldn't remember if they had ended the call.

Hope entered the office and spied Ashley's work phone open on the floor. She picked it up and thought she heard someone.

"Hello?" she said.

"Ashley? What's going on over there? Is everything okay?"

"Mr. Tennant?"

"Who is this?"

"It's Hope, Hope Halladay."

Hope couldn't believe he was still on the line.

"Where's Ms. Wallingford?"

"She's…" Hope stopped herself. She didn't know if Ashley had told Oscar that she was pregnant. Probably not. "Ms. Wallingford's dealing with an emergency and had to rush off. But she asked me to follow up with you."

Not a total lie.

"Good. Maybe you'll be a bit more reasonable. As I was telling Ms. Wallingford, Gemma's been under the weather and won't be able to get you the new book by the end of the month."

Hope frowned. She knew Ashley didn't want to extend the deadline again.

"Can you send me what you have? At least then we could…"

"I can't do that," he said, interrupting her.

"Why not?"

"Gemma doesn't work that way. You'll have the manuscript when it's finished."

"And when will that be?"

"I don't know. As I said, she hasn't been feeling well."

"I hope it's not serious," said Hope, trying to sound sympathetic.

Oscar mumbled something, which sounded to Hope's ears like, "I hope so too."

"If you could just send me a few chapters…"

"I told you," said Oscar. "Gemma…"

"I know what you said, Mr. Tennant," said Hope, trying to channel her boss and sound assertive. "But we need that manuscript. We've already blown the pre-Christmas publication date, and Herstory gave Ms. Lovegood a significant advance against royalties."

Hope almost smiled at how much like her boss she sounded. Ashley would be proud of her.

"I'll see what I can do," Oscar responded. "Good day, Ms. Halladay."

Had Oscar just hung up on her? Hope frowned. Well, he might have had the last word for now, but if she knew her boss, Herstory would get that manuscript even if Hope had to fly to England to get it.

She walked back to her office, her brain buzzing. On the way, she was stopped several times by editorial staff asking her if Ashley was okay. She told them what the paramedics had said and wished she had an actual office so she could close the door. Instead, like everyone else who wasn't a full editor, she had a glorified cube. And people kept poking their heads in, asking about Ashley.

Thankfully, it was soon lunchtime, and the office emptied. Hope used the quiet to get some work done. Or at least she tried to. She couldn't stop thinking about Ashley. Finally, she sent a text to Ashley's husband, asking how Ashley was. No reply. She tried not to worry, but it was hard.

Hope stared at the pile of manuscripts from literary agents and prospective authors on her desk. Vetting them was one of Hope's main responsibilities. She picked up the manuscript at the top of the pile. The title was *A New Beginning.*

Per the summary attached to the manuscript, it was about a big city lawyer who gets burned out, moves to the country, winds up working on a farm, and falls in love with farm life and the hot widowed farmer and his kids.

Hope had read plenty of books with a similar theme, but there was always room for one more if it was well written with likable characters and would appeal to their audience. Herstory specialized in books for women written by women.

Hope put the summary aside and began to read.

It was only after her phone had rung several times—Hope had been too absorbed in the manuscript—that she realized someone was calling her.

"Hope Halladay," she said, not bothering to look at the caller ID.

"Finally."

"Ashley?" Hope couldn't believe it. "How are you? Is everything okay? Did you have the baby?"

"Everything's fine."

"Thank goodness you're all right! And the baby?"

"She's sleeping right now. So I only have a minute to…"

"How big is she? Do you have a name?"

Hope heard Ashley sigh.

"She's nineteen inches and just over seven pounds, and we're still deciding on the name. Now, if you're done asking questions, I need you to listen."

Hope closed her mouth and nodded, not that Ashley could see her.

"As I was saying earlier, I want you to go to England, find Gemma, and get that manuscript."

"I spoke to Oscar after the paramedics took you to the hospital. He said that Gemma's been under the weather and the manuscript isn't ready."

"He's been saying that for months."

"I take it you don't believe him."

"I do not. Which is why I want you to go to England."

"But what if she really is ill and can't write?"

"Then we'll figure something out. But I have a feeling Mr. Tennant is lying."

"Why would he lie?"

"I can think of several reasons. In any case, I need you to get over there and find out what's up, no more fobbing us off with excuses."

"I understand, but if I go to England, who will take care of things here?"

"Fiona can handle the administrative work." Fiona was Ashley's editorial assistant. "And I believe they have internet in England. Let your authors know you'll be away for a bit but checking email. And take your computer with you."

"Okay," said Hope. "So, when do you want me to go to England?"

"As soon as you can get over there. Call Good Vibes Travel as soon as we get off the phone and have them book you a flight to London, rent you a car, and find a place for you to stay in Cupid's Bow."

"Got it," said Hope. "By the way, you left your work phone here. Do you want me to hold onto it until you get back from maternity leave?"

"No, have it messengered over to my apartment."

Hope was going to say something but stopped herself. Telling Ashley not to think about work was like telling her not to breathe.

"Okay. So did the doctor say when you could go home?"

"I'm planning on leaving tomorrow."

"Tomorrow? Isn't that a bit fast? Did the doctor say it was okay?"

"It was an easy delivery and the baby's healthy. And I'd rather be at home than lying in some hospital bed. Now go call Good Vibes and text me when they've booked your flight."

"Will do," said Hope.

They said goodbye, and Hope called Ashley's travel agency.

"Good Vibes Travel," answered a cheery male voice. "This is Peter. Where can we send you?"

It amazed Hope that there were still travel agents, what with so many DIY travel options. But Ashley claimed she was too busy to handle her own travel. And the woman who ran Good Vibes was a sorority sister of Ashley's.

"Hey, Peter. This is Hope Halladay at Herstory. I work with Ashley Wallingford, and I need to book a flight to London."

"When does Ashley want to go?"

"Actually, the reservation's for me. Ashley's having me go there to meet with an author while she's on maternity leave."

Oops. She didn't mean to say that. Well, too late now. Besides, Ashley's sorority sister probably already knew about the baby. Or she would soon.

"Ooh! Which author?"

"I can't say. Ashley also told me to rent a car. Can I take the train to Cupid's Bow, assuming a train goes there, and rent a car when I get there? And I also need to find a place to stay."

"Hold up. Did you say Cupid's Bow? Is that a real place? It sounds made up."

"I know, but it's real. It's in Devon."

"Okay. So, when do you need to go?"

"ASAP."

"And when will you be coming back?"

That was a good question.

"I'm not sure."

"Okay. I can get you a one-way ticket to London for

now. Let me see what's available. Can I call you back in a few?"

"Sure. Let me give you my cell phone number."

Hope gave him her number, and he said he'd call her back.

Less than fifteen minutes later, her cell phone rang. It was Peter.

"So, there's a flight from JFK to Heathrow Wednesday night with a couple of seats left."

"This Wednesday?"

"You said ASAP."

She did.

"Okay, book me on it." It was Monday evening. So she had a couple of days to go over everything with Fiona and get ready. That should be enough time, shouldn't it?

"And there's a train from London that goes to Exeter in Devon. Exeter's not exactly close to Cupid's Bow. So you'll definitely need to rent a car."

"Can I rent one in Exeter? And can you see if they have automatics?" The last time Hope was in England, it seemed everyone there drove cars with manual transmissions.

"I'll check."

"Thanks. What about a place to stay? Is there a nice bed and breakfast in Cupid's Bow? I don't need anything fancy."

"I'm looking into it. Cupid's Bow isn't very big."

"Okay. Let me know what you find."

"Will do. Hey, can I ring you back tomorrow? I've got to go to a meeting. But I'll book you on that flight before I go."

"Tomorrow's fine," said Hope. "Enjoy your meeting!"

"Thanks."

They ended the call, and Hope sat back in her chair. She was really going to England.

CHAPTER 2

Hope picked up Thai food on her way home. She was feeling too tired to cook and she had a lot to do to prepare for her trip to England. As she ate, she scrolled through her Instagram feed. There was a new post from her friend Edward, who lived in London. She and Edward had dated when Hope had been at university there, and they had stayed in touch.

The photo was of Edward's dog, a shaggy black mixed breed named King Arfur, running on a beach. The caption read, "Arfur loves the beach and his new home!" The location tag said Devon.

Huh. The last time Hope checked, Edward was living in London with his girlfriend, Lucy. Had something happened? Edward was originally from Devon. Had he moved back? Was his new home near Cupid's Bow? Hope immediately sent Edward a message.

"Are you back in Devon?" she typed. "I'm going to be in a little village called Cupid's Bow there for biz this week. Would love to see you if you're around."

She hit *send* and resumed eating her pad thai. A minute later, her phone started buzzing. Edward had messaged her back.

"How long will you be here for and where are you staying?"

"Not sure on both fronts," Hope replied. "Will know more tomorrow. So when did you and Lucy move to Devon?"

"We broke up."

"What?! When?!"

"Long story. I'll tell you when I see you. When do you arrive?"

"I get into London Thursday morning. Then I was planning on taking a train to Exeter and renting a car."

"Okay. Message me tomorrow when you know where you'll be staying. Though it may be tough finding a place. There's a festival this weekend."

"I'm sure my travel agent can find something."

"Well, if not, let me know."

"I will. Hey, I just realized it's pretty late over there. I should let you go. I'll message you tomorrow."

Hope put down her phone and caught Morris, her big orange tabby cat, eating her pad thai. Weirdo. She looked at him. Right. She'd need to find someone to watch him while she was gone. Fortunately, she knew just the person, her friend Dani.

Dani lived in Astoria, Queens, with two other women, and Hope figured she'd be happy to have a place of her own for a few days. Also, she and Morris had a thing.

"Hey," Hope texted her. "I have to go to England for work. Could I get you to stay at my place and look after Morris while I'm gone?"

Dani replied a few minutes later.

"When do you leave?"

"Day after tomorrow."

"Day after tomorrow?!"

"Yes."

"Why the rush?"

"Boss's order."

"How long will you be gone for?"

"Not sure. A week? Maybe two? I'll pay you," Hope added when Dani didn't reply right away.

"How much?"

Hope thought. She was letting Dani use her apartment, which was close to Dani's work. So really Dani should be paying her. But Hope knew Dani was doing her a favor.

"$25/day?"

No response. Should she offer Dani more?

"$30?"

"Sweet. I'll do it. And you don't have to pay me. You know I love Morris. And it'll be nice not having to deal with my roommates and being able to walk to work."

"Thank you. You want to come over after work tomorrow? I'll give you the spare key and go over everything."

"Sounds good."

Hope was at work before eight-thirty the next morning. She had a lot to do and not a lot of time to do it before she left. As soon as Fiona got in, Hope grabbed her.

She explained to Fiona that she would be going to England for a week, possibly longer, and that Ashley wanted Fiona to manage things while the two of them would be gone. Hope could see that Fiona was excited. She had been champing at the bit for more responsibility. Though Hope cautioned her not to get too excited. Their authors could be difficult, she warned, as could the other departments. Fiona said she knew that but could totally handle things.

Fiona taken care of, Hope went over to her manuscript pile. She would take several with her and give some to Fiona.

As Hope was going through her pile, her phone rang. It was Peter from Good Vibes.

"You find me a place to stay?" she asked him.

"That's why I'm calling. Every place in or near Cupid's Bow is booked solid through Monday. Apparently, there's some big festival happening near there this weekend."

"So I've heard. What about Airbnbs?"

"Also booked."

Hope frowned.

"I'll keep checking," said Peter.

"What about a train ticket?"

"All taken care of. Though I'm having trouble finding you a rental car."

"Because of the festival?"

"Uh-huh."

Hope frowned again. What was she supposed to do when she got to Devon, take an Uber to Cupid's Bow and sleep on a park bench? Maybe Edward knew someone with a spare room.

"It's just a bad weekend. But I'll keep looking."

"Thanks," said Hope.

As soon as they ended the call, she sent Edward a message.

"You happen to know anyone with a spare room to let in or near Cupid's Bow starting Thursday?"

"As a matter of fact I do," he replied a few minutes later.

"That's great!" wrote Hope. "Can you book it for me?"

"Consider it booked."

"Wow. So, where is it? And how much do they charge?"

"No charge."

Hope eyed her phone suspiciously.

"No charge?"

"You're staying with me. I have a guest room that's currently unoccupied."

"I can't stay with you."

"Why not?"

Hope tried to think of a reason.

"Stay. It'll be fun. I'll even pick you up at the train station."

"You don't have to."

"Did you rent a car?"

"No, they're all booked."

"How did you plan on getting here?"

"They have car services there, yes?"

"Good luck getting a ride during the festival. I'll come

get you. Let me know when your train gets in."

Hope wanted to tell him he really didn't have to. But what was the alternative?

"Fine," she finally wrote. "Thank you."

"My pleasure. I have to go. Send me your details when you have them."

He had added a kiss emoji. What did that mean?

Hope stared at her phone for several more seconds.

"Don't overthink it," she said aloud and pushed her phone away.

A few minutes later, her cell phone dinged. It was an email from Peter with her travel information. She thanked him and told him that she had found a place to stay, at least through the weekend, and wouldn't be needing a car.

Hope had silenced her phone so she could focus on work. When she finally checked it, she saw that she had multiple messages from her friend Ava, wanting to know when Hope was planning on telling her she was going to England.

Hope immediately called her.

"I cannot believe you didn't tell me!" said Ava.

"Sorry," said Hope. "I was planning on telling you."

"When?"

"I only found out yesterday."

"Still, you should have told me."

Hope rolled her eyes.

"Who told you, Dani?" Dani was the only friend Hope had told.

"What is Herstory having you do over there?"

"Hunting down a missing author and manuscript."

"Sounds intriguing. Though why isn't Ashley going?"

"She's on maternity leave."

"She had the baby?"

"Yesterday."

"So, who's the author? Wait, let me guess. You said England. Could it be Gemma Lovegood?"

"I'm not at liberty to say."

"It is her!" Ava crowed. "I love her books. And I'm not even into historical romance. What's the new one about?"

"I can't say."

"Come on, just between the two of us. I promise I won't say a word."

"Sorry, my lips are sealed."

"Boo. You're no fun."

"No fun at all. And right now, I need to get back to work. I have a lot to do before I leave tomorrow."

"I can't believe you're going to England! Message me when you get there. And post pics!"

"I'm going to be working, Aves."

"Yeah, yeah, yeah."

Hope said goodbye to her friend and went back to work.

CHAPTER 3

Dani came over to Hope's place that evening. Hope showed her where everything was, though Dani had been to Hope's place a dozen or more times. Then she went over the instructions for Morris.

"Everything's here," she said, handing Dani a piece of paper with the instructions. "I'll also email them to you. And if you have questions about anything, just message or call me. Though remember, I'll be five hours ahead."

"I've got it," said Dani. "Just go and have a good time."

"I'm not going there to have a good time. I'm going there to work."

Dani rolled her eyes.

"You can't work all the time, Hope."

"I know, but I'm not there to sightsee. I'm on a mission."

"To find Gemma Lovegood."

"Ava told you?! I told her not to say anything!"

"Don't be too hard on her. She didn't mean to let it slip."

"Uh-huh. Just don't tell anyone else, okay?"

"My lips are sealed. So how do you plan on finding her?"

"I'm going to go see her agent and demand that he tell me where she is."

"And if he refuses?"

Hope frowned.

"I'll think of something."

"Well, good luck."

"Thanks."

"You know…"

"What?"

"If you can't find her, you could always try writing it."

Hope stared at her friend.

"Pretend to be Gemma Lovegood?"

"Don't look at me like that. You've edited and read dozens of romance novels. And you have a master's degree in Victorian Literature. You could totally do it."

Hope shook her head.

"No way. Gemma's unique. And editing a manuscript isn't the same thing as writing one."

"You don't give yourself enough credit. Haven't you always wanted to write a book?"

"I've thought about it, sure. But I'm no Gemma Lovegood."

"You don't know that. You should give it a shot."

"I've tried writing a novel. It didn't go well."

"Maybe you should try again. Anyway, let's get something to eat. I'm starving."

"I should really pack."

"You need to eat. It's not good to pack on an empty stomach."

Hope knew better than to argue with Dani.

"Fine. Where do you want to go?"

"You choose."

"There's that pizza place around the corner that we like…"

"Say no more. You know I never say no to pizza."

Hope smiled.

"I just need to go to the bathroom. Okay, ready," she said when she emerged. She got to the front door, stopped, and detoured to the kitchen. "Here," she said, handing Dani the set of spare keys. "This one's for the door to the building. The little one's for the mailbox. And these two are for my door."

"Got it," said Dani. "Now let's go get some pizza."

Hope said goodbye to Dani after dinner and went back home to pack. The forecast for Cupid's Bow called for temperatures in the low-to-mid-50s, with temps in the 40s at night. And England could be rainy.

Hope wanted to pack light, but she didn't want to be cold. She pulled out her carry-on bag along with a week's worth of underwear, socks, some nicer shirts and pants, stuff to sleep in (an old concert tee and a pair of pajamas), running clothes and a pair of sneakers, in case she wanted to run, a couple of sweaters, and a pair of loafers. She'd wear jeans and a shirt, plus a sweatshirt, boots, and her down jacket, on the plane.

She thought about packing a dress or two, but that would mean packing pumps, and her carry-on bag was already full. Though there was always her backpack. But that would be filled with her computer, manuscripts, books, toiletries, and a change of clothes, in case the airline made her check her carry-on.

Well, if she needed a dress or more clothes, she could always buy something there.

She closed her suitcase so Morris wouldn't try to sleep in it. (He had a habit of climbing into her suitcase and napping there whenever she was about to go away.) She would load up her backpack in the morning.

Hope looked at the clock. It was nearly ten. But she wasn't tired. She was too wired. However, she knew she should get a good night's rest. Tomorrow would be a long day. She would go to the office in the morning, get as much work done as possible, come home in the afternoon, and then head to JFK around six, her flight to London Heathrow not being until nine-thirty.

Hope hadn't been able to decide which manuscripts to take with her, though she had narrowed it down. All of the manuscripts were on her computer, but she always printed out the files of the ones she felt were the most promising. She liked to hold them in her hands and be able to make notes in the margins.

Finally, she picked three. Now it was Fiona's turn.

Hope went over to Fiona's cube and asked if she had a minute to go over a few things. Fiona said she needed a few minutes, and Hope told her to come to her office when she was ready.

A few minutes later, Fiona poked her head into Hope's cubicle.

"What's up?"

"How would you feel about reading some manuscripts while I'm gone?"

"Seriously?"

"Seriously. You want to pick a few from the pile?"

Fiona looked over at Hope's manuscript pile.

"May I?"

Hope nodded, and Fiona began going through the manuscripts.

"Ooh, this one sounds interesting," she said.

"Which one is it?" said Hope, who had been looking at something on her phone.

Fiona held up the manuscript.

"It's yours," said Hope.

"Really?"

"Yup."

Fiona beamed.

"Tell you what, why don't you take the rest to your cube?

You can let me know later which ones you want to review."

"Will do," said Fiona. She picked up the stack of manuscripts and paused. "You hear from Ashley since she got home?"

"No, but I'm sure I will before I leave."

Fiona nodded.

"Anything else?"

"No. I think we've covered everything. And if something comes up, you can always email or message me."

Hope had left herself plenty of time to get to JFK, opting to take the train instead of a car service. She made it to the airport in good time and practically breezed through security. As she headed to the gate, she realized she was hungry. She had been too busy to eat lunch, and she didn't have time to eat dinner before heading to the airport. She stopped at an eatery and got herself a sandwich. Then she filled up her water bottle at a water fountain and found a seat by the gate.

An hour later, her flight began to board. Hope was seated near the back of the aircraft and was in one of the last groups to board. She didn't mind. She was just happy Peter had been able to get her a seat—and a window seat at that. She settled in, taking out a manuscript to read. Thirty minutes later, the plane lifted off the runway and she was on her way to London.

Hope hadn't realized she had fallen asleep until she heard the announcement that the plane had begun its initial descent into Heathrow. Forty minutes later, they were at the gate. After deplaning, Hope stopped in a bathroom to freshen up. Then she made her way to the Heathrow Express, which would take her to Paddington Railway Station. From there, she would catch the train to Exeter. She arrived at the railway station with time to spare. So she grabbed a cappuccino and a croissant and found a place to sit.

As she sipped her cappuccino and ate her croissant, Hope checked her messages. Everyone she knew back home would still be asleep. Or so she thought. Apparently not Ashley, who wanted to know if Hope had made it to England.

Hope knew that her boss had a newborn and probably wasn't getting a lot of sleep, but didn't she have better things to do than helicopter parent Hope? Hope quickly replied, letting Ashley know she was at Paddington Station, waiting for her train.

Ashley immediately wrote back, instructing Hope to let her know when she got to Cupid's Bow. Hope rolled her eyes but told Ashley that she would.

Finally, it was time to board her train. She found her seat and settled in, taking out the manuscript she had started on the plane. The journey to Exeter St. David's would take a little over 2.5 hours. And there was no one sitting next to her to interrupt her.

Hope watched as the train pulled out of the station and passed through London. She wished she could have spent a few days there. Maybe if she found Gemma quickly, she could go to London for a couple of days before she flew back home. But something told her that finding Gemma and getting the manuscript wouldn't be so easy.

Hope sighed and turned back to the manuscript.

The train pulled into Exeter St. David's a little after two-thirty. She pulled down her suitcase from the overhead rack, swung her backpack onto her back, and made her way off the train.

She saw Edward right away. He was standing on the platform, waiting for her. As soon as he saw Hope, he smiled and waved. Hope waved back.

Edward insisted on taking her suitcase, even though Hope said she could handle it. It wasn't very big or very heavy. Her backpack probably weighed more. But she kept it on her back.

He led her out of the station to the car park.

"That's my car over there," he said, pointing to a Mini Cooper. He popped the trunk—or boot—and placed Hope's suitcase inside. Then he waited as Hope removed her backpack and placed it next to her suitcase.

"Cupid's Bow is just under an hour from here," he told Hope as he started the car. "Do you want to stop by Gemma's place first or go to my place?"

Even though she had freshened up at the airport, Hope didn't feel she was ready to go to Gemma's or deal with Oscar.

"Let's go to your place. I'll deal with Gemma and Oscar tomorrow."

As they headed out of the car park, Edward asked Hope about her flight and the train ride down.

"They were fine," she told him.

He tried to engage Hope in conversation, but she wasn't in a chatty mood.

"Sorry," she said. "It's the jet lag."

"Have you eaten?" he asked her.

"I had a cappuccino and a croissant at Paddington this morning."

Edward frowned.

"No wonder you're tired. You need food. There's a good fish and chips shop near my place. Shall we stop there and get you something to eat?"

At the mention of fish and chips, Hope perked up.

"Actually, that would be great. Though, do you mind? You probably had lunch already."

"I always have room for fish and chips," he said. "We should be there in just over half an hour. Can you hold out?

I might have something in the glove compartment if you're starving."

"I can wait." Hope gazed out the window. She had been expecting rain, but the sun was shining. Maybe it was a sign.

"You brought the good weather with you," said Edward, as though reading her mind. "It's supposed to be sunny the next few days and above average, temperature-wise."

"I'm sure the festivalgoers will be happy."

"Indeed." Edward glanced over at her. "If you want to shut your eyes, go ahead."

"I took a nap on the plane."

"Ah. Go ahead and put on some music then if you like."

"Here we are!" said Edward, parking the Mini outside of a little fish and chips shop.

Hope looked over at it. It didn't look like much.

"Don't let the size fool you," said Edward. "They serve the best fish and chips in town."

Hope glanced around. There were a few shops and a pub, but that was about it.

"Looks like the only fish and chips shop in town," she said.

"That may be true, but I doubt you'll find better fish and chips in all of Devon."

"We'll see about that."

Edward got out of the car.

"Shall we?" he said.

"Let's," said Hope.

CHAPTER 4

Hope was immediately hit by the smell of fried fish and malt vinegar upon entering the shop. Her stomach let out a low growl in anticipation. When she had lived in London, she had enjoyed eating fish and chips, especially after a couple of pints at the pub near school.

She asked Edward what he recommended, and they both ordered the fried cod. Then they took a seat at one of the wooden tables and waited. They didn't have to wait long. As soon as the food was on the table, Hope shook some malt vinegar onto her fish and took a bite.

"Mm," she said. The cod was nice and crispy on the outside, moist and flakey on the inside.

"You like it?" asked Edward.

"I do. It's hot but really good." She took another bite.

"I told you. You'll not find better fish and chips in all of Devon."

Hope gave him a look.

"It's true. Tony's family catch the fish themselves, been doing it for generations. That's why his fish is so good. He gets it fresh off the boat."

"What about the chips? Does his family own a potato farm?"

"Nah," said the man behind the counter, who must have been Tony. "We get our potatoes from a farm up north. And I'd wager they're far better than what you lot eat over in the States."

"I don't know. McDonald's french fries are pretty darn tasty."

"McDonald's," said Tony, making a face. "You call those things chips? I bet they don't even use real potatoes."

Hope smothered a smile.

"Don't antagonize Tony," said Edward. "I want to keep eating here."

Hope took a bite of a chip and felt Edward and Tony watching her.

"Well?" said Edward.

"I need to have another one before rendering judgment." She took another chip and popped it into her mouth. The men were waiting. "Best chips I've had in Devon."

Edward smiled, and Hope thought she heard Tony mumble something uncomplimentary about McDonald's.

They finished their fish and chips, and Edward called out his thanks to Tony, who had gone into the back.

"How far is your place from here?" Hope asked Edward as they stood outside the fish and chips shop.

"It's just up the hill."

They drove the short distance, Edward parking the Mini in front of a tidy-looking, white semi-detached rowhouse.

"Here we are!" he said.

He got out and went around to the trunk.

"I can get my bags," said Hope. But Edward had already taken them out.

She followed him into the house.

"Welcome to my humble abode," he said. "It's a bit of a work in progress."

Hope glanced around. In front of her was a living area and just beyond was a dining table and chairs next to a large picture window. To the left of that was a small kitchen.

"There's a cloakroom—or bathroom—over there if you need it," he said pointing to a door. "The bedrooms and family bathroom are upstairs."

Hope headed towards the picture window. It looked out onto rooftops and in the distance you could see water.

"Is that the…"

"Channel? It is. It's why I chose this place, for the views. Plus it's only a fifteen-minute walk to the beach."

"Nice."

"Would you like to see your room? You can see the water from there too."

Hope followed him up the stairs.

"I use this room as my office, but I moved my desk into my room. So it's all yours."

Hope felt a pang of guilt.

"I didn't mean to kick you out of your office."

"You didn't. It's supposed to be a guest room. I just haven't had any guests yet, so I've been using it as my office."

"If you're sure it's all right. I can always sleep on the couch downstairs."

"Don't be ridiculous. There's plenty of room in my bedroom for the desk and a chair."

Hope looked like she didn't believe him.

"Come, I'll show you. That's the bathroom, by the way," he said as they passed by it. "And this," he said, stepping inside the next room, "is my bedroom."

Hope stepped inside. It was larger than her room, with a desk and a chair placed in front of one of the windows.

"See?" he said. "No problem. Plenty of room."

Hope let out a yawn.

"Do you want to lie down?"

"Actually, I'd love to go for a walk."

"Are you sure?"

"Positive. All I've done is sit for the last twenty-four hours. I could use to stretch my legs. Just tell me how to get to the beach."

"Better yet, I'll show you."

"You don't need to work?"

"That's the thing about being the boss." Edward had left his job in London to become a consultant. "I get to decide when to work and when not to. Mostly," he added with a smile.

"If you're sure."

"I am. Come."

They were headed downstairs when Hope realized something.

"Where's Arfur?"

"Poppy's watching him."

"Poppy?"

"My neighbor. She watches him when I have to go up to London or need to be gone more than a few hours."

"That's very nice of her."

"I pay her. She's a pet sitter. Well, when she isn't teaching first years."

"She's a teacher?"

Edward nodded.

"Though she's on break this week. Come, I'll introduce you. Then we can take Arfur to the beach. That is if you don't mind."

"Not at all. Let's go get him."

They left Edward's and headed down a couple of rowhouses, to a place that looked a lot like Edward's from the outside.

"Here we are," he said and rang the bell.

Immediately, they heard barking.

"That'd be Arfur," said Edward.

Then they heard a woman's voice telling Arfur to shush.

The door opened to reveal an attractive woman in her mid-twenties, dressed in a pair of jeans and an oversized sweater, her blonde hair in braids, and a shaggy-looking black dog barking behind her.

"Down, Arfur!" Poppy commanded. But Arfur was having none of it. He was jumping up and down, ready to rocket out the door.

"Come here, boy!" said Edward. Poppy made a face as

Arfur bolted out the door, heading straight for Edward.

The dog jumped on Edward, and Edward smiled as he rubbed the dog's head.

"Daft dog," said Poppy. "Could do with some obedience lessons that one."

"I promise to take him," said Edward.

"You've been saying that for weeks."

Poppy turned to Hope.

"I'm Poppy," she said. "You must be Edward's friend from the States."

"I am," said Hope. "Hope. Nice to meet you."

"Good luck with that one," said Poppy, looking at Edward and Arfur. Hope wasn't sure which one she meant. "Edward tells me you're here for work."

"That's right," said Hope.

"What do you do?"

"I edit books."

"I love to read! What sort of books do you edit?"

"Mostly women's fiction."

"Anyone I might have read?"

Arfur was jumping up and down.

"We should take him for a walk," said Edward. He turned to Poppy. "You have his leash?"

"I'll go grab it."

She returned a minute later with the leash, and Edward attached it to Arfur's collar.

"Thanks for watching Arfur."

"My pleasure."

"Nice to meet you," said Hope.

"Same," said Poppy.

Then they were off.

"So, how do you know Poppy?" Hope asked Edward as they headed down to the beach.

"We met at the pub."

"She seems very nice. Pretty too. You two…?"

"No, we're just friends. I'm not ready to start dating again."

"You miss Lucy?"

"Some days."

"What happened? If you don't mind me asking."

"We wanted different things."

"What did she want?"

"To hang out with her posh crowd, doing posh things."

"And you didn't?"

"Not really. I found most of her friends to be snobs and didn't like the clubs or parties they favored."

"I see. Though I thought you liked living in London."

"I did, but it got to be too much. I prefer living down here, where I can walk to the sea and Arfur can run around."

They had reached the beach, and Hope was glad she had worn her down jacket. It was chilly by the water and windy.

Edward picked up a stick and threw it for Arfur, who charged after it. He placed it in his mouth and came trotting back, depositing the stick at Edward's feet.

"Good boy, Arfur!"

Edward threw the stick again. Arfur dashed after it, returning the stick to Edward a minute later.

"He could do this all afternoon," said Edward. He threw the stick a couple more times and then stopped. "Come, Arfur," he commanded and began to walk.

The beach wasn't very big. And Hope imagined it must get quite crowded during the summer.

Edward looked up. The sky had become overcast.

"We should probably head back," he said.

"You think it's going to rain?"

"It wasn't supposed to. But it's England. You never know."

They headed back towards Edward's place.

"I forgot to ask, what do you like to eat? I have eggs and bread and yogurt and milk, as well as coffee and tea and beer, but not much else. We can stop at the corner shop and pick up something or go to Tesco tomorrow."

"As long as you have coffee, I'm good. Though I wouldn't mind checking out the local Tesco."

"We'll do that. Now, about dinner…"

"I'm not that hungry. We had a rather late lunch."

"Well, if you get hungry later, we can grab something at the pub."

"You're not going to cook for me?"

Edward looked startled, and Hope grinned.

"I'm kidding. I don't expect you to cook for me. If anything, I should cook for you."

"You don't have to do that."

As they walked up the hill, the sun came out. The sun's rays shone on Edward's blond hair, giving it a golden glow. For a second, Hope thought that she saw a halo. Edward really was an angel to have invited her to stay with him. But he had always been kind and thoughtful.

She had met him shortly after arriving in London, at a mixer for visiting students. She had seen him chatting with a group of girls and thought he was cute. Clearly, so did they. She watched them for a few minutes, and then Edward turned and smiled at her. She smiled back, and before she knew it, he was walking over to her.

He introduced himself, and they wound up talking for over an hour. Then one of his friends pulled him away. But before he left, he asked Hope for her number, and she gave it to him. She wasn't really expecting him to text her, but he did the next morning, asking her out for a drink. She didn't want to sound too eager, but she accepted his invitation—and had been glad that she did. Edward was easy to talk to, as well as easy on the eyes.

Drinks had led to dinner, then to brunch. Before she

knew it, Hope was spending nearly all of her free time with Edward. She had told him early on that she wasn't interested in a long-term relationship. She would be going back to the States at the end of the school year. And he had seemed fine with that.

However, after a few months, as their relationship deepened, Hope started to think about staying in England. It was a crazy idea, but she loved living in London—and possibly Edward too. Then her mother fell ill. Hope told her parents that she would fly home right away. But her parents convinced her to finish up in London. There were only a few more weeks to the term. So Hope stayed, feeling guilty the entire time.

Hope spent her last night in London with Edward. They promised to keep in touch and visit each other. But, as often happens, life got in the way, and they never managed to meet up. Though they stayed in touch, mainly via social media.

Hope often wondered what would have happened if she had stayed in England. Would she and Edward have continued to date? None of Hope's relationships since Edward had worked out. Was Edward the one who got away?

"Penny for your thoughts," said Edward.

"Hm?" said Hope.

Edward smiled.

"You had a faraway look."

"I was just thinking."

"So I gathered. What about?"

Should she tell him?

"I was recalling how we met."

"Ah," he said and smiled.

"I had seen you chatting with those girls, and I thought to myself, 'I'm not here to get a boyfriend. I'm here to study.' Then you came over and chatted me up and asked for my phone number."

"Smartest thing I ever did."

"I doubt that. Though I've always wanted to know, why me? There were loads of pretty girls at that mixer, dying to land an English beau."

"But not you."

"Definitely not me."

"Maybe that's why I liked you."

"Because I wasn't interested in you?"

He shrugged.

"I just saw you and I knew."

"Knew what?"

"That I liked you."

"You could tell that just by looking at me?"

"I'm an excellent judge of character. My only mistake was not begging you to stay."

"Though you knew I had to go home."

"I should have persuaded you to come back when your mother went into remission."

"But by then I was back at school in the States."

"I know. And I should have come to visit you."

"Why didn't you?"

"School. Life. Work."

"So it's no one's fault," said Hope. "And here we are, still friends. Who knows? We might have come to hate each other if I had stayed or come back."

"I doubt that."

"Anyway," said Hope, wanting to change the subject, "we've both done all right for ourselves."

"True."

They had reached Edward's door, and Arfur was scratching to get in.

"He wants his dinner," said Edward.

"By all means, let's feed him."

CHAPTER 5

They had wound up going to the pub for a beer a little after eight. When they got back to Edward's an hour later, Hope brushed her teeth and went straight to bed, falling asleep immediately. When she woke up, it was light outside. Hope wondered what time it was. She turned on her phone and saw that it was nearly eight o'clock. She couldn't believe she had slept that much. She never slept that much at home. Must be the sea air.

She got up and went to the bathroom. On her way back to her room, she noticed that Edward's door was open. She knocked, but he didn't answer. She poked her head in, but he wasn't there. He must be downstairs. Though she didn't hear Arfur. Maybe they had gone for a walk.

Hope headed downstairs to the kitchen. There was a pot of coffee on the counter. Hope reached into a nearby cabinet and retrieved a mug, Edward having shown her where everything was last night. She poured herself some coffee and went to get milk and sugar.

She was leaning against the counter, sipping her coffee, when she heard the front door open and Arfur's bark. He ran into the kitchen and jumped on Hope, causing her to spill a few drops of coffee.

"Down, Arfur!" Edward commanded. Then he turned to Hope. "Sorry about that."

"It's all right," said Hope, putting down her mug. "No harm done."

"It's not all right. Poppy's right. I need to take Arfur to obedience school."

Arfur was looking up at Hope with those big brown eyes, his tongue hanging out and his tail wagging. Hope couldn't resist petting him.

"You're just encouraging him," grumbled Edward.

Hope continued to pet the dog for another minute.

"Thanks for making coffee."

"My pleasure. Is it all right? I'm more of a tea drinker."

Hope was going to tell him it was a bit on the weak side but said it was fine instead. She would make it the next morning.

"Did you have breakfast?" she asked him.

"No, I was waiting for you."

"Do you mind if I take a shower first? I'll be quick."

"Take your time," he said.

Edward made them scrambled eggs and toast.

"And here I thought you didn't cook," said Hope.

"I wouldn't consider this cooking," he replied.

He slid some eggs and a piece of toast onto a plate and handed it to Hope, putting the rest on his plate.

"Mm," she said, taking a couple of bites of egg. She was hungry.

"All right?"

"Better than all right. The eggs are scrambled perfectly."

Edward beamed.

They finished breakfast and Edward asked Hope when she wanted to go to Cupid's Bow.

"I emailed Oscar that I would be stopping by Gemma's cottage this morning, but I didn't hear back from him."

"You still want to go?"

"Absolutely."

"You want to call over there first?"

Hope thought about it.

"Let's just go. Knowing Oscar, he'll make up some excuse to keep me away."

"What if she's truly ill?"

"Then I'll apologize. Look, you said Cupid's Bow wasn't far. If you need to work, I can get a car service to take me."

"I'll take you. I just think you should let them know you're headed over there."

"I already told Oscar I planned on stopping by this morning."

"Did you write to Gemma?"

"I don't have her email address. Per Oscar, she doesn't have one."

"No email? What about texting her?"

"If I'm to believe Oscar, which I don't, she doesn't text either."

"Does she at least have a cell phone?"

"I assume she must, but he refused to give Ashley her number."

"That's insane. How does she communicate?"

"Via Oscar."

Edward frowned.

"I know," said Hope. "Why don't I clean up? Then we'll head to Cupid's Bow."

"If you insist."

"I do."

Hope wondered if she should have phoned Oscar before she and Edward headed to Cupid's Bow. Well, too late now. They were nearly there.

Edward pulled up in front of what Hope would describe as a quintessential English country cottage. The house was white with a thatched roof and a little garden in front.

Hope stayed in the car.

"You're not going to get out?"

"I just need a minute."

She glanced around.

"I don't see a car. Do you think that means there's no one here?"

"It could be parked in back. Or maybe she doesn't drive."

"Right."

Hope waited another minute and then opened the door.

"Wish me luck."

"Good luck."

Hope took a few steps and then turned around.

"You don't have to wait for me."

"What if no one's home?"

"Good point. Okay. I'll go ring the doorbell. If she's there, I'll get a car service to take me back to your place."

"And if she's not?"

"I'll call Oscar."

"Okay," said Edward.

Hope walked to the front door and rang the doorbell. Then she waited. The house seemed quiet, as though no one was there. She rang the doorbell again. This time, she thought she heard someone. A few seconds later, the door was flung open.

A disheveled-looking man was standing there, glaring at her.

"Yes?" he said.

"Oscar?" said Hope. She had looked him up online and seen a picture of him. He was quite good-looking. And, in addition to being Gemma's agent, he was a playwright who had had a play produced at the Edinburgh International Festival.

"Yes?" he said, continuing to glare at her.

"I'm Hope, Hope Halladay, from Herstory? I sent you an email."

"I didn't receive it."

"Did you check your spam folder?"

Oscar glared at her.

"What do you want?"

"To see Ms. Lovegood."

"She isn't here."

"Where is she?"

"Elsewhere."

"Well, I'm not leaving until I've met with her and discussed the manuscript."

Oscar smirked.

"Then you may be here a while."

"I'm serious, Mr. Tennant."

"So am I, Ms. Halladay."

They eyed one another, like a couple of prize fighters sizing each other up.

"Did you tell her I was coming to England to see her?"

"As I said, I didn't receive an email from you."

"You must know how to reach her. Can you let her know I'm here?"

"I'll do that," he said and started to close the door. Hope put out her hand to stop him, which earned her a dirty look.

"What do you want, Ms. Halladay?"

"I told you, to meet with Ms. Lovegood and see the manuscript for the new book."

"And I told you over the phone, it's not finished."

"I understand, but could I at least see what she's written so far?"

"No."

"Why not?"

"I told you, she doesn't let anyone see her work until it's finished."

"Even you?"

Oscar didn't reply.

"Look, we can't keep extending the deadline."

"Why not?"

"Because we have a schedule to keep."

"So, change the schedule."

"I can't do that."

"Why not?"

"I'm not in charge of scheduling."

"Well, speak to whoever is."

Hope frowned.

"Ashley doesn't want to change it. Marketing's already made plans."

Now it was Oscar's turn to frown.

"Look, Oscar, you and Gemma signed a contract with Herstory that called for two more books. Herstory has extended the deadline for the new book twice now. And if we don't have the manuscript by the end of the month, there's a good chance Herstory will sue."

Hope didn't know that for sure, but maybe the threat of a lawsuit would motivate Oscar to motivate Gemma.

"Contracts can be broken."

"What about the advance? You do realize, you'll have to pay it back if you don't deliver the manuscript."

That seemed to do the trick.

"Fine. I'll get you the manuscript."

"Before the end of the month?"

"Yes. Now good day, Ms. Halladay."

He went to close the door again. Again, Hope stopped him.

"What about Gemma?"

"What about her?"

"I'd like to speak with her."

"That's not possible."

"Why not?"

"I'll let her know you stopped by," he said. This time, he managed to shut the door.

Hope stood there fuming. She was about to knock, but what would she say? She waited a few seconds. Then she turned and headed back to Edward's car.

CHAPTER 6

"No luck?" said Edward.

Hope shook her head.

"He said Gemma wasn't there, and he doesn't have the manuscript."

"What are you going to do?"

"I don't know. He said he'd get me the manuscript by the end of the month."

"I take it you don't believe him."

"I do not. I want to speak with Gemma."

"Did he say when she'd be back?"

"No. And I can't go home without at least speaking to her or seeing some chapters."

"So now what?"

"I keep trying."

"I need to do a call. Shall we head back to my place?"

"I suppose," said Hope.

As they drove away, Hope looked back at the cottage. What was Oscar doing there? And where was Gemma?

Hope was surprised to find an email from Oscar the next morning, telling her to call. Was Gemma back? His signature included a phone number. Hope immediately called it.

"It's Hope Halladay," said Hope as soon as Oscar answered. "I got your email. Is Gemma back?"

"She's not here, but she agreed to let me show you a few chapters."

"Great!" said Hope. A few chapters were better than nothing. "Can you email them to me?"

"No."

"No?"

"You need to come here."

"I do. Why?"

"Do you want to read the chapters or don't you?"

"Fine. I'll come over. When?"

"What are you doing right now?"

"Now?"

Hope looked at the time. It was eight-thirty. She was dressed and had had her coffee, but she'd need to have Edward drive her to Cupid's Bow.

"I could be there at nine, nine-thirty at the latest."

"Fine. I'll see you then."

Before Hope could say another word, Oscar had ended the call.

Hope raced up to Edward's room, knocking on the door. Arfur immediately started barking.

"Yes?" said Edward.

"May I come in?"

Edward said that she could.

"I just spoke to Oscar. He communicated with Gemma, and she's agreed to let me see the first few chapters of her book."

"That's great! Is she back?"

"No, but he has the chapters and said I should come over."

"He can't email them to you?"

"No. They're probably paranoid about me sharing them with anyone."

"Really?"

"I know. Look, I hate to ask, but can you drive me over

there? I'll get a car service to drive me back. I just need to get over there as soon as possible."

"In case Oscar changes his mind?"

"Something like that."

"Just give me a minute."

A few minutes later, they were headed to Cupid's Bow.

Oscar let Hope in and escorted her up the stairs to what Hope assumed was Gemma's office. There were two desks, a more modern-looking one with a laptop computer on it and a wooden one with a typewriter. There was also a comfy-looking armchair with a reading lamp and several bookcases crammed with books and photographs.

"Is this Ms. Lovegood's office?" asked Hope.

"And mine," said Oscar. "We share it."

Interesting, thought Hope. She didn't realize they shared an office. Wasn't that a bit unusual? Did Ashley know?

"Is that her typewriter?" Hope asked, looking over at it. Gemma supposedly typed her first drafts, someone else— Oscar?—retyping them into Word on a computer.

Oscar nodded.

Hope went over to the bookcases. On one of the shelves was a photo of a young man and a young woman. They looked to be in their twenties. And judging by the way they were dressed and the woman's hair, Hope guessed that the photo had been taken sometime in the 1940s.

"Who are they?" she asked Oscar, holding up the framed photo.

"Gemma's parents. It was taken on their honeymoon."

"Ah," said Hope. She gazed at the picture for another moment and then returned it to the bookshelf.

"Here are the chapters," he said, holding out a small pile of paper.

"Thank you," said Hope. "I'll let you know what I think after I've read them."

She made to leave, but Oscar stopped her.

"You need to read them here."

"Excuse me?" said Hope.

"I said, you need to read them here."

"I'll bring them back."

But Hope could tell from Oscar's expression and body language that the pages were not to leave the room.

"Fine," she said. She went over and took a seat in the armchair. Oscar hadn't moved. "Do you plan on watching me?"

Oscar looked like he was thinking about it.

"I'll go get some coffee."

Hope was going to ask him to bring her a mug but thought better of it. She settled into the chair and began to read. It didn't take her long. As if sensing she had finished, Oscar returned.

"Well?" he said.

Hope collected her thoughts before speaking. The chapters weren't bad, but they were missing something.

"That bad?" he said.

"They're not bad," Hope slowly replied.

"But they're not good."

Hope wasn't a very good liar.

"They could use a little something."

"Like what?"

"I'm not sure. Some of that Gemma Lovegood wit? They were a little…"

"Flat?"

Hope nodded.

"Well, I'm sorry to inform you, but Gemma hasn't been feeling particularly witty recently."

"Because of her health?"

"Something like that."

"Maybe if she took another look…"

"I don't think it would help."

"Why not?"

"She hasn't been herself."

"I'd be happy to work with her. I've helped several of our authors and...."

Oscar cut her off.

"Thank you, but no."

"No? Shouldn't it be up to Gemma to decide?"

"Gemma's done."

"What do you mean *done*?"

"I mean, I'm afraid the old girl just doesn't have it in her."

"But the contract..."

A phone was buzzing. It was Oscar's. He looked down at the screen.

"I need to go."

"Okay, but..."

"Which means you need to leave."

Hope followed him out of the office and down the stairs. He grabbed a jacket and a bag and was headed out the door.

"Wait," said Hope, putting on her jacket. "Where are you going? We need to discuss the book!"

"I need to get to Ruby's Place. I'm already late."

"Ruby's Place? What is that? Is that where Gemma is?"

"No, it's a horse farm."

"Oh, I love horses," said Hope.

Oscar looked at her.

"Fine. You can come with me."

"I can?" said Hope.

"Yes, they can always use help."

"Okay," said Hope and followed him out the door.

"How far is it Ruby's Place?" Hope asked Oscar as they drove to the farm in Oscar's car.

"Not far," he replied.

A few minutes later, he turned off the road and headed

down a long driveway. Hope saw horses in the distance, some with riders and some just grazing.

"Is this the farm?" Hope asked.

"The horses give it away?"

Smart-ass, thought Hope.

Oscar parked the car, and they got out.

"Welcome to Ruby's Place," he said.

"So people come here to ride?" said Hope, watching a young girl on a horse being led around a ring.

"They do. But it's not just a riding stable. Ruby's Place provides equestrian therapy to children and adults with physical, mental, and behavioral challenges."

"So they teach people with disabilities to ride?"

"To ride and to take care of the horses."

"That's wonderful. And what do you do here?"

"I'm a volunteer."

"Do you teach people how to ride?"

"Occasionally. All of us volunteers do a bit of everything."

Hope followed Oscar over to a barn, where he was met by a woman who looked to be in her forties or early fifties. Hope hung back, feeling a bit shy, as Oscar and the woman spoke. Then Oscar indicated for Hope to come over.

"This is Anne," he said to Hope. "She and her husband Bert run the farm. This is Hope," he said to Anne. "She's visiting from the States."

"Nice to meet you, Hope," Anne said with a smile. "What brings you to Devon?"

"Work."

"Well, nice of you to volunteer your free time."

"Happy to help out. I love horses."

"So Oscar says. He said you volunteered to clean the stalls with him."

"Oh he did, did he?" said Hope, looking at Oscar, who was doing his best to look innocent.

Anne looked concerned.

"No problem," said Hope, turning to Anne. "I used to muck out stalls back when I rode in Connecticut." *Take that, Oscar!*

Anne smiled.

"I thought you looked like a horsewoman. Though did you bring a change of clothes? I wouldn't want you to get those things dirty."

Hope looked down at what she was wearing. While not fancy, her outfit was too nice to be shoveling manure in.

"I'm afraid not."

"Hm," said Anne. "You're about my daughter Emerald's size. I'll go get you some of her things. Be back in a tick."

She went off to get Hope some suitable clothes. As soon as Anne was gone, Hope turned to Oscar.

"You're going to have to try harder if you want to scare me off," she informed him.

"I wasn't trying to scare you off."

Hope didn't believe him.

"So, how long have you been volunteering at the farm?"

"Going on a year now. It helps me clear my head."

"How long has it been here?"

"Around four years now. Anne and her husband started it to help their daughter Ruby."

Hope waited for him to say more.

"She's on the spectrum."

"You mean the autism spectrum?"

Oscar nodded.

"Ruby found it hard to be around people when she was younger, but she loved animals, especially horses. Anne and Bert took her to an equestrian stable that worked with kids like her. Ruby loved it. Unfortunately, the place wasn't close to here. So they decided to start their own farm for special needs children and adults."

"That's amazing," said Hope. "It must have taken a lot of work."

"It did. And money."

"But if they've been here four years now, they must be doing all right."

"Ruby's Place is a registered charity. It's survived because of donations and volunteers."

Just then Anne returned with a pile of clothes and a pair of boots.

"Go see if these will work," she said to Hope. "There's a changing room in the barn."

"Is Emerald okay with me wearing her things?"

"She's at university. I doubt she'd care."

"Okay," said Hope. "I'll be right back."

CHAPTER 7

Hope emerged from the barn a few minutes later, dressed in Emerald's gear.

"How do I look?"

Anne smiled at her.

"Like you're ready to muck out a stable."

Hope smiled. Then she turned to Oscar.

"Ready?"

"Ready," he replied.

Then they headed to the stables.

Oscar began to explain how to muck out a stall, but Hope stopped him.

"I've done this before," she reminded him.

"You don't need a refresher?"

"It may have been a while since I've cleaned a stall, but it's not something you forget. I can shovel shit with the best of them."

Oscar smiled. He had a rather nice smile, Hope thought. And was that a dimple?

They got to work, keeping to themselves. But during a break for water, Hope asked Oscar about Ruby.

"She's at university, studying to be a vet," he explained. "She and Emerald work here in the summer and during school breaks. Ruby loves this place."

"I'm sorry I won't get to meet her. She sounds like an extraordinary young woman."

"She is. Being around horses really helped her. The farm has helped a lot of people."

"That's wonderful. So, how often do you volunteer?"

"A couple of days a week, more if I can."

They finished drinking their water and went back to work. When they were done mucking out the last stall, Oscar put their pitchforks and shovels away. Hope had forgotten what hard, smelly work cleaning a stable was, but she had enjoyed it.

"You can go change," he told her.

"Thanks," said Hope. "Though I could use a shower."

"There's one in the bathroom."

"That's okay. I don't have a towel. I'll just wash my hands and face and take a shower when I get back to my friend's."

"Suit yourself."

Hope went to the bathroom to wash up. Then she changed back into her clothes, placing Emerald's now sweaty and smelly clothes in the hamper, her boots next to it. She emerged from the bathroom to find Oscar chatting with Anne.

"I left Emerald's clothes in the hamper in the bathroom," she told Anne. "I hope that's all right."

"Perfect. Thank you. So, you enjoy yourself?"

Hope didn't know if Anne was kidding or serious.

"I did," Hope answered truthfully. "I've missed being around horses."

"Would you like to take one out?"

"You mean for a ride?"

Anne nodded.

"That is if you're not too tired from cleaning the stable."

Hope looked at Oscar.

"Is that okay? I'd love to go for a ride. It's been ages."

Oscar looked at Anne.

"Go on," she said to him. "The horses could use the exercise. Have your friend take Percy. You can take Lightning."

Oscar led Hope over to a brown horse with a black mane and tail.

"Hello, Percy," said Hope, holding out her right hand for Percy to sniff.

Percy sniffed her hand and made a snuffling noise.

"He was probably hoping for a bit of apple or a carrot," said Oscar.

"Oh," said Hope, feeling bad that she didn't have either.

"Hold on. Let me see if I can rustle up something. I'll be right back."

He disappeared, returning a few minutes later with a couple of carrots.

"Here, offer him this."

Hope held out the carrot. Percy took a big bite, and Hope smiled.

"Where's Lightning?" she asked.

"Over there," said Oscar, pointing.

Hope turned to see a large jet-black horse with what looked like a white lightning bolt on his forehead.

"Well, I can see why they named him Lightning."

Oscar walked over to Lightning and offered him a carrot, which the horse greedily ate.

"Shall we?" he said when the horses were done with their treats. "We just need to saddle them."

Oscar helped Hope saddle Percy. Then he placed a saddle on Lightning and went to get riding helmets.

"Here," he said, handing one to Hope.

"Thanks."

She put it on and then looked at Percy. Suddenly, she felt nervous. She hadn't been on a horse in years. But it was just like riding a bicycle, right? Once you learn, you never forget. But horses weren't bicycles. They could sense fear—and throw you.

"You need help?" asked Oscar.

"I'm good," said Hope. Then she changed her mind.

"Actually, if you wouldn't mind."

Oscar smiled and came over.

"Up we go," he said, lifting Hope into the saddle.

His hands felt warm against her body, and Hope could feel herself blushing. *Stop that!* she told herself.

"Thanks," she said.

Then Oscar swung himself onto Lightning's back.

"Let's go," he said and headed off.

"Where are we going?" Hope asked.

"There's a trail over there. Follow me."

They didn't speak as they rode, which was fine by Hope. She had been nervous at first, having not ridden in so long. But the horses clearly knew where they were going and were used to inexperienced riders. Not that Hope was inexperienced, just rusty. And she quickly became more comfortable in the saddle.

She gazed at Oscar upon Lightning. They made a handsome pair. Oscar looked good on a horse. She pictured him in a proper riding habit, his jodhpurs hugging his strong thighs as he spurred his horse on. *Stop it!* she told herself a second time.

When they got back to the barn, Oscar dismounted and looked over at Hope.

"I've got this," she said, slipping off Percy.

It wasn't the most graceful dismount, but at least she hadn't landed on her bottom.

Two volunteers came over to take the horses. Hope thanked them and asked where she should leave the riding helmet she'd borrowed. The woman who took Percy said she'd take it.

Hope really needed a shower now. Though Oscar looked fresh as a daisy. Curse the man.

She followed him back to his car.

"Do you mind giving me a lift?" she asked him.

"Where to?"

"My friend's. His place isn't far from Cupid's Bow."

Oscar said that he would drop her off. No doubt he was eager to get rid of her.

Hope gazed out the window as they drove. She had questions for Oscar, but she was feeling tired and didn't have the energy to get into it with him.

They arrived at Edward's, and Hope turned to Oscar.

"Thank you for taking me to the farm. I enjoyed it."

He looked at her as though trying to discern if she was telling the truth.

"I mean it," she said. "It was nice being around the horses. I didn't even mind mucking out the stalls."

Oscar didn't say anything.

"Well, thanks again," said Hope. Then she got out.

As soon as she was on the pavement, Oscar took off.

"So?" said Edward. "Did you meet with Gemma?"

"She wasn't there."

"But you were gone for hours."

"I was with Oscar."

"For over three hours?"

"We went to his horse farm."

"He has a horse farm?"

"It's not his. He volunteers there. Look, do you mind if I get a shower? I could really use one."

"Fine. But I want to hear more about this farm when you're done."

Hope went to take a shower and put on fresh clothes. Then she headed to the kitchen to get something to eat. Edward was there.

"What are you having?" she asked him.

"A cheese sandwich. You want one?"

"Sure."

"So, tell me about this farm," he said as he fixed her a sandwich.

"It's called Ruby's Place, and it's for special needs children and adults."

"And you say Gemma's agent works there?"

"Volunteers. Yes."

"And you spent the morning there, with him."

"Pretty much."

"What about the manuscript?"

"Oscar showed me a few chapters before we left."

"And?"

"They weren't very good."

"But you can edit them, yes?"

"He won't let me."

"What do you mean, he won't let you? Isn't that what an editor does, edits things?"

"Yes, but Gemma won't let anyone touch her work until she's done."

"So, when will she be done?"

"He doesn't know. Possibly never."

"Never? Never's a long time."

"Tell me about it." Hope sighed. "He claims that Gemma's lost her mojo."

"Her mojo? He said that."

"Not in so many words, but it's what he meant."

"So now what?"

"Now I have to tell Ashley."

"But it's Saturday. And isn't she on maternity leave?"

"Try telling her that. She texted me a little while ago, wanting to know what was up. I said I'd call her."

"Eat your sandwich first."

CHAPTER 8

Hope was dreading talking to Ashley. Though what was the worst that could happen? Hope didn't really think Ashley would fire her. It wasn't Hope's fault that Gemma was MIA and had only written a few chapters.

"Is now a good time?" Hope texted her boss, hoping she wouldn't reply.

No such luck.

"Give me a minute," Ashley replied.

A few minutes later, Hope received a request to video chat. *Oh great*, she thought. If a phone call with her boss was bad, a video chat was worse.

"Hi, Ashley!" Hope said, trying to look cheerful.

"So, did you meet with Gemma?" Ashley asked her.

Leave it to Ashley to cut to the chase.

"Actually…"

"Is there a problem?"

"She's not here."

"Where is she?"

"Oscar won't tell me."

Ashley frowned.

"But he did allow me to read a few chapters of the new book."

"And?" Hope didn't reply right away. "Come on, Hope. Spit it out. How were the chapters? I take it from your expression that they need work."

"They do. Quite a bit."

Ashley continued to frown.

"Did you offer to help?"

"Of course I did. But Oscar refused."

"What do you mean, he refused?"

"He said Gemma didn't like anyone editing her work until she was finished."

"Usually her work doesn't need much editing, at least by the time I get it. So, is she planning on rewriting the chapters?"

Hope hesitated.

"What aren't you telling me?"

"Gemma appears to be suffering from writer's block."

"You need to meet with her."

"I know but…"

"I knew I should have gone over there as soon as Oscar told me the manuscript would be late," Ashley said, more to herself than to Hope. "Now we've wasted months." She looked back at Hope. "Did you tell Oscar that if Gemma didn't produce a manuscript by the end of the month Herstory would sue?"

"I did actually."

"And?"

"He said we'd have something by the end of the month. But…"

"You don't believe him."

"I'd like to, but he also said Gemma was done, that she didn't have it in her. So I'm not sure what to believe. Should I just head back?"

"To New York? No. I want you to stay there, find Gemma, and talk to her. Find out what's going on from her, not Oscar."

"You want me to stay here in England?"

"Did you not hear me?"

"I just…"

"Listen to me, Hope. This book is very important to

Herstory. And I know you've been wanting me to promote you. Well, this is the way to get that promotion, by getting me that book."

"But…"

"No buts, Hope. Find Gemma. Talk to her. And get me that manuscript."

Hope thought she heard a baby crying in the background.

"I need to go," said Ashley.

"Is the baby all right?"

"She's fine."

"Have you decided on a name?"

"We have."

"What did you name her?"

"Elizabeth Gemma, after Derek's mother and my most valuable author."

Hope winced. Now she really needed to find Gemma.

"Keep me posted," said Ashley. Then she ended the call.

"Everything all right?" said Edward.

Hope hadn't noticed him there.

"Not really."

"What happened? Is Ashley upset?"

"You could say that."

"What did she say?"

"That I'm not to return without getting Gemma's manuscript."

"She said that?"

"She did."

"So you'll be here for a while?"

"Looks that way. Ashley's giving her until the end of the month."

"And if she hasn't finished the manuscript by then?"

"She says Herstory will sue."

Edward whistled.

"Hopefully, it won't come to that."

"So, I guess you'll be here for a while."

"I guess so. I should look for an Airbnb and rent a car."

"Nonsense. You can stay here and borrow mine."

"That's very kind of you, Edward, but I can't stay here. And don't you need your car?"

"Why can't you stay? I like having you here, and I rarely use my car."

Hope was dubious.

"What about work? I'm staying in your office."

"Guest room. And I'm perfectly fine working out of my room or at the dining table."

"I don't know…" Then she looked down at Arfur, who had come over and rested his head in her lap. She looked down at his shaggy head and began petting him.

"Now you have to stay," said Edward. "Arfur would miss you."

"Well, in that case."

Speaking of pets, Hope needed to check in with Dani.

"I should text my pet sitter, make sure Morris is okay."

"Do that. Then do you want to go for a walk with me and Arfur?"

"Sure."

Edward went upstairs, and Hope opened her texting app and sent a text to Dani, asking how things were going.

"All good," Dani replied. "How are things there? Please tell me you're not working today."

Hope didn't reply right away.

"You are working, aren't you?"

"I spent the morning at a horse farm."

"Ooh, a horse farm! Did you go riding?"

"I did."

"How was it?"

"Good."

"You meet a cute British riding instructor?"

Hope immediately thought of Oscar.

"No."

"Bummer. Oh, btw, you have a new neighbor."

"I do?"

"You do. He's cute, single, and has a cat named Livingston. I'm thinking about arranging a playdate."

"For Morris or for you?"

"For both of us. Hey, I've got to run. I'm meeting friends for brunch. Morris sends his love."

"Give him some scritches for me."

"I will. Ciao for now!"

"Ciao."

Hope put her phone away and went to see Edward.

Edward suggested they go to the dog park, which was ten minutes away. There were several dogs there, of varying sizes, and it looked like Arfur knew all of them. Hope watched as Edward let Arfur off his leash to run around and play with his friends.

"So it's okay to let him off his leash? He won't run off or bite anyone?"

"Arfur? Nah. He's a good boy. Just keep an eye on him, make sure none of the bigger dogs get too rough."

Hope watched the dogs play.

"That's Cole," said Edward, pointing to a black standard poodle. "And that's Charlie," he said, pointing to an English springer spaniel.

"And who's the pug trying to get Arfur's attention?"

"That's Archie."

"What's Arfur, by the way? I've been meaning to ask."

"Some kind of poodle mix. Lucy wanted to have his DNA tested, but I didn't care. What difference would it make?"

They continued to watch the dogs play.

"So what did your pet sitter have to say? All good at home?"

"Yeah, and apparently I have a cute new neighbor who

has a cat. Dani's planning on arranging a playdate."

"Do cats have playdates?"

"I guess I'll find out."

Edward smiled.

"You sure you don't mind me crashing at your place a bit longer?" said Hope. She had glanced at Airbnb listings, but there wasn't anything available in or near Cupid's Bow.

"Mind? I'd be delighted. I told you, *mi casa es su casa*. And I like having a roommate."

"You do?" Hope preferred living alone. Though she had liked her college roommates.

"I suppose I'd gotten used to living with someone. Living on my own feels a bit lonely."

"But your family lives near here. And you still have friends in Devon, yes?"

"I do, but it's not the same."

"Well, l don't want to wear out my welcome. But if you don't mind me staying a bit longer…"

"I told you, stay as long as you like."

"Thank you."

They heard two dogs barking and turned to see what was up. Arfur and Cole were chasing each other. They seemed happy.

"We should head back," said Edward.

He whistled for Arfur, who bounded over. Arfur placed his paws on Edward's legs and looked up at him.

"Who's a good boy?" said Edward, looking down at Arfur.

Arfur's tongue was hanging out.

Edward reached into his pocket and pulled out a dog treat. Arfur scarfed it down and then waited for another.

"That's it for now," Edward told him.

Arfur looked dejected. Hope smothered a laugh. She would need to be careful. If it had been up to her, she would have given Arfur several treats.

When they got back to Edward's, he gave Arfur some food and fresh water and told Hope he'd walk Arfur again later but that she needn't come with them.

"So, what would you like to do tomorrow?" he asked her. "And please don't tell me you need to work. It's Sunday."

Hope had been planning on doing some work.

"I guess I could take a little time off to sightsee," she said. "I don't know this part of England."

"Well, allow me to be your tour guide. I know Devon like the back of my hand. And I know just where to take you."

"Where?"

"That's for me to know and you to find out. I just need to see if Poppy can watch Arfur."

"Are dogs not allowed where we're going?"

"Probably not. In any case, I think it best we don't take him. I'll just shoot Poppy a text."

"You're not going to tell me where you're thinking of taking me?"

"It'll be a surprise."

Hope wasn't crazy about surprises, but she didn't say anything.

"Now about dinner…"

"I'm not really hungry."

"Neither am I. But you'll want something later. And I don't feel like eating in tonight."

"What do you suggest?"

"There's always the pub. There's also a pretty good Indian place not too far away and an Italian trattoria."

"Any of those are fine. Do you want to make a reservation? It is Saturday."

"The pub doesn't take reservations. And I don't think the Indian place does either. Shall I try the Italian?"

"Sure."

"Okay, I'll call over there now. Shall we say seven?"

"Seven's fine."

CHAPTER 9

"You ready to hit the road?" Edward asked Hope the next morning after they'd had breakfast.

"I just need to grab my bag."

They got in the car and Edward set off.

"I've got a confession to make," he said as they headed out of town.

"A confession?" said Hope.

"I'm a Gemma Lovegood fan."

"You are?"

He nodded.

"Lucy thought she was the bee's knees. So I decided to check her out."

"You read both books?"

"I did."

"And?"

"I rather enjoyed them. I particularly liked that Captain Ripley fellow."

Captain Ripley was the love interest in Gemma's first book, *Belle of the Ball.*

"Well, what do you know," said Hope. "Say, would you mind detouring to Cupid's Bow? Do we have time?"

"Why do you want to go there? Did Oscar text you? Is Gemma back?"

"No. It's just a feeling."

Edward didn't say anything, just drove to Cupid's Bow.

There was a car parked in front of Gemma's place. Could it be Gemma's? It wasn't Oscar's. Hope had thought about texting him on the way over but had decided not to.

Edward parked behind the other car.

"You want to come with me?" Hope asked him.

"Really?"

"You said you were a big Gemma fan."

They got out of the car and headed to the door. Hope rang the bell and waited. A minute later, the door opened to reveal a tall, attractive woman around Hope's age. She looked a bit like a young Kate Middleton, aka Catherine, Princess of Wales.

"Good morning," said Hope. Could this woman be Gemma Lovegood? Hope had always pictured Gemma as short, plump, and in her sixties. This woman was the opposite. "Are you Gemma Lovegood?"

The woman snorted.

"Hardly." She turned and called out to Oscar, letting him know they had company.

Oscar appeared a minute later. He didn't look happy to see them.

"We were in the neighborhood and thought we'd stop by, see if Gemma was in," said Hope.

"She's not here," said Oscar.

"Oh," said Hope, disappointed. "We saw the car and…"

"That's my car," said the Kate clone.

Hope turned to Oscar.

"Have you spoken with Gemma, told her I was here?"

"Not yet," said Oscar. "I've been a bit busy. Now if you wouldn't mind?"

He made to shut the door, but Hope stopped him. Oscar looked annoyed.

"So you haven't discussed the…?" Hope didn't want to say too much in front of the Princess of Wales clone.

"I told you I would speak with her and that you'd have

the manuscript by the end of the month."

"What's going on?" said the Kate clone.

"Nothing," said Oscar.

"It doesn't sound like nothing."

Oscar sighed.

"It's about *Gemma's* new book."

"Oh," said the Kate clone.

"Well, when you do speak with Gemma, tell her I need to speak with her and that I'd be happy to work with her," said Hope.

"I told you…" said Oscar.

He was dressed in a pair of jeans that hugged his hips and a black t-shirt that showed off his muscular arms.

"I know what you told me," said Hope, looking at him. "But I spoke with Ashley, and she wanted me to let you know that I'm here for you. I mean Gemma. You know what I mean."

The Kate clone looked amused.

"I think you should take the woman up on her offer," she told Oscar. "Maybe she can help."

"Stay out of this, Felicity."

Felicity rolled her eyes, and Oscar turned back to Hope.

"I'll let Gemma know you stopped by."

"Thank you."

"Now if you don't mind?"

Hope gave him a final look.

"Fine. I'm going." She turned and saw Edward staring at the Kate clone. She had forgotten about him, he had been so quiet. She headed to his car, Edward following her.

"I can't believe it," said Edward after they got in.

"I know. It's hard to believe someone could be that rude."

"No, I mean her."

"Her?"

"The woman who was there, Felicity. You didn't recognize her?"

"Should I have? I mean she looked a bit like Kate Middleton, or the Princess of Wales, but I know it wasn't her."

"You really didn't recognize her?"

Hope shook her head.

"I'm pretty sure that was Felicity Rogers."

"And who is Felicity Rogers?"

"You really don't know?"

"I haven't a clue. Who is she?"

"She's a model. She also dated Prince Harry before he hooked up with Meghan. It was a bit of a scandal, Felicity being so much younger than him."

"Huh," said Hope. "I never heard of her."

"And here I thought Americans were more into royal gossip than us Brits."

"Not this American. So Harry dumped her?"

"I believe she dumped him. She's currently dating some tech billionaire if you believe the tabloids. I wonder what she was doing with your friend."

"He's not my friend. He's Gemma's agent. So, where are you taking me?"

"I told you, it's a surprise."

"I hate surprises."

"You'll like this one. Promise."

"How far away is it?"

"Around an hour."

"Okay, let's go."

"We're here!" said Edward.

"Where's here?" said Hope as they drove down a long driveway.

"Greenway, Agatha Christie's holiday home."

"Really?" said Hope, staring at the big white house a short ways away that was surrounded by pretty gardens.

"I know how much you used to like her."

"I did." Though Hope hadn't read an Agatha Christie in years.

"I've never been to Greenway," said Edward, "but I heard it's worth a visit. It's managed by the National Trust. You can see where Christie and her husband spent summers and Christmases. She even wrote some of her books here."

"I don't recall you being a Christie fan," said Hope.

"I'm not really. Though I've read a couple of her books. And you dragged me to see *The Mousetrap* back at uni."

"Which you said you enjoyed."

"I did. But I went because you wanted to go see it."

"You didn't have to take me here."

"I know. But I thought it would be fun. The grounds are supposed to be very nice. And there's also a second-hand bookshop and a café."

"You've clearly done your research. I can't wait to see the place."

"Come. I believe there's a tour starting soon."

"That was so interesting!" Hope said to Edward when the tour had ended. "Thank you for taking me here! I had forgotten that Christie had been born in Devon. And I love that the place housed children during World War Two."

"And then was used by the U.S. Coast Guard afterwards," said Edward.

"Though she got it back on Christmas Day 1945. I'm amazed there was so little damage."

"What did you think of the library?"

"I loved it! Over five thousand books! And all of those first editions!"

"I liked her study."

"I liked that too. I liked everything! And I can't believe you can actually stay here!"

"I tried to book the apartment, but it wasn't available."

"That's all right."

"You hungry? Shall we get something to eat?"

"Sure. You have someplace in mind?"

"I do. There's a gastropub not far from here that's gotten good reviews."

"Let's go!"

They arrived at the gastropub a short time later.

"It's adorable," said Hope.

"You just have a thing for thatched roofs."

"I do. You don't really see them in the States. And they're so cute, like something out of a fairy tale."

They stepped inside the gastropub. The place was busy, but they didn't have to wait long for a table.

"What are you going to have?" Hope asked, eyeing the menu.

"I was thinking of getting the pork belly."

"That's what I was thinking of getting."

"Then I'll get the John Dory."

"You don't have to."

"It's fine. I could go for some fish."

"We could always share."

Edward eyed her.

"What?" said Hope.

Edward continued to look at her.

"You don't want to share?"

"I'm fine sharing. But I remember a certain someone suggesting we should share and then not wanting to."

"That was eons ago."

Edward continued to eye her suspiciously.

"I promise to share."

"Fine. Though if you change your mind…"

"I won't."

Edward smiled at Hope. Then he signaled to a server.

Lunch had been delicious. And true to her word, Hope had shared her pork belly with Edward and had eaten some of his John Dory. She had also had half a pint of hard cider and was feeling sleepy as they drove back to his place.

"We're here," said Edward, gently nudging Hope awake.

Hope opened her eyes and looked around.

"How long was I out for?"

"Not long."

"Why didn't you wake me?"

"You looked so peaceful."

"Hm," said Hope. She hoped she hadn't snored.

"I should go retrieve Arfur and take him for a walk."

"I'll go with you."

"You don't have to."

"I'd like to. I could use a walk too."

Edward smiled.

They headed down the street to Poppy's place. As soon as Edward rang the bell, they heard barking.

"Do you think Arfur knows it's you?" Hope asked.

"I don't know. He always barks when he hears a doorbell."

Poppy opened the door, and Arfur strained to get past her.

"Sit, Arfur!" Poppy commanded.

Arfur did not sit.

"We're still working on that," said Edward. "So, did he behave?"

Poppy looked down at the shaggy black dog.

"Have you been a good boy, Arfur?"

"Arf!" barked Arfur, his tongue hanging out of his mouth.

Everyone laughed at that.

"I'll take him off your hands," said Edward.

"That's all right," said Poppy. "Arfur and I had a right good time. Didn't we, boy?"

Arfur looked up at Poppy and barked.

"Did you take him to the dog park?"

"We did. I think Archie has a crush on him."

"I'll let you get on with it," said Edward.

"I'll go fetch his leash."

Poppy returned with the leash and fastened it to Arfur's collar.

"Here you go," she said, handing Edward the lead.

Arfur bolted out the door and jumped on Edward.

"You miss me, boy?"

"Arf!" barked Arfur, continuing to jump.

Edward laughed as Poppy and Hope shook their heads.

"Thanks again, Poppy."

"No worries."

CHAPTER 10

"Mind if we head down to the beach?" Edward asked Hope. "I think Arfur could do with a bit of exercise."

"Sure," said Hope.

It was chilly by the water, though that hadn't stopped townspeople from gathering there to sun themselves or take a walk.

"Are you cold?" Edward asked Hope, seeing her shiver.

"A bit," she replied.

Arfur, on the other hand, didn't look the least bit cold. Probably because of all the running around he was doing.

"I don't know where that dog gets his energy," said Edward. "Hopefully, he'll nap when we get home. I have some work I need to do."

"On a Sunday? I thought you didn't work on Sunday."

"It's just bits and bobs."

"That's okay. I should probably do some work too."

"Oh, I forgot to mention, my mum invited us over for dinner."

"Tonight?"

"Sorry. It slipped my mind. Is that okay?"

"It's fine. I just wish I'd known before I'd eaten that big lunch."

"It wasn't that big. And we won't be eating dinner for a few hours yet."

"Well, I'd love to see your family. So you told them I was here?"

"That's why they invited us. Mum's very excited to see you."

"Remind me again what your sister and brother-in-law do," said Hope as they drove to Edward's parents' house.

"Alice is a doctor, and William is a solicitor."

"Thank you."

Edward parked the Mini in his parents' driveway. His sister's family was already there, as evidenced by their Range Rover. They got out and rang the doorbell, which was immediately answered by Edward's mother. Hope wondered if she had been lying in wait for them.

"Edward!" she said, kissing him on each cheek. She stood back and looked at him. "Have you not been eating? You're as thin as a rail."

"I'm fine, Mum. I've just been a bit busy."

"I'd be happy to drop something off. Can't have you starve."

Hope grinned. She had forgotten how Edward's mother doted on him.

"And Hope!" said his mother, seeing her. "Just as pretty as I remember you. No, prettier. Here, come and give me a hug!"

Hope went over to her.

As Edward's mother hugged her, Hope saw his sister. She looked amused.

"Let poor Hope breathe, Mum," Alice admonished her mother.

"It's okay," said Hope. "It's nice to see you again, Mrs. Wilson."

"Please, call me Joan."

Hope smiled at her.

"Come," said Joan and led them into the living room. "Dinner will be ready in a bit. Have a seat and make yourselves comfortable while you wait."

"Can I help with anything?" Hope asked her.

"Just sit and relax." Joan turned to her daughter. "Come, Alice."

"Yes, Mother."

"Where did your father and husband hare off to?" Joan asked Alice as they headed to the kitchen.

"They took Charlotte to the playground."

"Right. Well, tell them Hope and Edward are here and to scoot on home."

"I'll let them know."

They disappeared into the kitchen, and Hope turned to Edward.

"You should go see if they need help."

"I'm sure they're fine."

Hope gave him a look. Edward sighed and headed to the kitchen.

As soon as he had gone, Hope took a look around. Edward's parents' house had a homey, lived-in feel to it, the living area filled with cozy-looking sofas and armchairs, a wood burner, a coffee table, and wooden end tables covered with photographs.

Hope went over to look at some of the pictures. There were framed photographs of Joan and David, Edward and Alice's parents; their parents and grandparents; Alice and Edward through the years; and photos of Alice's family. There was even a picture of Edward and Lucy. Had he not told his mother they had broken up?

The front door opened a few minutes later, and Hope heard a happy squeal. It was Alice's daughter Charlotte. She ran into the living room but stopped in front of Hope. Hope thought she must be four or five.

"Who are you?" said the little girl.

"I'm Hope. I'm a friend of Edward's."

"Are you his girlfriend?" asked the little girl.

"Now Charlotte, what have we said about asking people personal questions?" said her father. He turned to Hope and apologized.

"That's all right," said Hope.

"I'm William," he said.

"Nice to meet you," said Hope. "I'm Hope."

"So I gathered."

"And to answer your question, Charlotte, your uncle Edward and I are not dating. We're just friends."

"Oh," said Charlotte, sounding disappointed. "Mummy didn't like Edward's last girlfriend and hoped he'd find a nice new one."

"Charlotte!" said her father.

"What?" said the little girl, looking up at her father with innocent, big blue eyes.

He just shook his head.

"Nice to see you again, Hope," said Edward's father.

"It's nice to see you, too, Mr. Wilson."

"Please, it's David."

"There you are!" said Edward's mother, emerging from the kitchen. "Take off your jackets and go wash your hands. We're about to eat."

David saluted, and his wife playfully swatted him.

"Come, Charlotte," said her father. "Let's go wash hands."

"You sit here next to me," Edward's mother said to Hope. "I want to hear all about what you've been up to since you left us."

"I, uh…" said Hope. She looked over at Edward, but he was talking to his father.

Joan turned to her husband.

"David, help me with the platters."

He stopped talking and followed his wife into the kitchen. They emerged a minute later with several trays of food.

"I made you a proper Sunday roast," Edward's mother told Hope, "with Yorkshire pudding and green beans."

"It looks delicious," said Hope.

"I asked Edward if it was okay. His last girlfriend was a *vegan*." She said the word as though *vegan* was some sort of disease.

"There's nothing wrong with being a vegan," said Alice. "It's much better for people and the planet."

"There's nothing wrong with a little meat," replied her mother.

"I love roast beef!" said Charlotte.

"There, you see?" said Joan.

Alice and William exchanged a look.

"David, would you carve the roast beef?" Joan asked her husband, ignoring her daughter and son-in-law.

Joan peppered Hope with questions as they ate, asking her about her job and what it was like to live in New York City. Hope did her best to answer, though Joan kept interrupting her.

"Alice said your company only publishes books by women. Is that true?"

"It is," said Hope.

"Imagine that!" said Joan. "Any authors I might have heard of?"

"They publish Gemma Lovegood's books," said Alice.

"You do?!" said Joan. "I just love her. Will there be a new one soon? I finished the last one months ago."

"Hopefully," said Hope.

"You don't know?"

"She may not be in charge of Gemma's books," said Alice.

Joan looked at Hope.

Before Hope could respond, Charlotte got up and asked to be excused.

"You didn't eat your green beans," said her mother.

"I don't like green beans," said Charlotte.

"Since when?"

Charlotte made a face.

"She's tired," said William.

"Are you, darling?" said Alice. "You want to go upstairs and have a lie-down?"

"I want pudding."

Hope knew that meant dessert.

"I thought you wanted to be excused?" said Charlotte's father.

Charlotte wrinkled her face.

"Why don't you have a little lie-down, and we'll get you when it's time for pudding?" said her grandmother.

Charlotte looked as though she was thinking it over.

"Come," said Alice, getting up and holding out a hand.

Charlotte didn't move.

"You don't want to go upstairs and play with your stuffies while the grownups talk?"

"You promise to get me for pudding?"

"Promise," said Alice.

Charlotte silently moved toward her mother.

"Come here," said Alice, scooping her up.

Hope watched as the little girl wrapped herself around her mother, resting her head on Alice's shoulder. It was quite sweet.

"She's really a very good girl," said Joan, after Alice had taken Charlotte upstairs.

"I have no doubt," said Hope. "She's adorable. How old is she?"

"She'll be five next month."

Alice returned a few minutes later.

"Is she taking a nap?" Hope asked her.

"Doubtful. She was playing with her stuffies." She took a sip of water and then turned back to Hope. "So, how long are you here for?"

"I'm not sure. It depends."

"On what?" asked Alice.

"On when she completes her assignment," said Edward.

"You make her sound like a spy," said Alice. "You're not secretly a spy, are you, Hope?"

"I am not."

"Though I doubt she'd tell us if she was," said William.

They chatted for a few more minutes, making small talk. Then Hope helped to clear the table.

CHAPTER 11

"It was nice seeing your family again," said Hope as they drove back to Edward's place.

"I'm glad you enjoyed it. Sorry about all of the questions."

"It was fine."

Hope looked out the window.

"What are you thinking?"

"Nothing important."

"Not everything has to be important."

Hope turned to face him.

"I was thinking how nice your family is, and how I wished mine was more like that."

"Yes, well, everyone was on their best behavior this evening. We're not always so nice."

"I doubt that," said Hope. "I've met them before."

"And your family's not so nice?" Edward had never met them.

"They're fine. Things just haven't been the same since my mother's cancer. And my brother and I aren't exactly close."

"He's older than you, yes?"

Hope nodded.

"By five years. He's an emergency room doctor."

"That must be quite stressful."

"It is."

Hope looked out the window again, and Edward let her be.

As soon as Edward put his key in the lock, Arfur began to bark.

"It's all right, Arfur," he called to the dog.

He opened the door and Arfur pounced, nearly knocking Edward over.

"You'd think we'd been gone a few days instead of a few hours," said Hope.

"I should take him for a walk," said Edward, putting the food his mother had given him on the counter. "You want to come?"

Hope thought about it. It was late, and she was feeling sluggish from the roast beef and Yorkshire pudding, but a short walk sounded good.

"Sure. Let's put all the food your mother gave us away first."

"She thinks I don't eat enough."

"Well, I think it's sweet. And she's a good cook."

"I'll give her that."

They put away the food and then headed out with Arfur, taking him for a walk around the neighborhood. When they got back, Hope said she should do some reading and headed up to her bedroom.

Hope had stayed up late reading a manuscript. As a result, she slept until nearly nine. As she crossed the hall to go to the bathroom, she heard Edward talking to someone on the phone. He was still on the phone when she emerged.

She took the manuscript downstairs to the kitchen. She would start her report after she'd made herself some coffee. She knew where everything was now and how to make her coffee just the way she liked it in Edward's coffee maker.

She was hunched over her laptop when Edward came downstairs.

"You're up," he said.

"I am," she replied.

"You sleep all right? I was worried Arfur would wake you. He was a bit noisy this morning."

"I didn't hear him."

"Good. What time did you get up?"

"A little before nine. I was up late reading."

"Good book?"

"Manuscript. And yes, I think so."

"So you're going to give it the green light?"

"I plan on recommending we publish it, yes."

"How many books does Herstory typically publish?"

"In a year?" Edward nodded. "It depends. Last year I think we published around three hundred titles. However, we received more than ten times that in submissions. We're a pretty small publisher, but we're growing and always looking for new authors."

"Wow. So you giving something the green light is a pretty big deal."

"I guess."

"You ever think of writing a book?"

"Once in a while. I'm happy being an editor." Hope looked around. "Where's Arfur?"

"Asleep in my room."

"You take him for his morning walk already?"

"I did. You good down here? Have everything you need?"

"I do. I just need to type this report."

"Okay. Well, I need to do some work myself. Give a shout or message me if you need anything."

Hope said that she would and returned to her laptop. She was working on her report when her phone began to ring. It was half past eleven in Devon, half past six in New York. Who could be calling her? She looked down at her phone. Of course, it was Ashley.

"Hi, Ashley. What's up?"

"I just had a chat with Oscar."

"He called you?"

"No, I called him."

"Why? I told you I…"

"I know what you told me, but Gemma is my responsibility, and I wanted to make sure she understood what the legal ramifications were should we not receive her latest manuscript."

"I did tell Oscar that Herstory would sue and ask for the advance back should Gemma not deliver. And he said we'd have the manuscript by the end of the month."

"I just wanted to hear it from him."

"Did he say anything about Gemma, like where she is? I stopped by her house again, but there was no sign of her."

"He said she was in London, taking care of a sick friend."

"I thought he said Gemma was the one who was sick."

"Apparently, she's better."

"Okay," said Hope. "So, do you want me to go to London?" Hope wouldn't mind a trip there.

"Actually… I want you to go to Gemma's."

"I told you, she's not there."

"Oscar gave me the impression that she would be back later today or else tomorrow when I told him I'd send you to London."

"He did?"

"He did."

"So you want me to go over there later or first thing tomorrow and see if she's returned?"

"Actually, I'd like you to stay there."

"I don't understand."

"I want you to pack your things and go stay at Gemma's."

Hope stared at her phone.

"You want me to stay there? I doubt Oscar will agree to that."

"He already has."

"He has?" Hope couldn't believe it. "What did you say to him?"

"Does it matter? We have a lot of money invested in Ms. Lovegood and this new book. And we've already given her and Oscar too much leeway. I want you there keeping an eye on things, making sure she's hard at work."

"Yes, but to live with them? That's a bit unusual." More than a bit. "Maybe I could find a place in Cupid's Bow and just stop by occasionally."

"I've already told Oscar you'd be staying there until the manuscript's finished."

Hope wanted to tell her boss that was insane, but she knew better. Once Ashley got an idea in her head, there was no dissuading her.

"And where am I supposed to sleep?" Hope suddenly had a vision of a nearly naked Oscar lying in bed, then shook her head to clear it.

"There's a guest room on the first floor."

"Oh. So will Oscar text me when Gemma's back?"

"Actually, I told him you'd be going there later today."

"But I'm in the middle of working on a report."

"A report?"

"On Millicent Brown's latest."

"Did you like it?"

"I did."

"Good. I was hoping you would."

"You read it?"

Ashley rarely read manuscripts anymore.

"No, but the pitch was quite promising. And her first book did quite well."

"She self-published that one, yes?"

"She did."

"Did you ask her agent why Ms. Brown wasn't self-publishing this one?"

"I did."

"And?"

"She said Millicent wanted to reach a broader audience. She's also expecting a baby and has a full-time job. So I'm guessing she doesn't have the time or energy to deal with production, distribution, and marketing this go round."

"Probably not. Well, I should have the report done by this afternoon."

"Good. Send it to me when it's ready. And let me know when you've settled in at Gemma's. I'm counting on you."

They ended the call and Hope laid her head on the table. The idea of staying at Gemma Lovegood's was insane. She wasn't a babysitter or writer sitter. What was she supposed to do, hang out in Gemma's office and watch her type?

She lifted her head and reached for her coffee, but it was cold. She thought about making more but was feeling too lazy. Besides, the caffeine would likely make her even more stressed.

She heard the sound of human and canine feet on the stairs.

"You okay?" said Edward.

"Not really," said Hope.

"Have you eaten?"

"Not yet. I've been working."

"Well, get yourself dressed. I'm taking you out for lunch."

"We have food here."

"Arfur and I could use some fresh air, and there's a café down the road that has good salads and sandwiches."

"What about Arfur?"

"We can take him with us. They allow dogs. Well, if you sit outside."

"Is it warm enough to sit outside?"

Hope looked out the picture window. It seemed nice enough out, but it could be chilly.

"We'll bundle up."

"Could I grab a quick shower?"

"Of course. Go shower and get dressed and we'll go."

Hope saved her report and closed her laptop. She'd finish her report after lunch. (She was in no hurry to go to Gemma's.) As she headed upstairs, she sent Oscar a text. "We need to talk. When are you available?" Then she went into the bathroom and started running the shower.

CHAPTER 12

"You're really going to stay there?" said Edward, as he and Hope ate their sandwiches. They were seated at a little table just outside the café, Arfur lying at Edward's feet.

"I don't have much of a choice."

"Of course you have a choice. You could have told her no."

"You don't know Ashley. And I've imposed on you enough."

"You haven't. Besides, I like having you around."

Hope placed a hand on top of his.

"And I've liked hanging out with you and Arfur. But you'd probably get sick of me if I stayed much longer."

"I doubt that."

Hope studied Edward's face. Did he still have feelings for her? *Those* kinds of feelings? She had enjoyed their time together, but her heart hadn't zinged when she saw him again, not like it had when they had dated 10 years ago. Though she found him attractive, and he made her smile.

"Well, it's not as though you're getting rid of me. I'll be just down the road in Cupid's Bow. That is, assuming Oscar and Gemma actually let me stay there."

"You think they won't?" He looked hopeful as he said it.

"I mean, it's a possibility. I don't know what exactly Ashley said to Oscar, but I can't imagine he's thrilled about us being roommates."

"Well, you let me know if he won't let you stay there."

"I will. And even if I do wind up staying there, we can still get together. It's not like I'll be a prisoner." Though it felt a bit that way to Hope.

"Good. I'll make sure to rescue you."

Hope smiled at that. She could just picture Edward in a suit of armor.

"What?" said Edward.

"I was just picturing you in a suit of armor, riding up to Gemma's place to rescue me from the evil Oscar."

Now it was Edward's turn to smile.

"Who knows? I might just do that. Medieval History was my specialty, after all."

They finished their sandwiches and walked back to Edward's.

Hope checked her phone as soon as they got back. Oscar hadn't replied to her text. A part of her was relieved, but another part was annoyed.

"What's up?" said Edward, seeing the expression on Hope's face.

"Oscar didn't get back to me. And I don't want to just show up there with my things."

"If he doesn't reply, does that mean you can stay here?"

"For now. Ashley was pretty insistent that I go there."

"You could always lie to her, tell her you're there when you'll really be here."

"And what happens when she asks me something about Gemma's place, or the manuscript, or Gemma?"

"You could make something up."

"I'm not that good a liar. If he hasn't gotten back to me by tonight, I should probably just go over there in the morning. You mind driving me over after breakfast?"

"I have a call at ten. But as long as I'm back by then… Are you going to bring your things?"

Hope thought about it.

"First, let's see if Oscar and Gemma are there. If they are, I'll come back and get my things."

"And if he and Gemma aren't?"

A part of Hope hoped that they weren't. But then Ashley would be furious.

"I don't know."

Oscar still hadn't replied to Hope's texts by the time she went to bed that evening, and she was starting to wonder if something had happened to him. Could he have been in an accident? Or was he just blowing her off? Hope suspected the latter. Though he must know that Ashley would not be happy if he didn't let Hope stay at Gemma's.

When there was still no word from him the next morning, Hope called him. But the call went immediately to voicemail. She left him a message saying she was on her way over. Then she went to get Edward.

"I need to go to Gemma's," she told him.

"Did Oscar get back to you?"

"No."

"Then why do you want to go over there?"

"I think he's ignoring me, and I refuse to be ignored."

"Can you give me a few?"

"That's fine. I should eat something and shower. We can go after."

"Okay," said Edward. "I just need to be back by ten."

It was a lovely spring morning, with flowers starting to bloom all around Cupid's Bow. Edward pulled up to Gemma's cottage, and Hope got out. There wasn't a car parked in front, but that didn't mean anything. Oscar's car could be in back.

She rang the bell, but no one answered. She waited a minute and then rang the bell again. Still nothing.

"Oscar?" she called.

Hope walked around to the back of the house. Oscar's car wasn't there. Was he out? And where was Gemma? She looked up to where his and Gemma's office was, but she couldn't see anything.

Hope went back to the front of the house and rang the doorbell again. Then she pounded on it.

"Oscar?" she called. "Are you in there?" No reply. She knocked again, louder this time. "Gemma? Anyone?" Still nothing. Where could they be?

"Nobody home?" said Edward. He had gotten out of the Mini and was standing a few feet away.

"It would appear so."

"Did you tell him you were coming over?"

"I did, just before we left."

"You think he did a runner? Maybe Ashley scared him off."

Hope made a face. It was possible. She took out her phone and tried calling him—and was surprised when he picked up this time.

"Where are you?" she said. "I've been trying to reach you!"

"I'm in London. Did you not get my email?"

"No. Did you not get my texts or messages?"

"I misplaced my phone and just found it." *A likely story,* thought Hope. "Check your spam folder."

"What are you doing in London? I thought Gemma was coming back here. Didn't Ashley tell you I was to stay at Gemma's?"

"She did, but something came up."

"Is it Gemma? Is she all right? Ashley said she was in London, looking after a sick friend."

"She's fine. She just decided to stay in London a bit longer."

"Why?"

"She's to be the guest of honor at the Historical

Romance Society Ball here this weekend."

"Excuse me?" said Hope. Was Oscar pulling her leg? Hope had never heard of the Historical Romance Society. "There's really such a thing as the Historical Romance Society?"

"There is. I'm surprised you don't know about it."

"And they're throwing a ball?"

"They are."

"And Gemma is to be the guest of honor? I thought she didn't do public appearances."

"Special case. A bit of a one-night-only deal for a friend. It's for a good cause."

"Why didn't you tell me about this before?"

"It slipped my mind."

Hope sincerely doubted that.

"How can I get a ticket?"

"You can't. It's sold out."

"Will you be there?"

"Of course."

"So take me as your plus one."

"I'm afraid I can't."

"Can't or won't?"

Oscar didn't reply.

"Surely, you can scrape up a ticket for me? After all, I'm Gemma's editor."

"Ms. Wallingford is her editor. And I sent her an invitation. She didn't respond."

"When did you send her this invitation?" Ashley hadn't said anything about a ball in London to Hope. Hope would have remembered. She had a feeling Oscar was lying to her.

Oscar didn't say anything.

"Well, as Ashley is on maternity leave, and I am acting editor, I should get a ticket."

"You can try. But I doubt you'll able to get one."

"You won't help me?"

Hope heard him sigh.

"I'll see what I can do."

"Thank you. So you're going to be in London through the weekend?"

"That is the plan."

"Have you spoken with Gemma, told her everything?"

"We've spoken."

"And? Is she working on the manuscript?"

"Yes. Look, I need to go."

"Fine. Will you call or text me if you manage to get me a ticket?"

"I will, but don't get your hopes up. Good day, Ms. Halladay."

Hope was about to say something, but Oscar had already ended the call.

"Everything okay?" said Edward.

"No," said Hope.

"What's up?"

"Oscar is in London, as is Gemma. She's apparently to be the guest of honor at some ball this weekend."

"What ball?"

"Some ball being given by some organization called the Historical Romance Society, which I've never heard of."

"Oh."

Hope looked at him.

"What?" She could tell something was up.

"I actually have tickets."

"You do?" Hope was staring at him.

"Lucy's a member. We bought tickets a while ago for ourselves and some friends. The ball raises money for some shelter that supports abused women and children."

"Lucy didn't keep the tickets?"

Edward looked a bit embarrassed.

"She wanted to, but I insisted we split them as I paid for them."

"Do you still have the tickets?"

"Probably. I don't remember throwing them out."

"Let's go home and look for them!"

"Why?"

"So we can go to the ball, of course!" She went over to Edward and kissed him on the cheek. He blushed.

"What was that for?"

"For not throwing away the tickets and for being such a good friend."

"You seriously want to go?"

"Of course I want to go! Gemma will be there!" She paused. "Oh. Lucy will be there too, yes?"

"Probably."

"Okay. I totally understand if you don't want to go, but I should."

Edward stood up straight.

"I shall be delighted to escort you to the Historical Romance Society Ball, Ms. Halladay. Just one thing."

"Yes?"

"It's a costume ball."

"So?"

"We'll need to rent costumes."

"Fine. We'll rent costumes. Is there a place around here where we can rent Victorian formalwear?"

"Not that I know of."

"What about London? I'm sure there's someplace there."

"I'm sure, but it's a bit last minute. Everything's probably been rented already."

"How big is this ball? I'm sure we can find someplace with a costume or two."

"Okay," he said and looked down at his watch. "We should head back. I have a call."

They walked to Edward's car and got in.

"I'll start looking for costume shops as soon as we get back," said Hope as they drove back to Edward's place.

"And I'll call Raj."

"Raj?"

"You remember Raj from uni."

"That Raj?"

"One and the same."

"You two are still friends?"

"We are."

"What's he up to? I haven't thought about Raj in years. Does he live in London?"

"He does. Though he travels a lot. He works in the City and has a place in Shoreditch. I'll shoot him a text and see if we can crash there."

"That would be amazing. Though I could ask Ashley if Herstory would pay for a hotel for a couple of nights."

"Let me reach out to Raj first."

They parked in front of Edward's building and went in, Arfur nearly knocking Edward over. Edward petted him and then the two of them went upstairs as Hope headed to her laptop.

She opened up her browser and did a search for costume shops in London.

CHAPTER 13

There were a half-dozen or so costume shops in London. Hope found one called Lords and Ladies Fancy Dress Hire that looked promising. They had dozens of period outfits, including Victorian-style ball gowns. And Hope saw several she liked. But she had no idea if they were available or how much they cost. Or if they came in her size, Hope being much taller, at five-foot-nine, than the average Victorian woman.

The website said to call or email for more information. So Hope picked up her phone and called them.

"Lords and Ladies Fancy Dress Hire," said a female voice.

"Good morning," said Hope. "I'm hoping you can help me. I'm looking for a gown to wear to the Historical Romance Society Ball this weekend. Something Victorian. And my friend Edward also needs an outfit."

"I'm afraid we have very little left," said the woman. "Most of our Victorian-style gowns were rented weeks ago."

Hope's face fell.

"There must be something I could wear. I'll take anything."

"Can you come by the shop later?"

"I'm afraid I can't. I'm in Devon right now, and I won't get to London until later this week."

"Oh dear."

"Please. I have to go to the ball. I'm an editor and one of

my authors is the guest of honor. Maybe you've heard of her, Gemma Lovegood?"

Hope hated to name-drop, but she was desperate.

"Your Gemma Lovegood's editor? Margaret and I simply adore her. Tell you what, send me your measurements and those of your friend, and I'll see what I can do."

"Thank you," said Hope. "I'll send them to you later this morning. What's your email? Oh, and I didn't catch your name."

"It's Eleanor. And you are?"

"Hope, Hope Halladay."

"Nice to meet you, Hope."

"Same, Eleanor. And thank you for helping us out."

"I haven't helped you yet. As I said, we're quite low on stock right now. But send me your measurements, and I'll see what I can do. You say you'll be here at the end of the week?"

"Yes. Either Thursday or Friday." Though she hadn't discussed with Edward when they would go.

"Very good. Send me an email as soon as you know so we can schedule an appointment for a fitting. That is, assuming we find something."

"I'll do that. And thank you again."

Hope put her phone down and went to look for a tape measure. Where would Edward keep one? She looked for a toolbox but couldn't find one. She went upstairs to Edward's room. She could hear that he was on the phone. She thought about knocking but sent him a text instead. He replied a minute later. As far as he knew, he didn't own a tape measure.

Hope made a face. Then she started typing.

"Is there a hardware store in town?"

"No," he replied. "I'll need to take you there."

Hope frowned and then typed *OK*.

She went back downstairs to do some work. Though she

wasn't very productive. She was too antsy.

Half an hour later, Arfur came bounding down the stairs, Edward behind him.

"You off your call?" Hope asked him. Though, obviously, he was.

"Yes, and I have good news. I found the tickets!"

"Hurrah! Where were they?"

"In a box. Why do you need a tape measure?"

"To take our measurements. I found a costume shop in London that might have something. However, since we won't be in London until later this week, and they don't have much left, the woman I spoke with suggested I send her our measurements."

"Got it."

"So, where does one go to get a tape measure around here?"

"There's a DIY shop not far from here."

"Perfect. Let's go. That is if you're free."

"I have time."

On the way, Edward reported that Raj had gotten back to him, and he would be delighted to host them for a few days.

"When can we leave?"

"I told Raj we'd be there Thursday. Is that all right?"

"That's fine." Though Hope wouldn't have minded going sooner.

"What about your work?"

"I can do it anywhere."

Hope took Edward's measurements as soon as they got back. Then she took her own. That done, she sent the information to Eleanor, including pictures of her and Edward. Couldn't hurt. Then she went back to the manuscript she'd been reading.

A little after one, Edward came down the stairs.

"Have you eaten?" he asked Hope.

"Not yet," she replied.

"Shall we go grab a bite?"

"We have food here."

"Right." He didn't seem excited.

"Come on," said Hope. "I'll fix us something. We have all of that food from your mother."

Edward begrudgingly agreed to have lunch at home, and Hope went to the refrigerator. She took out the container of stew his mother had given them and went to heat it up. As they ate, Hope asked Edward about work. When they were done, they took Arfur for a walk.

There was a message from Ashley waiting for Hope when she got back, asking if she was at Gemma's. Hope replied that Gemma was in London and that she, Hope, would be going there that weekend to see her. Then she put her phone on silent, turned it over, and returned to her manuscript.

Hope had started to worry when she hadn't heard back from Eleanor by dinnertime. Had she not received Hope's email? Or maybe they didn't have any costumes left in her size. Edward said to give it until the morning and then call the shop.

That night, Hope dreamed she was at a masked ball. The ballroom was full of people, some dancing, others talking. And Hope had felt shy and nervous, standing off to the side watching everyone. Then a tall, handsome stranger with a mane of dark brown hair had asked her to dance. They had danced a waltz, and her whole body had thrummed as the stranger's hand pressed against her waist and his other held her hand.

They continued to dance, the stranger holding her close.

Then Hope said that she needed some air. He led her outside onto a balcony. The air was cool, whereas the ballroom had been quite warm. Hope closed her eyes and breathed in.

She sensed the handsome stranger looking at her. And when she opened her eyes, she saw that he was. And that look… It made her whole body tingle.

"You're very beautiful," he said.

Hope gazed up at his face and had a sudden desire to kiss him. It seemed the stranger had the same idea as his face started to lower to hers. And then…

Hope was awakened by the sound of Arfur barking. She silently cursed and looked at the time. It was a little after seven. She tried to go back to sleep but was unable to. So she went downstairs to make herself coffee. Edward was there drinking a mug of tea.

"Did Arfur wake you?" he asked. "I told him to be quiet but…"

"It's all right," she said.

As she waited for the coffee to brew, she asked Edward what he was up to today.

It was half past ten and still no word from Eleanor. Hope was about to pick up her phone and call the shop when she received an email notification. Eleanor had finally gotten back to her. As luck would have it, a woman about Hope's size had sent an email canceling her order shortly after Hope had called. Eleanor had just needed to confirm the cancellation and make sure that there wasn't a waitlist for the gown. The good news was, if Hope wanted the gown, it was hers.

Eleanor had included a photo of the dress. It was a rich burgundy, low cut, with cap sleeves, a fitted bodice, and a bustle with a train. It was beautiful and came with a matching mask.

Hope wondered who had ordered the dress and why she had canceled.

Eleanor had also included a costume for Edward, basically the Victorian version of a tux. Hope forwarded the email to him and asked him if the outfit was acceptable. He wrote her back a few minutes later saying that it was.

Hope immediately phoned the shop and asked to speak with Eleanor.

"We'll take them!" Hope told her.

Eleanor chuckled.

"I just hope they fit. You're lucky that customer canceled. We only have one other dress that might do, but it's not as nice as that one. And the burgundy is just like the one Lady Emily wore in *Balls Aren't Just for Men*," she said, conspiratorially.

Hope had forgotten. She would need to reread, or at least skim, Gemma Lovegood's books before they attended the ball.

"Right," she said. "Could I see the other one anyway? What color is it?"

"Blue."

"I like blue. So how can I reserve them? Can I give you a deposit? How much for each dress?"

Hope was a bit stunned when Eleanor told her how much the dresses and menswear cost to rent. But she gave Eleanor her credit card information. Hopefully, Herstory would reimburse her.

Thursday morning Edward took Arfur to Poppy's place. Then they drove to Exeter to catch the train to London.

Hope read one of her manuscripts on the train ride while Edward worked on a whitepaper. A few hours later, they arrived in London. Edward suggested they grab a bite to eat before heading to Lords and Ladies.

As soon as they were done with lunch, they headed to the costume shop. Eleanor greeted them and led them to the fitting rooms, where she had placed their costumes. Hope looked at the two dresses hanging on opposite sides of the fitting room. They were both beautiful, though her eyes immediately went to the burgundy gown.

She took a quick look into Edward's fitting room, which contained two Victorian-style tuxedos.

"Let me know if you need any help," Eleanor said to them.

"I'm good," said Edward.

Eleanor turned to Hope.

"The dresses have zippers, but if you need help, just call. Oh, and I left a corset for you."

"Thank you," said Hope. She had never worn a corset before.

She went into the fitting room and closed the curtain. Then she removed her clothes, leaving on her underwear. She donned the corset, which required a bit of work, and then stepped into the blue dress. She tried to zipper it but was having trouble. She poked her head through the curtain and called to Eleanor. Eleanor immediately came over and zipped her up.

Hope turned and looked at herself in the three-way mirror. Then she turned to Eleanor.

"What do you think?"

"It's very nice," Eleanor replied.

"But?" said Hope. She had a feeling Eleanor didn't love it.

"It's just that it was made for someone…"

"Younger?"

"Yes. Though it looks quite nice on you."

Hope studied herself in the mirror again. She was about to go change when Edward stepped out of his fitting room.

"What do you think?" he said.

"Very dashing," said Hope.

Edward turned from side to side.

"You don't think it too tight? It feels a bit snug."

"That was the style," said Eleanor. "But if it feels too tight, try on the other suit."

Edward continued to look at himself in the mirror. Then he turned and looked at Hope.

"Is that what you plan on wearing?"

"I haven't decided. I still need to try on the burgundy gown. What do you think?"

"It's okay but… It seems a bit frilly."

"I agree," said Hope. "I think it was intended for someone younger than me. I'll go try on the other gown."

She turned to Eleanor and asked if she would unzip her. That done, Hope changed into the burgundy dress, Eleanor again zipping her up.

"What do you think?" Hope asked as she stood outside the fitting room.

"It's like it was made for you," said Eleanor.

Edward agreed.

"Definitely that one," he said.

"You don't think it's too lowcut?"

"Not at all," said Eleanor. "That was the style. You look just like Lady Emily."

Hope studied herself in the three-way mirror, piling her hair on top of her head. She did look a bit like Lady Emily, or how she imagined Lady Emily had looked. She wondered if she would meet Lord Dashingly, the Earl of Winslow, at the ball. He was the alleged rake who had captured Lady Emily's heart. Though she didn't know who he was when she had danced with him.

"What are you thinking?" asked Edward.

"Hm?" said Hope.

"I asked what you were thinking."

"I was imagining being at the ball," she replied. "So this one?"

"Yes," said Edward and Eleanor in unison. Hope smiled. "This one it is then."

Hope and Edward went to change back into their clothes. Then they handed their costumes to Eleanor, who went to wrap them in tissue paper. Edward offered to pay, but Hope insisted, saying Herstory would reimburse her. After all, the only reason they were going to the ball was because of Gemma. Though Hope was secretly, or not so secretly, thrilled to be going.

They thanked Eleanor for her help and then Edward arranged for a car to pick them up. No way were they riding the Tube with such precious cargo.

Raj had texted Edward the code for his apartment and informed the doorman that they'd be staying there for a few days. He would be leaving for Hong Kong straight from work that evening, but he hoped to see Edward next time he was in town.

"Just wait until you see his flat," Edward told Hope.

"Nice?" said Hope.

"Nice doesn't begin to describe it."

CHAPTER 14

"Wow. You weren't kidding," said Hope as they stepped inside Raj's apartment. "This place is amazing. And you say he's barely here?"

"I know, right?

Hope walked around. You could see all of London from the floor-to-ceiling windows. Or it felt that way.

"If I had a place like this, I'd never leave."

"Let me know which bedroom you want."

"How many are there?"

"Two."

"Raj is okay with one of us sleeping in his bed? I can sleep on the sofa. It looks plenty big."

"No one's sleeping on the sofa. Go take a look at the bedrooms and let me know which one you want."

"If you insist."

"I do."

Hope left her things on the sectional that took up most of the living area and went to explore the rest of the apartment.

"I'll take the guest bedroom," she said upon her return.

"You sure?"

"Positive. I feel weird sleeping in his bed."

"Suit yourself. I have no qualms about it. Did you see his bed? It's massive! A family of four could fit in it with room to spare."

Hope immediately thought of the family bed in *Charlie and the Chocolate Factory*.

"Have you ever slept in it?"

"Once. We had all had a bit too much to drink and wanted to see how many of us could fit in it."

"How many of you are we talking about?"

"There were four of us. And we could have fit two more."

Hope looked over at the sectional.

"We should hang up our costumes. We wouldn't want them to get wrinkled."

"And after that?"

"I should probably do some work. What about you?"

"I suppose. What about dinner? I should probably make us a reservation somewhere."

"Where were you thinking?"

"How do you feel about Indian food these days?"

"I love it. Is there a good Indian place near here?"

"There is."

"And we need to make a reservation?"

Most of the Indian places Hope had gone to when she lived in London were quite casual. Though that was years ago.

"This place is a bit upscale."

"We don't have to go someplace fancy."

"It's not fancy, just popular. Shall I make us a reservation for eight? That is, assuming they have a table."

"Eight is fine."

Edward took out his phone.

"All set," he said a few seconds later. "Are you sure you don't want to take a walk and explore the neighborhood?"

"I should do some work. Maybe later?"

"Later it is. I suppose I should do some work too."

"Shall we reconvene at five?" Hope suggested.

"Sounds good," said Edward.

"Nice place," said Hope, looking around the Indian restaurant.

"Raj says they serve the best Indian food in Shoreditch."

They had gone for a long walk earlier, and Hope was starving. She looked down at the menu. Everything sounded good. A few minutes later, a server came over to take their drink order. Edward ordered an Indian beer, and Hope ordered a tamarind margarita.

"So, aside from work, is there anything you'd like to do while we're in London?" Edward asked Hope.

"Too many things. But as you said, I do need to do a bit of work while I'm here."

"You could always play hooky. It is the weekend."

"Not quite. But I suppose I could squeeze in some sightseeing," she said with a smile.

Edward smiled back at her.

"So, where would you like to go?"

"Well, I'd love to see the new exhibit at the Tate Modern… and go on the London Eye."

"Done and done. What else?"

"Hm… I'll take a look at Time Out and see what's on."

"Do that and let me know what you want to do."

"You know, I'm perfectly capable of entertaining myself. You don't have to play chaperone."

"I know I don't have to. But it would be my pleasure to show you around London. The city has changed a lot since you were last here."

"I know. I just thought that maybe you'd like to see some of your friends. Did you tell them you'd be here?"

"Actually…"

Just then the waiter came over to deliver their drinks.

The table was covered with several half-eaten plates of food.

"I don't think I could eat another bite," said Hope, leaning back. "Do you think they have to-go boxes?"

"Only one way to find out," said Edward.

He signaled to their waiter and asked him if he could package up the rest of their meal.

"That was delicious," said Hope as the waiter cleared away their dishes. "I haven't had goat in ages. And I'm glad we ordered the peshwari naan."

"You have room for dessert?"

"Do you?" Hope couldn't understand how Edward wasn't full.

"I always have room for dessert."

"I'm too full. But you go ahead."

"You sure?"

"Positive."

"On second thought, I'll just get the check."

"You sure?"

"Positive."

The waiter returned with their leftover food placed in little boxes and Edward asked him for the check. Hope tried to pay, but Edward refused. Dinner was on him.

As they walked back to the apartment, Hope looked up at the sky.

"You can't really see the stars here, not like in Devon."

"I know," said Edward. "That's one of the things I like about living there."

"So you don't miss living in London?"

"Honestly?"

Hope nodded.

"A little. I miss being able to pop into a museum—and the variety of restaurants. But I'm happier in Devon."

"Because you can see the stars at night?"

Edward smiled.

"That and I like being able to walk to the beach, knowing my neighbors, and having family nearby. But sometimes…"

"Yes?" said Hope.

"It feels too quiet."

"You could always invite friends down."

"I have. But everyone's so busy. What about you?"

"What about me?"

"Are you happy in New York? Do you ever wonder what would have happened if you had stayed here?"

He was looking at her so intently.

"I've thought about it, but I like living in New York. My friends are there. And I like my job."

"Are you seeing anyone?"

This was the first time Edward had asked her that. And Hope was surprised it had taken him this long.

"Not right now. My last two relationships didn't end so well. So I decided to swear off men for a while and focus on work."

Edward didn't say anything.

They had arrived back at Raj's and took the elevator upstairs.

"Thank you again for dinner."

"You're welcome," said Edward.

"I should call Dani, check in with her. I told her I'd call when I got to London."

"Okay."

Hope paused.

"Are you all right?" Edward seemed a bit sad or preoccupied. She wondered if it was being back in London. Or maybe he missed Lucy more than he wanted to admit.

"I'm fine."

"Okay. Just checking. I'll see you in the morning."

"See you in the morning. And Hope?"

She stopped and waited for him to go on.

"Sweet dreams."

Hope smiled at him.

"Same to you," she said. Then she headed to the guest room.

She pulled out her phone and sent a text to Dani.

"Yo," she typed. "You available?"

A few seconds later, Dani replied.

"What's up?"

"I made it to London. Just got back from dinner. You want to talk?"

A few seconds later, Hope's phone rang.

CHAPTER 15

"So you promise you won't make fun of me?" Hope asked Edward over coffee—made in Raj's fancy espresso machine—the next morning.

"I promise," said Edward. "What did you decide?"

"You'll think it horribly touristy."

"As long as we don't have to go to Madame Tussauds, I'm game."

"No Madame Tussauds, but I would like to visit some museums."

"Which ones?"

"The Tate, as I mentioned. And the V and A. There are several exhibits there I want to see. And I'd like to visit the National Gallery too."

"Okay."

"You don't have to go with me. I'm fine going on my own."

"I don't mind. But going to museums isn't what I'd consider horribly touristy. Where else did you want to go?"

"I'd really like to go on the London Eye. And go see the Houses of Parliament, and Big Ben, and Westminster Abbey. And Buckingham Palace."

"What, no Tower of London?"

"If there's time."

He smiled.

"I told you, it's horribly touristy," said Hope. "But I

don't know when I'll be here again, and I want to see everything."

"In three days."

"You can pack a lot into three days."

"Don't forget about the ball."

"I haven't. But that's at night."

"And work?"

"I'll work it in."

"Sounds like you have it all planned."

"As you noted, we only have three days."

"We could stay longer."

"What about Raj?"

"I'm sure he wouldn't mind."

Hope wasn't so sure about that.

"What about Oscar?"

"What about him?" said Hope.

"Did you tell him you're here?"

"Not yet."

"Does he know you'll be at the ball?"

"No, and I don't plan on telling him. He never got back to me about a ticket. And I don't want him and Gemma to disappear on me."

"I doubt Gemma will disappear when she's to be the guest of honor."

"True. Still, why take chances?"

"So, when do you want to head out?"

"You're coming with me?"

"I was planning on it. Unless you don't want me to."

"No, I'm happy to have you tag along. That is, if you won't be bored."

"I never get bored."

Hope wasn't sure she believed that.

"How's Arfur?" she asked. "You talk to Poppy?"

"We texted last night. He's fine."

"She doesn't mind watching him?"

"She loves Arfur. Sometimes I think she hopes I'll forget about him and just leave him there."

"She could get her own dog."

"She says she doesn't want the responsibility. She's happy sharing Arfur."

"She seeing anyone?"

"Why do you ask?"

"Just curious."

"I don't know."

"You never asked?"

"It's none of my business."

"You ever think about asking her out?"

"Not really. I told you, I'm taking a break from dating."

"I think she likes you."

"She likes Arfur."

"Uh-huh."

"Why all the interest in Poppy?"

"No reason."

"Mm. You're trying to fix me up, aren't you?"

"It's just that you seem so compatible."

"You deduced this after seeing us together for all of five minutes?"

"More than that. Anyway, I won't bring it up again as it clearly makes you uncomfortable."

"It doesn't make me uncomfortable. Poppy's a nice girl, but I told you, I'm not interested in dating anyone right now."

"Okay," said Hope. "Why don't we both get a little work done before we go sightseeing?"

An hour later, Hope closed her laptop and went to look for Edward.

"Edward?" she called, knocking on his door.

No reply. She knocked and called his name again. Still no

reply. She opened the door a crack. Edward was on his computer, earbuds in his ears. She walked over and tapped him on the shoulder. He jumped.

"Sorry," said Hope.

Edward removed his earbuds and told her it was okay.

"You still want to go sightseeing with me?" she asked him.

"I do. Just give me a minute."

"Take five," said Hope. "I'll be in the living room."

Five minutes later, Edward appeared.

"You good?" he asked Hope.

"I am!" she replied.

"So, where do you want to go first?"

"I was thinking the Tate. Then we could have lunch someplace. Then after lunch, we could go on the London Eye and then stroll past Big Ben and Westminster Abbey and visit King Charles and Camilla."

"Visit King Charles and Camilla, eh? Are they expecting you?"

"No, but I'm sure they'd be happy to see us," said Hope. "I hear Camilla's a big fan of Gemma Lovegood's."

"That wouldn't surprise me. You should probably purchase tickets for the Eye before we leave."

"Good point." Hope took out her phone and typed *London Eye tickets* into the search engine. "What time do you think?"

"Up to you. You said after lunch."

"I'm getting us fast-track tickets for two-thirty. That should give us enough time. That work for you?"

"Fine by me."

Hope tapped away.

"Done! All set. Okay, let's go."

They spent over an hour at the Tate Modern and then found a café nearby to have lunch. Then they walked along the

Thames to the London Eye. It was a mostly clear day, and they could see all the way to Buckingham Palace and the Financial District from the large Ferris wheel, as well as Big Ben, Westminster Abbey, and the Houses of Parliament.

Hope had felt a touch of vertigo as their carriage swayed gently back and forth at the top of the wheel and had reached out and grabbed Edward's hand. He had smiled and had given her hand a reassuring squeeze. Then they slowly started to descend.

"Where to now?" he asked her when they had disembarked.

"Let's walk across Westminster Bridge and head to Buckingham Palace. What time do you think they do the changing of the guard?"

"You don't know?"

"I didn't check." Hope whipped out her phone. "Hm. It says the changing of the guard takes place at eleven. And you should get there early if you want a good view." She frowned.

"We could go tomorrow," said Edward.

"Do they do it every day?" She went back to her phone to check. "Hm, it says the next one is Sunday."

"We could always go before we leave."

"True. Okay, let's do that."

"So, what do you want to do now?"

They were standing in front of Big Ben.

"The National Gallery isn't far. You okay going to another museum? And there's the National Portrait Gallery."

"Wherever you want to go," said Edward.

They arrived back at Raj's a little after five. Hope was tired from all of the walking and sightseeing.

"So, where shall we dine tonight?" Edward asked her.

"You pick. Just nothing fancy or too far. I'm exhausted."

"What are you in the mood for?"

"What's good around here?"

"There's a good Vietnamese place and a couple of good Italians. I don't think either of them are fancy."

"Let's do Vietnamese. That is if that's all right with you."

"Vietnamese it is. I'll make us a reservation. What time?"

"How about seven-thirty?"

Edward had his phone out.

"Seven-thirty it is."

"Great," said Hope. "I'm going to lie down for a bit. Would you knock on my door at seven, make sure I'm awake?"

"Will do."

CHAPTER 16

It was the evening of the Historical Romance Society Ball. Earlier that day, Hope and Edward had gone to the Victoria and Albert Museum where there had been an exhibit on 200 years of formal wear. While men's fashions hadn't changed that much, at least to Hope's eyes, women's evening wear had changed dramatically.

As she wandered through the exhibit, Hope wondered what the other guests at the ball would be wearing. Would everyone come in period costumes? Per the invitation, guests were to dress as a character from their favorite Regency or Victorian-era romance, basically the entire 1800s. But she guessed that some of them would show up in more modern attire that referenced clothes from the Regency or Victorian period. Well, she would soon find out.

Thankfully, the corset she had wound up purchasing from Lords and Ladies was of recent vintage and much easier to get into than an original one. Though as she breathed in to fasten it, she wondered how her ancestors could have functioned with their rib cages and waists bound so tightly. Then again, many women still wore restrictive corset-like garments, now referred to as shapewear, to give them the appearance of a slimmer waist. So much for women's liberation.

Hope eyed her dress before stepping into it. It really was lovely. Get rid of the bustle and the train and she could see someone wearing it to a modern gala.

She stepped into the crinoline underskirt first. Then she carefully pulled on the dress, so as not to disturb her hair and makeup, which she had spent over an hour doing. Eleanor had helped zipper the dress at the shop, but Hope felt that if she could angle her arms just so, she could do it herself.

She had gotten the zipper most of the way there but gave up near the top and went to Edward's room for help.

"Yes?" he said, poking his head out the door in response to Hope's knock.

"Can you help me zip up my dress?"

He came out and finished zipping it, fastening the hook and eye at the top.

"There," he said, stepping back. "All set."

"Thank you." Hope turned around and frowned. "Why aren't you dressed?"

"I was about to when you knocked."

"But we're to leave soon."

"It won't take me long. I'll be ready in ten minutes tops."

How nice for him, thought Hope.

Ten minutes later, Edward announced he was ready.

"Shall we?" he said, offering his arm to Hope.

"We shall," said Hope, taking it.

"You look lovely, by the way," said Edward as they drove to the ball. He had insisted they take a car service, and Hope hadn't objected. Though it might have been amusing to have taken the Tube there.

The ball was being held at an event space in Mayfair, one of the posher neighborhoods in London. The building dated back to the late 1700s. But it had been updated and converted into a townhome for an aristocratic family a hundred years later. The family sold the building after the

Second World War, and it had since become a popular place to hold weddings and events.

Hope knew all of this because she had looked up the place.

As they approached the venue, Hope saw a line of cars waiting to drop off guests. She wondered if Gemma Lovegood was in one of the vehicles. Not that Hope would be able to tell, having never laid eyes on the famously shy author.

Finally, it was their turn. They thanked their driver as he pulled up in front of the building and got out, Edward helping Hope. They stopped on the sidewalk to admire the building and put on their masks. Then they headed inside.

There were two footmen in period uniforms stationed just inside the imposing front door checking bags. And just beyond them was the check-in table. Edward went over to the three women seated there and gave them his name.

"Has Ms. Lovegood arrived?" Hope asked the women.

"Not yet, but we are expecting her any minute," replied one of the women, who was dressed in a forest green gown.

"Thank you," said Hope. Then they stepped aside.

Hope eyed the walls and ceilings. They were covered with ornamental plaster work, reminding Hope of the grand mansions and homes you would see on a PBS or BBC period drama. No doubt that was why the Historical Romance Society had chosen this place to host the ball.

To the left and right were reception rooms, all of them filled with people dressed in period costumes, their faces covered by masks, some of the masks quite elaborate. Hope saw several women who resembled Lady Eugenia and Lady Emily, the leading ladies in Gemma Lovegood's two books. Though, to be honest, the women could have been characters from any number of historical romances. As for the men, there were several who reminded her of Captain Ripley and Lord Dashingly.

As she gazed at the men, she wondered if Oscar was there. She could see him dressed as Captain Ripley or Lord Dashingly. Both men were tall with wavy brown hair and hazel eyes, like Oscar. Hope wondered if Gemma had based them on him.

"Shall we get something to drink?" asked Edward.

Hope nodded and followed him to a bar that had been set up at the end of the hallway, near doors that led to a courtyard.

"Do you think they have regular drinks or are they only serving drinks that would have been served in the 1800s?" she asked him as they approached the bar.

"Good question," said Edward.

"What can I get for you, sir?" said the bartender when it was their turn. He was dressed in a period costume but wasn't sporting a mask.

"What do you have?" asked Edward.

"We have red and white wine as well as sparkling wine and punch."

"Anything nonalcoholic?" asked Hope.

"There's lemonade."

"What's your fancy, milady?" Edward asked Hope.

"I'll have a sparkling wine, please."

Hope had thought about getting lemonade but decided to throw caution to the wind.

"Make that two," said Edward.

"You're not going to try the punch?" asked Hope.

"Maybe later."

The bartender handed them their drinks, and they moved away.

"A toast," said Edward, holding up his glass.

"To what?" said Hope.

"To a memorable evening."

They clinked glasses and drank.

"I'd love to take a look around the rest of the mansion,"

said Hope. "I saw pictures of it online, but…"

"It's not the same."

"No, it isn't."

Edward offered Hope his arm, and they explored the rooms on the first floor.

"How many people are here, do you think?" Hope asked him.

"I don't know," he replied. "Maybe a couple hundred?"

Having explored the various reception rooms, they made their way up a grand marble stairway.

"This must be where dinner and dancing will be held," said Hope, looking into what looked like a ballroom. It was filled with beautifully decorated tables and reminded Hope of some wedding venues she had been to.

"And that must be where the orchestra will play," said Edward, looking over at a raised platform. "Though orchestra is probably the wrong word. I doubt you could fit more than a quartet on that stage."

"They're not expecting us to dance like they did back then, are they?" said Hope.

"Back then?"

"You know what I mean."

"I'll have you know that the most popular dances during the Victorian era were the waltz, which you must know, and the galop and polka."

"The galop? Like what horses do?"

Edward smiled.

"Exactly."

"You think people here know how to galop?"

"You might be surprised."

"Do you know how to?"

"Lucy dragged me to a dance class the Society sponsored right before we broke up."

"And you learned how to galop?"

"It's not actually like what horses do."

"So you did learn!"

"I wouldn't say *learn*. I saw how it was done."

"What about the other dances?"

"My mother made me and Alice take dance lessons when we were little."

"Did they teach you to waltz and do the polka?"

"They did."

"I'm impressed!"

"Not like I remember."

"I only know how to waltz."

"There you go. However, I doubt they're expecting people to dance like they used to back then. This isn't *Bridgerton*."

Though looking around, that's exactly what Hope thought of.

"Let's go back downstairs," she said.

They descended the stairs, and Hope noticed that there were a lot more people. Suddenly, she felt a bit overwhelmed.

"Are you okay?" asked Edward.

"I could use some air."

"Let's go to the courtyard," he suggested.

They headed to the courtyard. It was warm for April though still a bit chilly. But the cool air felt good. Hope was gazing at the fountain in the center of the courtyard when she felt Edward squeeze her arm. She turned and looked at him.

"What is it?"

Then she saw what, or rather who, Edward was looking at. Lucy. Despite the mask, Hope recognized her from Edward's Instagram feed. Lucy was wearing a low-cut blue satin dress that showed off her curves, her blonde hair piled on top of her head. She was with a man Hope would describe as tall, dark, and handsome, with dark brown hair. Lucy was touching the man's arm and whispering in his ear.

"Are you all right?" Hope asked Edward.

"Perfectly fine," he replied. But Hope could tell he was not.

"You want to go back inside?"

"No." He then led Hope over to Lucy and her date.

"Edward!" said his ex upon seeing him. "I'm surprised to see you here."

"Why? You know I'm a fan of Gemma Lovegood's. And I did buy the tickets."

"Yes, but I didn't expect you to use them." Lucy turned and looked at Hope, as though just noticing her. "And who is this?"

"I'm Hope," said Hope, holding out her right hand.

Lucy looked down at it. Then she looked up at Edward.

"An American. How sweet."

Hope felt an instant dislike for Edward's ex.

"Where did you find her, Edward?"

"We dated at uni."

"Oh, *that* Hope."

Lucy took a more interested look at Hope.

"And you came all this way to go to the ball?"

"I was here for work, and Edward invited me. Wasn't that sweet?" She squeezed his hand and looked lovingly at him, which clearly irritated Lucy. "Who's your friend?"

"This is Gabriel," said Lucy, pronouncing it the French way.

"Are you French?" Hope asked him.

"*Oui*," said Gabriel.

"Where in France are you from?"

"*Bretagne*. Saint-Malo."

"I've always wanted to go there," said Hope. "I hear it's very beautiful."

"It is."

"Gabriel's family has lived there for generations," said Lucy.

"And what brings you to London?" Hope asked him.

"Work."

Gabriel didn't appear to be much of a talker. Or maybe his English wasn't very good.

"Gabriel works for LVMH, the big luxury brand," explained Lucy.

"What do you do for them?"

"He's in finance," said Lucy.

"And how did you two meet?"

Hope didn't know why she was asking so many questions.

"At a party. We saw each other from across the room and…" Lucy gazed up at Gabriel. "We just knew." She gazed up at Gabriel for several more seconds, then she turned to Hope. "And what do you do?"

"I'm an editor."

"Her company publishes Gemma's books," said Edward.

"Really?" said Lucy.

"Yup."

"How interesting. You wouldn't happen to know when the new one will be out?"

"If I told you, I'd have to kill you," said Hope, smiling at Lucy.

Lucy frowned. Clearly, she didn't get the joke.

"Come, Gabriel," she said to her date. "Let's go inside and get something to drink."

"Nice meeting you!" called Hope. But Lucy ignored her.

CHAPTER 17

"You okay?" Hope asked Edward after Lucy had gone.

"I am. You know you didn't have to do that."

"Do what?" Hope asked innocently.

"Get under Lucy's skin."

"Did I do that?"

"You know you did."

"Do you mind?"

"Not at all. She deserved it."

Hope smiled.

"I think she was jealous."

"You do?"

"Definitely."

Edward looked thoughtful.

"Let's get another drink," said Hope. "I'm thirsty."

They went over to the bar, and Edward got a gin punch while Hope asked for a lemonade. Then they took their drinks to a room that looked like a study, its walls lined with books.

"You think the books are real?" asked Hope.

"They look real," said Edward. He went over and pulled one out. "Definitely real."

"I wonder if Gemma has arrived."

"You want to see?"

Hope nodded, and they left the study.

"Excuse me," said Hope to one of the women at the check-in table. "Has Ms. Lovegood arrived?"

"Not yet," the woman replied. "She should be here any minute now." Though she looked nervous as she said it.

"Will she be signing books?"

Hope had noticed several women discreetly carrying Gemma Lovegood books.

"Did you purchase a VIP ticket?"

Hope had no idea what kind of tickets Edward had purchased and looked over at him.

"Do we have VIP tickets?"

"No, just the regular ones."

Hope looked back at the woman.

"I'd be happy to pay for a VIP ticket."

"I'm sorry, but they sold out weeks ago."

"But it's critical I see Ms. Lovegood."

The woman gave her a sympathetic smile.

"I'm sorry, Miss…"

"Halladay. So there's no way to see her? I came over three thousand miles just to meet her. I'm her editor."

The woman gave Hope a funny look.

"If you're her editor, you must see her all the time."

Hope frowned. How could she explain the situation to this woman?

"Let's go," said Edward, gently laying a hand on Hope's arm. "We'll find a way to see Gemma."

"Do you think someone would sell us their VIP ticket?" she asked Edward.

"I don't know. Though…"

"Yes?" said Hope.

"There's always Oscar. You could message him, tell him you're here and demand to see Gemma."

It wasn't a bad idea. She started to take out her phone, but the room began to buzz. Hope and Edward looked to see what all of the excitement was about.

"Excuse me," said Hope, touching the arm of the woman in front of her.

"Yes?" said the woman.

"Do you know what's going on?"

"Ms. Lovegood just arrived."

Hope and Edward exchanged a look, then Hope grabbed his arm.

"Come on!" she said.

"Where is she?" said Hope, straining to see around all of the people.

"Do you know where Ms. Lovegood went?" Edward asked a woman standing near him.

"To the VIP room," the woman replied.

"Where is that?" he asked her.

"Upstairs. Though you'll need a VIP ticket to enter."

"Come on," said Edward, heading over to the stairs.

"But we don't have VIP tickets."

"We'll figure out something."

They stood on the marble staircase, trying to avoid being crushed by Gemma Lovegood fans.

"This is ridiculous!" said Hope. "I'm her editor! I should be in there with her!"

"Excuse me," said a pretty young woman in a pale pink dress who was standing near them. "Did I hear you say you were Gemma Lovegood's editor?"

"That's right," said Hope.

"That must be so exciting! What's it like working with her?"

"Uh," said Hope.

The young woman waited.

"I, uh…"

"What Hope means," said Edward, "is that there are no words to describe how thrilling it is to see a Gemma Lovegood manuscript for the first time and find yourself transported to another world full of romance and intrigue and balls."

"So true!" said the young woman. "So do you know when the new one will be out? Will it be about Lady Eliza, Lady Eugenia and Lady Emily's sister? She hinted at that in the last book."

"I'm afraid I'm not at liberty to say," Hope replied. "It's a secret."

"Right. Of course. I was just wondering. Well, maybe Gemma will give us a hint when we meet with her."

"You have a VIP ticket?"

"Of course! Don't you?"

"I, uh…"

"There was a bit of a mix-up," said Edward. "We just have regular tickets."

"Oh, that's too bad. Strange, though. I would think as her editor you wouldn't even need a ticket."

"To be honest," said Hope. "This was a last-minute trip. And by the time I learned about the ball, all of the VIP tickets were gone. And my boss, who probably could have called in a favor, is on maternity leave. So…"

"That's too bad," said the young woman. "Though as her editor, you can always see her another time."

The VIP line moved, and the young woman hurried up the stairs.

"If only I had realized one needed a VIP ticket to see her," said Hope, looking forlorn.

"It's my fault," said Edward. "I didn't think to look when Lucy handed me two tickets."

"Please. How could you have known I'd show up on your doorstep and want to go to the ball and see Gemma?"

"True but… You are her editor."

"Excuse me," said a woman in a green ball gown. "I don't mean to eavesdrop, but are you really Ms. Lovegood's editor?"

"I am. Well, technically, I'm the acting editor. My boss, who's her normal editor, is on maternity leave." Hope realized she was oversharing, but too late now.

"And they won't let you into the VIP room?"

"Not without a VIP ticket."

"Hm," said the woman, who Hope thought to be around her age. "Well, if her editor isn't considered a VIP, I don't know who is."

She turned to her date and whispered something in his ear. He nodded, and the woman turned to Hope.

"Come with me," she said, taking Hope's hand.

"You have an extra VIP ticket?"

"I do. Well, it's Teddy's. But he agreed to loan it to you."

Hope looked back at Teddy.

"Thank you," she said.

"I just have one condition," said the woman, pausing on the stairs.

"Yes?" said Hope.

"You have to promise to send me a signed copy of Gemma's new book when it comes out."

"I…" Hope was about to say she couldn't promise that. But this could be her only shot of getting into the VIP room and talking to Gemma. And surely she could figure out a way to get a signed copy. "Of course," she replied, mentally crossing her fingers. "No problem."

"Excellent. We have a deal then. I'm Caroline, by the way."

"Very nice to meet you, Caroline. I'm Hope."

They reached the top of the stairs and Caroline gave her name to a woman holding a clipboard.

"And this is my plus one, Hope…"

"Halladay," said Hope.

"It says on the list your plus one is Theodore Wilkinson," said the woman, giving Hope a suspicious look.

"Yes, well. He couldn't make it," said Caroline. "Food poisoning. So I invited Hope instead. I did pay for two VIP tickets. And Hope's ever so eager to meet Ms. Lovegood."

The woman with the clipboard eyed Hope. Hope smiled at her and sent up a prayer to Aphrodite, the goddess of love.

"Very well," said the woman.

"Thank you," said Caroline and Hope together.

"The VIP room's over there."

Hope and Caroline hurried away in case the woman changed her mind.

"I'm so excited!" said Caroline. "I've been waiting months for this."

They entered the room. It was filled mainly with women, ranging from their early twenties to somewhere in their seventies or eighties. There were a handful of men too. Hope wondered if they were Gemma fans or had been dragged here by their dates.

She peered around the room and saw Lucy chatting with another woman but didn't see Gemma. Not that she knew what Gemma looked like. However, there was a long table against the far wall with two stacks of Gemma's books on it and two chairs, no doubt one of which was meant for the author.

"Where is she?" asked Caroline.

"I don't know," said Hope.

A door opened near the table and chairs and out stepped Oscar. At least Hope was pretty sure it was Oscar. He was dressed in formal clothes and wearing a mask. Hope saw several women's heads swivel at the sight of him. She didn't blame them. He cut quite a dashing figure.

"Ladies—and gentlemen," said Oscar, addressing the crowd. "If you would please form a line. Ms. Lovegood will be out momentarily. Thank you."

"Another line?" said Caroline. "Really?"

Caroline wasn't the only one who was grumbling. But everyone did as they were told. Of course, Lucy had somehow managed to be at the front of the line.

A few minutes later, the door opened again to reveal a

woman dressed in a buttercup yellow Victorian-style gown with lace trim. Her mostly gray hair was piled on top of her head. She smiled at the people gathered there, and Oscar led her over to the table.

That must be Gemma, Hope thought. Who else could it be? She was a good head shorter than Oscar, and Hope doubted Gemma was wearing a corset, her full figure filling out the yellow gown.

"Thank you all for coming this evening," Gemma said to the crowd. "To be honest, I didn't realize there would be so many of you. I feel a bit overwhelmed."

Oscar placed a reassuring hand on Gemma's arm.

"Do you think he's her lover?" Hope heard the woman in front of her ask her friend.

"It wouldn't surprise me," said her friend. "You remember Lady Josephine? She was in her fifties and had a lover half her age. Gemma could have modeled her on herself."

"He's actually her agent," said Hope. "He handles her affairs."

"I wouldn't mind him handling my affairs," said the first woman. And she and her friend giggled.

Hope watched as Oscar pulled out a chair for Gemma. Once she was comfortably seated, he turned to address the crowd.

"I know you all are eager to have a word with Ms. Lovegood and have her sign your books. We just ask that you limit your time with her as there are many people here who would like a word. And dinner will be served soon.

"And for those who would like to purchase a book, please see Phoebe at the end of the table first. You can use Visa, Mastercard, or Apple Pay to pay."

The line moved slowly, and Hope was feeling impatient. Finally, it was almost her turn, Caroline having gone to get her book signed by the author.

"Good evening, Oscar," Hope said.

"Do I know you?" he replied.

Hope smiled.

"I should *hope* so."

"Hope?"

Hope felt his eyes on her, taking her in, and felt her skin grow warm.

"You look…"

"Yes?" she said, a bit breathlessly. His Victorian garments suited him, showing off his lean form.

"What are you doing here?"

"I came to meet Gemma, just like everybody else. Is there a problem?"

"I… How did you get a ticket?"

Hope smiled.

"A good friend." Then she turned to Gemma, who was chatting with Caroline. "Ms. Lovegood," she said, taking advantage of a pause in their conversation. "So nice to finally meet you. I'm Hope Halladay."

Gemma looked confused.

"I work with Ashley Wallingford at Herstory."

Gemma continued to look confused.

"Your editor?"

"Oh, of course!" said Gemma. "So nice to see you again, dear."

Hope glanced over at Oscar. He seemed on edge.

"You're American," said Gemma.

"I am," said Hope. "As is Ashley."

She caught Gemma looking over at Oscar.

"Of course. How silly of me. What brings you to this side of the pond?"

Had Oscar not told Gemma about her? He said that he had, but clearly, he had lied.

"You, actually," said Hope.

"Oh?"

Oscar swooped in.

"You can chat with Ms. Lovegood later, Ms. Halladay. This session is for her fans. Now, if you wouldn't mind?"

Hope didn't move. Though she could hear the people behind her grumbling.

"If you would kindly step aside and let someone else have a turn," said Oscar.

"I wasn't finished," said Hope.

"You can speak with Ms. Lovegood later," he said, more brusquely this time.

"When?"

"After dinner."

"You promise?"

"Yes," he said.

Hope was aware she was causing a bit of a scene.

"Fine," she said. "After dinner then."

She moved to where Caroline was waiting.

"Is everything okay?" she asked Hope.

"Everything's fine," Hope lied.

"What's the deal with you and Lord Dashingly?"

"Lord Dashingly?"

"The man with Gemma. You should have seen the way he looked at you."

"What way?"

"Like he wanted to rip your clothes off."

"More like my head."

"Is something going on between the two of you?"

"Between the two of us?"

"It's just a coincidence that you're dressed like Lady Emily and he's dressed like Lord Dashingly?"

Hope stared at her.

"Anyway, we should go," said Caroline. "Teddy's probably wondering what happened to us."

CHAPTER 18

Edward and Teddy were waiting for Hope and Caroline outside of the ballroom.

"How did it go?" Edward asked Hope. "Did you speak to Gemma?"

"Briefly. Oscar would barely let me talk to her."

Teddy turned to Caroline.

"Did she autograph your books?"

"She did!" said Caroline.

Caroline opened *Belle of the Ball*, and everyone looked at Gemma's signature.

"What is it?" said Edward, noticing the expression on Hope's face. She was frowning again.

"Nothing," said Hope.

Caroline closed the book, and Hope asked her what she and Gemma had chatted about.

"I told her how much I enjoyed her books and hoped she was working on a new one."

"And what did she say?"

"She just smiled and said she was glad that I liked them."

"She didn't say anything about the new book?"

"No."

"We should go into dinner," said Edward.

Inside the ballroom there was a section for VIPs and another for those with regular tickets.

Hope and Edward were about to head to the non-VIP

section when Caroline stopped them.

"I need to give you my address," she said to Hope, "so you can send me Ms. Lovegood's new book when it comes out. You promised to send me a signed copy."

"Right," said Hope. She had forgotten.

Caroline pulled out her phone.

"What's your number? I'll text you my information."

"I have a better idea," said Hope, taking out her phone and opening her contacts. "Fill in your contact information. I'll add you to the list."

Caroline took Hope's phone and began to type.

"There," she said when she was done. "You won't forget, will you?"

"I won't. But it's going to be a while. Probably not until early next year."

"That's okay," said Caroline. "I can wait."

"Don't let her fool you," said Teddy. "She's been prattling on for months, wondering when Ms. Lovegood would have a new book, saying she couldn't wait."

Caroline shot him a look.

"I promise, you'll be among the first to know when the new book is out," Hope told her.

"Enjoy the rest of your evening," Edward said to the couple. Then they all headed inside the ballroom.

Hope and Edward were seated at a table with a group of older women, friends who had come to the ball together.

The women had welcomed Hope and Edward, making a fuss over Edward.

"It's so nice to see so many young men here," said one of the women.

"I told you there'd be men," said another.

"Well, wild horses couldn't have dragged my Ernie here," said a third.

"My Sam likes a good bodice ripper," said the fourth woman. "But he's not one for balls other than the two he's got."

Her friends laughed at the joke.

"Well, I'm not ashamed to say I enjoy a good bodice ripper," said Edward. "And I'm looking forward to dancing later."

"Good man!" said the first woman. She turned to Hope. "You've got a good one there, love."

Hope smiled at her.

A few minutes later, the first course, Mulligatawny soup, was served. Hope took a few sips and then pushed it aside.

"Not a fan of Mulligatawny soup?" said the woman seated next to her.

"Not really," Hope replied.

The main course was either chicken, mutton, or something vegetarian, guests having indicated their preference beforehand.

"What did you order?" Hope asked Edward as the main course was being served to other tables.

"I don't remember. Lucy said she'd order for everyone. If you don't like what she ordered, we can switch."

Their meals came out, and a white-gloved server placed a plate of mutton in front of Edward and what looked to be pasta primavera in front of Hope.

"Do you want to switch?" he asked her.

Hope looked over at Edward's plate.

"I'm good."

They began to eat, the group of friends mostly chatting amongst themselves. Hope tried to see Gemma. But it was a big room, and she and Edward were seated toward the back.

"Would you excuse me?" she said to Edward.

"Is everything all right?" he asked her.

"I just need to find the ladies' room. I'll be right back."

Hope excused herself and asked one of the servers where

the ladies' room was. She didn't really need to go. She just wanted an excuse to find Gemma.

She made her way out of the ballroom, heading down the hall. She stopped at the open door by the VIP section and peered in. There was Gemma, Oscar seated next to her.

"Can I help you?" asked a server.

Hope turned to the young woman, smiled, and said she had just wanted to get a peek at Ms. Lovegood.

"Do you have a VIP ticket?" asked the server.

"Just a regular one, I'm afraid."

"Then I'll have to ask you to move along."

So much for sneaking in. Though even if she had managed to sneak in, Hope doubted Oscar would let her have a word with Gemma. She would just have to wait until after dinner.

She started to head back to the table but figured she might as well go to the loo while she was up.

Unfortunately, the stalls in the ladies' room were quite small. And it took some maneuvering for Hope to be able to pee, what with her dress and underskirt taking up so much space. But she eventually managed.

She was heading to the sink to wash her hands when the door opened and who should walk in but Gemma Lovegood. Here was her chance!

Hope thought it best to wait until Gemma had finished doing her business. So she took her time washing her hands and checking her face in the mirror. Finally, Gemma emerged from the stall.

"Ms. Lovegood!" said Hope, as Gemma approached the sink.

"May I help you?" said the author.

"We met earlier," said Hope. "I'm Hope, Hope Halladay, from Herstory?"

"Oh yes. You must forgive me dear. This whole evening's been a bit overwhelming for me."

"I can imagine. If I could just have a moment of your time to discuss the manuscript."

Hope noticed several women looking at them. Perhaps it wasn't such a good idea to have this conversation in the ladies' room.

"Could we step outside?" she asked Gemma.

"May I wash my hands first?"

"Of course," said Hope, feeling embarrassed.

Gemma proceeded to wash her hands.

"Shall we?" said Hope, indicating the door. Gemma followed her to a quiet nook.

"It's about the manuscript," said Hope, once she was sure no one was around.

"The manuscript," Gemma repeated.

"Oscar showed me some chapters. And I wanted to assure you, I'm here to help you in any way I can. We just need you to finish by the end of the month."

"The end of the month," Gemma repeated.

"I know it's asking a lot, but you've already blown through two deadlines, and Ashley, my boss, really wants that manuscript."

"She does."

"Yes, she does. And if she doesn't get it, Herstory will sue."

"It will?"

"For breach of contract."

"I see."

"Oscar didn't tell you?"

"No, he did not."

As if hearing his name, Oscar appeared. He looked angry.

"There you are," he said to Gemma. "I was beginning to wonder what happened to you."

Gemma patted Oscar's arm.

"You worry too much. I'm fine. I was just chatting with Hope. She was asking me about the new Gemma Lovegood."

Did Oscar just flinch?

"She said that my publisher will sue me if they don't have the new manuscript by the end of the month."

"Nothing for you to worry about," said Oscar. "Now let's go back to the ballroom. They're about to serve the pudding course."

He started to lead Gemma away, but Hope stopped him.

"What?" he said. Then he turned to Gemma. "You go in. I'll be right there." Gemma hesitated. "Go," he commanded. And she hurried towards the ballroom.

Hope turned on Oscar.

"You didn't tell her, did you?"

"Tell her what?"

"Everything! About me and the new deadline and Herstory suing."

They glared at each other.

"I need to get back."

"Do you deny it?" said Hope.

"I'm going," he said.

"We're not done," said Hope. But Oscar was already heading back to the ballroom.

"Is everything all right?" Edward asked Hope when she had returned to the table.

"Everything's fine," she replied.

"You don't seem fine."

She leaned over, so the other people at the table wouldn't hear her.

"I ran into Gemma in the ladies' room."

"And? Did you talk to her?"

"Briefly. Oscar showed up and stopped us."

"He showed up in the ladies' room?"

"No, in the hallway. It was too crowded in the ladies' room. So I took Gemma to a quiet nook down the hall. Then Oscar interrupted us."

"Were you able to ask her about the manuscript?"

"I did but…"

"But what?"

"She didn't know about the new deadline or that Herstory would sue if she didn't hand in the manuscript by the end of the month."

"Maybe Oscar was protecting her."

"Maybe. I really need to chat with her, without Oscar looming over her."

"You'll get your chance. Didn't you say he'd arrange for you to speak with her after dinner?"

"I doubt he'll let me speak with her now."

The wait staff were busy serving dessert, and the musicians had returned from their break. Soon, the dancing would begin. Which gave Hope an idea.

CHAPTER 19

Before the dancing could begin, however, there were speeches. The first one was quite short. It was to introduce the head of the Historical Romance Society, Patricia "Patsy" Campbell. The second speech, given by Ms. Campbell, was a bit longer. After thanking her colleague for the introduction, Ms. Campbell thanked everyone for coming to this year's ball. Then she gave a brief history of the society and the work it did and mentioned a couple of upcoming events. Finally, it was time to introduce the guest of honor.

"Tonight's guest of honor needs no introduction," she began. "But I'm going to give her one anyway."

There was polite laughter from the crowd.

"Gemma Lovegood is the author of *Belle of the Ball* and *Balls Aren't Just for Men*, both of which are set in the late 1800s. Ms. Lovegood's books have won several awards and topped the bestseller lists in over a dozen countries for weeks. As you may know, Ms. Lovegood is quite private and doesn't normally do appearances. However, when she heard about our little event and that the money raised this evening would be going to a cause dear to her heart, she accepted our invitation to be tonight's guest of honor.

"Now, without further ado, I give you Ms. Gemma Lovegood!"

There was a great deal of applause and some whooping as Gemma got up and made her way to the podium.

"Thank you, Patsy," she said. Then she turned to the audience. "And thank all of you for coming here this evening and supporting such a worthwhile cause.

"I'm not one for giving speeches," she continued. "And I know many of you are eager for the dancing to begin. So I shall be brief. Thank you for reading the books. I am truly astounded by their success."

She then turned to head back to her seat. But the audience wanted more.

"When's the new book coming out?" someone called out. It sounded like a man, but Hope wasn't sure.

"Yes! When can we expect a new book?"

That was definitely a woman, Hope thought.

Gemma paused and looked at Oscar, who was subtly shaking his head. She looked nervous, Hope thought. Sensing her distress, the head of the Historical Romance Society went over to Gemma, exchanged a few words with her *sotto voce*, and then returned to the podium.

"Ladies and gentlemen," she said. "Ms. Lovegood wants all of you to know that she appreciates your interest in her next book. But she's not at liberty to discuss it."

"We just want to know when to expect it!" a woman called out.

Hope thought it was the same woman as before.

There were murmurs of assent from the crowd.

The head of the society looked over at Gemma and Oscar, and Oscar got up. He made his way to the podium and addressed the crowd.

"Good evening," he said.

"Who are you?" someone called out.

"He looks like Lord Dashingly!" said a woman, which resulted in laughter from the crowd.

Hope was surprised by the shouting and laughter. It hadn't seemed like a rowdy crowd. Clearly, people had had too much gin punch.

"I represent Ms. Lovegood," said Oscar. "And I appreciate you wanting to know when her new book will be out. While I do not have a publication date, I can tell you that she has been hard at work on it. And as soon as the publisher has given us a date, we will share it with all of you."

Hope scowled.

"The cheek of him!" she said to Edward. "We had a publication date, but she blew right through it."

"You going to get up there and say something?"

Hope thought about it.

"No. But I'm going to have a word with Oscar and Gemma as soon as I'm able."

"How are you planning on doing that? Isn't their section VIPs only?"

Just then the orchestra began to play.

Hope looked over at it.

The orchestra was playing a familiar melody but in a classical style, and several couples had gotten up to dance. Soon, they were joined by more. Hope was watching them when Edward stood up and held out his hand.

"Come," he said.

Hope looked up at him.

"Are you asking me to dance?"

"I am."

After a moment's hesitation, Hope took Edward's hand, and he led her out onto the dance floor.

As they whirled around the ballroom, Hope kept her eyes on Oscar and Gemma.

"Would you like me to ask her to dance?"

"Who?" said Hope.

"Gemma."

"You want to ask Gemma for a dance?"

"Why not? That way I can ask her about the manuscript."

Hope stared at him.

"You would do that?"

He nodded.

"Not that she'd tell me anything but…"

"Go for it," said Hope. "If anyone could charm the truth out of her, it's you."

"You flatter me. Hey, don't look now, but a certain someone's looking at you."

"Who?" said Hope, glancing around.

"Oscar."

Hope looked over at him. He was glaring at her.

"He's just mad because I talked to Gemma without his permission and told her Herstory would sue."

"Mm," said Edward. "Oh look, someone has beaten me to the punch."

They watched as an older man led Gemma out onto the dance floor.

Hope watched Gemma and the man for a few minutes, then she told Edward to cut in.

Edward whirled them over to Gemma and her partner, and Hope announced that she needed a break. Then Edward turned to Gemma and asked to cut in. The older gentleman said something to Gemma, and Gemma nodded her head, smiling at Edward. He smiled back at her, and they began to dance. Hope stood off to the side, watching them.

"What do you think you're doing?"

It was Oscar. She hadn't noticed him approach.

"I'm watching the dancers."

"That wasn't what I meant. What's your friend doing with Gemma?"

"I believe they call it dancing."

Oscar frowned.

"Speaking of which, why aren't you dancing?"

He looked at her.

"I'm not a fan."

"Of dancing?"

He nodded his head.

"But it's a ball."

"What is your point, Ms. Halladay?"

"You should at least dance one dance." He frowned. "Oh, come on, Oscar. One dance won't kill you." Though judging by his expression, he clearly thought that it could.

"Very well," he said. "Let's go."

"Excuse me?"

"You insist that I dance one dance, so, let's dance."

Hope was going to object, but he had taken her hand and was leading her back out onto the dance floor. Despite his protestations, it was clear that Oscar knew how to dance. He commanded the dance floor, moving Hope effortlessly around it. And Hope could see people watching them.

"Where did you learn to dance?" she asked him.

"My mother made us take lessons as children."

"Us?"

"Me and my sister."

"You have a sister."

"You sound surprised."

"Sorry. Is she older or younger?"

"Younger. Technically, she's my half-sister."

"Is she here tonight?" Hope asked, looking around.

"No. She wanted to come, but she was unable to."

They continued to waltz around the dance floor, and Hope was suddenly very conscious of Oscar's hand on her back, pulling her close to him.

"You look quite beautiful tonight," he whispered into her ear.

Hope could feel her face grow warm.

"Thank you. You don't look so bad yourself."

She could sense him smiling.

The dance ended, and Hope said she could use some air.

Oscar guided her out onto the terrace.

It was dimly lit, light mainly coming from the ballroom and the moon. A few couples were milling about, but they took no notice of Hope and Oscar. Hope stood at the railing. The temperature had dropped, and it was quite chilly. She shivered.

"Are you cold?" Oscar asked.

He was standing so close to her, and she could feel the warmth of his body.

"I'm fine," she said.

"Are you sure? Here, take my jacket."

Before she could object, Oscar had removed his jacket and placed it around Hope's shoulders.

"Better?" he said.

"Yes, thank you."

They stood there silently, looking out, neither speaking, for what seemed like an eternity to Hope. Finally, she turned and looked at him. He cut a striking figure. For a moment, she had the urge to lean over and kiss him. Instead, she asked him about Gemma.

"Why didn't you tell her about Ashley's ultimatum?"

"I didn't want her to worry."

"She needed to know."

"No, she didn't."

Hope frowned.

"Is she really working on the manuscript?"

"She is."

"And we'll have it by the end of the month?"

"I told you that you would."

"Look, if Gemma needs help…"

"She doesn't need any help."

"I do have a master's degree in Victorian Literature. And I've edited dozens of books."

Oscar smirked.

"What?" said Hope.

"Nothing."

"No, you smirked. Why?"

"Do you really think that editing a book is the same thing as writing one?"

"I never said that it was. I just meant I can try to help her if she's having trouble."

"I told you…"

"There you are!"

It was Gemma. Edward was with her.

"We've been looking all over for you." She looked from Oscar to Hope. "Are we interrupting something?"

"No," they said in unison.

Hope turned to Edward.

"Where were you two?"

"Gemma wanted a drink."

Oscar cast a disapproving look at Gemma.

"Oh, relax, Oscar. It was just one little drink."

Oscar continued to look disapprovingly at Gemma. She sighed.

"I'm a bit tired. You think it's all right if we go?"

"I'm sure it's fine. I'll just let Ms. Campbell know. Don't go anywhere. I'll be right back."

"Where would I go?" said Gemma. But Oscar was already heading inside.

Hope couldn't believe her good luck. Had Oscar really just left her alone with Gemma? She glanced around the terrace. There were other people there, but none of them seemed to have noticed the author. They were too preoccupied.

"Did you ask her?" Hope asked Edward.

"I'm right here," said Gemma. "Ask me what?"

"About the manuscript," said Hope.

"I did but…"

"And I told him I wasn't at liberty to discuss my work," said Gemma.

"I tried," said Edward.

Gemma patted his hand.

"You do understand that Herstory will sue if you don't give them the manuscript by the end of the month," Hope said to Gemma.

"Can't they just extend the deadline?"

"They've already extended it twice."

Gemma sighed.

"I'll speak with Oscar."

"Speaking of Oscar, did he tell you that I'm to stay with you in Devon?"

"No, he did not. You're to stay at the cottage?"

Hope nodded.

"It was my boss's idea. She's worried about the manuscript and insisted I stay with you to make sure it gets finished."

"Honestly," said Gemma. "I don't need a babysitter."

"I'm not crazy about the idea either, but you know Ashley." Or maybe she didn't. "Once she decides something, there's no going back."

"We're all set." It was Oscar. "Is something wrong?"

"Ms. Halladay just informed me that she is to stay with us in Devon while I work on the manuscript."

Oscar scowled.

"Why didn't you tell me?"

"I was hoping to convince Ms. Halladay that it was unnecessary."

"Yes, well, according to Ashley, it's absolutely necessary," said Hope.

Gemma was looking up at Oscar. He ran a hand through his hair, forgetting about his mask.

"We'll sort something out."

"And where will she stay?"

"In Fe's… In the guest room downstairs."

"But…"

"I'll take care of it."

Hope wondered what was going on.

"When do you plan on moving in?" Gemma asked her.

"When will you be back in Devon?"

Gemma looked at Oscar again.

"We're heading down tomorrow afternoon."

"Then shall we say Monday?"

"I'm feeling quite tired, Oscar," said Gemma.

"Let's get you home. I told Patsy you were tired."

"It was very nice meeting you," Edward said to Gemma.

She turned and smiled at him.

"And you," Gemma replied.

Hope wondered if Edward had a little crush on the author and couldn't help smiling at the thought.

"Come," said Oscar, gently laying a hand on Gemma's arm.

Hope watched them leave. Then she turned to Edward.

"I'm feeling a bit tired too. Okay if we go?"

"Let's," he said.

CHAPTER 20

"So, you're really going to stay with them," Edward said to Hope on the train back to Devon.

They had gone to Buckingham Palace that morning to watch the changing of the guard and did a bit of last-minute sightseeing before leaving London.

"I am," said Hope.

"And you honestly think she'll pop out a manuscript in a couple of weeks with you there?"

"It's not like she's starting from scratch. Oscar said that she's been working on it."

Edward looked skeptical.

"And it doesn't need to be perfect. We just need something to work with."

"Will Ashley let you edit it?"

Hope had been thinking about that.

"Maybe? She did say to offer to help."

"And what about Oscar?"

"What about him?"

"Will he be there?"

"I don't know. Though he did say he was going back to Devon with Gemma."

"Does he always stay with her?"

"I have no idea. Maybe she likes having him around."

"Well, I don't like the idea of him being there."

"Why's that?"

"He seems very possessive."

"Of Gemma?"

Edward nodded.

"You saw how he was with her at the ball, treating her like a child."

"I don't think he treated her like a child. He was just looking out for her."

"Why are you defending him? I thought you didn't like him."

"Why are you so concerned about Gemma? Seemed to me like she could take care of herself. Anyway, I'm going to read," said Hope, reaching for her bag.

"Fine," said Edward and looked out the window.

Things continued to feel tense that evening. And the next morning, Hope had had enough. She would be heading to Gemma's later, and she didn't want to leave things the way they were with Edward. As soon as she had gone to the loo, she went to Edward's room.

His door was open, but she knocked anyway.

"Yes?" he said.

"May I come in?" Hope asked.

"The door's open."

Hope entered and saw Arfur curled up on the floor next to Edward's desk.

"Look, I'm sorry about yesterday," she said.

Edward turned and looked at her. It looked like he hadn't slept or hadn't slept well.

"I'm sorry too. I don't know what got into me. I guess it's just... I'm going to miss having you around."

Hope went over and sat on the edge of his bed.

"I'm going to miss you too. But as I told you the other day, you can come visit me whenever. And don't worry about Oscar. I can handle him. That is, assuming he's there.

For all we know, he could just be accompanying Gemma and then turning around and going back to London."

"I hope so," said Edward. "Have you had breakfast?"

"Not yet. I came to see you first. Have you eaten?"

"Not yet. Shall we go downstairs and get something?"

"Let's."

Hope smiled as they went downstairs, happy that she and Edward were on good terms again.

Hope had texted Oscar while Edward fixed breakfast, letting him know that she planned on moving in that afternoon. He didn't reply. Hope wrote to him again after lunch, saying she would be there around three. Again, he didn't text back.

"Are you sure they came back?" said Edward as Hope carried her bags downstairs. (She had insisted she could handle them.)

"He said they were coming back Sunday afternoon."

"But he hasn't replied to you."

"Not yet."

"Maybe you should call before we head over."

"Fine," said Hope. She put down her bags when they reached the base of the stairs and fished out her phone. She was about to leave a voicemail message for Oscar when he finally picked up.

"Yes?" he said. He sounded annoyed.

"It's Hope."

"I know."

"Is Gemma there? I'm about to head over."

"She's here."

"Excellent. I'll be there soon."

Oscar started to say something, but Hope ended the call. She didn't want to hear what Oscar had to say. He was likely going to try to convince her not to come. But Hope had already informed Ashley she was headed to Gemma's.

Hope said goodbye to Arfur, giving him a hug. She would miss him. Then she followed Edward out to his car.

"You know, you can always come back if things don't work out over there," Edward said as he placed Hope's bags in the trunk of his Mini.

"I know."

"And I'm just a phone call or text away if you need anything."

"I know."

"And you promise to phone me once you've settled in, let me know that you're okay."

Hope placed a hand on his arm.

"It's going to be fine, Edward."

Judging by the look on his face, though, Edward wasn't so sure about that.

"Really. You mustn't worry about me. I'm a big girl and am used to dealing with difficult authors."

"It's not Gemma I'm worried about."

Hope sighed.

"For all I know, Oscar won't be there."

"For your sake, I hope so."

"Can we go now?"

"Fine," he said, and they got in the Mini.

They arrived at Gemma's cottage a short time later. Oscar's car was parked in front.

Hope told Edward she would make sure Gemma was there before getting her bags and headed down the flagstone walkway to the front door. She rang the doorbell and waited. Oscar answered it a minute later. He didn't look pleased to see her.

"Hello, Oscar," she said.

He continued to frown.

"Who's at the door?" called a cheery female voice. Seconds later, Gemma appeared. "Oh, it's my editor! And my dance partner," she added with a smile upon seeing

Edward. Hope hadn't realized Edward had followed her. "Do come in, both of you."

Oscar didn't move.

"Oh do let them in, Oscar."

He begrudgingly stepped aside.

"Won't you have a seat?" Gemma said to Edward and Hope as they entered the living room.

They took a seat on the sofa while Oscar remained standing.

"Can I get you something to drink?" Gemma asked them. "Some tea or maybe something a bit stronger?"

Oscar shot her a look, which Gemma ignored.

"I'd love some tea," said Edward.

Gemma smiled at him.

"I'll be right back with it."

She disappeared, leaving Oscar glaring at Hope and Edward.

"You're not going to sit?" Hope asked him.

"I have work to do."

"Well, don't let me stop you."

He scowled at Hope and then headed up the stairs.

Gemma returned a few minutes later with a tray of tea and a plate of scones.

"Thank you," said Hope, as Gemma handed her a cup. Then she handed one to Edward.

"Please, take a scone."

Edward immediately took a scone, spreading jam and clotted cream on it. He took a bite and his face lit up.

"Mm!" he said.

Gemma smiled.

"You like it?"

He nodded, his mouth still full. He swallowed and told Hope to take one, insisting she add jam and clotted cream. Hope was still full from lunch but she obeyed.

"Wow!" she said after taking a bite.

"I'm so glad you like them. I made them myself—and the cream and the jam."

"You did?"

Gemma nodded.

Hope took another bite.

"This may be the best scone I've ever tasted. You could sell these."

Gemma smiled again.

"I used to."

"Used to?"

"I used to own a bake shop."

"You owned a bake shop?"

"I did."

"What happened to it?"

"I sold it."

"When?"

"Oh, years ago now. Though I still like to bake. It relaxes me."

Edward and Hope polished off their scones, washing them down with some tea.

"So, are you two dating?" Gemma asked them.

"We're just friends," they said simultaneously, which made Gemma laugh.

"I see," she said, taking a sip of her tea.

"We dated at university," Hope explained. "I studied here my junior year, of college, at the University of London."

"Did you enjoy it?" asked Gemma.

"I loved it."

Gemma looked over at Edward as she took a sip of her tea.

"And you live here in Devon?"

"Yes, in Farthingate."

"Farthingate's very nice. Right on the sea."

They continued to make small talk. Then Edward said he needed to go.

"My bags!" said Hope.

"Right," said Edward. "I'll go get them."

CHAPTER 21

Hope insisted on helping Gemma with the washing up.

"So how long have you lived here?" Hope asked her.

"I grew up here," said Gemma.

"That must have been nice."

"It was. My mother adored it here. She convinced my father to buy this cottage when we were little, even though they couldn't really afford it at the time."

"Did your father like it here too?"

"He did, though he was gone a lot. He was a fisherman. Died at sea."

"I'm sorry. How old were you when he died?"

"I was twelve, and Netta was fourteen."

"Is Netta your sister?"

Gemma nodded.

"What did you do after he died?"

"My mother opened a bake shop here in town to support us. Netta and I worked there when we weren't in school."

"And then you took it over?"

Gemma nodded.

"Did you sell it because of the books?"

Gemma looked confused.

"I meant because the books did so well."

"No. It was just time to sell."

"And your mother, is she still around?"

"No. She died almost ten years ago."

Hope realized she was being nosy, but she couldn't help it. She was naturally curious, and she knew nothing about Gemma.

"And your sister?"

"She lives in London."

They had finished cleaning and drying the tea things.

"I should get upstairs," said Gemma. "Thank you for helping."

"Of course," said Hope. "Thank you for the tea and scones. So, how's the manuscript coming along? I'd be happy to read it whenever. You don't have to wait until it's finished to share it with me."

Gemma gave her a funny look.

"Sorry," said Hope. "I'll leave you to it. Just know that I'm here for you."

"That's very kind of you," said Gemma. "And you let me or Oscar know if you need anything."

"He'll be staying here?"

Gemma gave her a funny look again.

"Yes, he…" She stopped herself. "Just let us know if you need anything."

"I will," said Hope.

After Gemma left, Hope snooped around the kitchen. It seemed as though Oscar and Gemma had gone shopping recently as the refrigerator and pantry were both full. Hope looked to see if they had bought coffee and was relieved to find a fresh bag along with a coffee maker.

Having familiarized herself with the kitchen, Hope went to her room. On the way, she stopped by the stairs. She didn't hear the sound of a typewriter, but maybe that was because the door to the office was closed. She waited a few more seconds and then headed to her room.

The room wasn't large. There was a queen-size bed with a night table and lamp, a rug, a chest of drawers, and a small wardrobe, the British not being big on closets. Fortunately,

Hope didn't have many things that needed hanging.

May as well unpack, she said to herself. She didn't have that much. Though she had bought a few things while she and Edward were in London. She would need to ask Gemma about a washer and dryer or else find a laundromat if she was going to be here for a couple of weeks.

Though would she really be here for two weeks? She couldn't imagine staying there that long.

She unpacked her things, placing most of them in the chest of drawers. She went over to the wardrobe. It looked old. When she opened it, she found a half-dozen dresses inside. They looked to be old. Vintage. Likely from the fifties and sixties. All in good condition. She wondered who they belonged to. She would ask Gemma later.

She gently moved them to the side and hung up the rest of her things.

"There," she said when she was done.

She glanced around the room and felt a pang of homesickness. She missed her apartment and her cat. Speaking of Morris… She sent Dani a text, asking how he was. Then she took out her laptop, wondering where to put it. She looked over at the chest of drawers. No, that wouldn't do. She looked over at the bed. It looked comfortable, but she made a point of never working in bed. Well, almost never. And the little table next to the bed was barely big enough to hold the lamp sitting on it.

She frowned. Clearly, she would need to find someplace else to work. She thought about asking Gemma if she could work in her office. But she recalled Oscar saying that Gemma didn't like having people around while she was writing. Though didn't Oscar say they shared the office? Not for the first time, Hope wondered about their relationship.

She took her laptop and went into the living room. There were two sofas and a couple of armchairs, as well as a coffee table and a couple of end tables. She looked at the coffee table. It was too low, and the end tables too high. Where would she work?

She felt her phone vibrating in her back pocket. She pulled it out and saw that she had a message. She unlocked the phone and saw that it was from Ashley.

"How are things at Gemma's?" Ashley had written.

"I just got here," Hope replied.

"You see the manuscript?"

"Not yet. Gemma's upstairs working on it."

"Good. Keep me posted."

Hope gave her a thumbs-up and put her phone away. It immediately started buzzing again. Hope was going to ignore it, thinking it was Ashley again. Then she thought better of it. It was Dani, replying to her message.

"Morris is Morris. So, you at Gemma's? What's it like? I have this vision of it being one of those cottages you read about in fairy tales or see on British TV shows, with whitewashed walls, wooden beams, a thatched roof, and a garden."

"That pretty much describes it," wrote Hope.

"Send me pictures."

"Later."

"OK. You good?"

"I'm good."

"Is he there?"

"He who?"

"You know who: Oscar."

"Unfortunately."

"Is he being a grouch?"

"Of course."

"Sorry."

"It's okay. I plan on ignoring him. I'm here for Gemma."

"She busy working on the book?"

"Yup."

"Let me know if it's any good."

"You know I can't discuss it."

"I'm not asking you to reveal any secrets. Just let me know if it's worth reading. Though I'll probably read it anyway."

Hope smiled.

"I need to go," wrote Dani. "Send pics!"

"I will. And send me a pic of Morris!"

Dani sent her a thumbs-up emoji.

Hope put her phone in her back pocket and glanced around the living room, looking for a place where she could set up her laptop. Her eyes went to a wall lined with bookcases. She went over to take a look. Many of the books looked old. She wondered if they belonged to Gemma's parents.

Many of the titles were by Victorian-era authors: the Brontë sisters, Lewis Carroll, Wilkie Collins, Sir Arthur Conan Doyle, Charles Dickens, Elizabeth Gaskell, Thomas Hardy, and Robert Louis Stevenson. There was also a full set of Jane Austen's books.

Hope wondered if Gemma's mother had read the books to her daughters. Maybe listening to them as a child or reading them had inspired Gemma to write her own Victorian tale.

Hope pulled out a copy of *Villette* by Charlotte Brontë. She hadn't read it since graduate school. She took it over to a comfortable-looking armchair and sat. On the title page was a stamp with the words "This book belongs to Gemma Lovegood." Hope smiled. She imagined Gemma reading this book when she was a young girl.

Hope flipped to the first page and began to read, forgetting all about work.

She had no idea what time it was when she heard someone coming down the stairs. It was Gemma. She stopped to put on a coat, not seeming to notice Hope.

"Are you going out?" Hope asked her.

Gemma froze.

"Sorry, I didn't mean to scare you," said Hope.

"That's all right," Gemma replied.

"Where are you off to?"

"I'm meeting a friend for dinner."

"Is it dinner time already?" Hope looked at her phone. How had it gotten to be so late? "Oscar not going with you?"

"Oh no. He's too busy working. Actually… would you make sure he eats something? Maybe have him take you to the pub? He forgets to eat when he's working, and I worry about him."

"I, uh…" Hope didn't know what to say. "Okay."

"Thank you. If he gives you any gruff, tell him I told you to drag him out."

Hope smiled at that.

"Well, I should get going," said Gemma.

"Have a good time!" said Hope.

Hope wondered who Gemma was meeting for dinner. Did she have a beau in town? Or maybe it was just an old friend.

She returned to *Villette*. She hadn't been reading for long when her stomach let out a growl. She put down the book and looked over at the stairs. She hadn't heard or seen Oscar. She was going to get something to eat in the kitchen when she remembered what Gemma had said and sighed.

She turned and headed up the stairs. The door to the office was closed. Hope knocked on it. No answer. She knocked again.

"Oscar?"

Still no answer.

She knocked again, louder this time.

"Oscar! It's Hope! You in there?"

Though where else would he be?

Hope thought about going back downstairs, but again she heard Gemma's voice in her head. She turned the knob. The door was unlocked. She opened it slowly, so as not to scare Oscar. But she doubted he heard her. He was sitting in front of his computer with noise-canceling headphones on his head.

She went over to him and cleared her throat, but it was as though she was invisible. She waved her hand in front of his face. He jumped and immediately shut his laptop.

"What the hell are you doing here?" he snapped. "Don't you know it's rude not to knock?"

"I did knock, several times. I even called your name. But you didn't hear me."

Oscar was scowling.

"Well, what do you want?"

"Gemma wanted me to make sure you ate."

"I'm not hungry."

"She thought you'd say that and said to drag you out of here."

Oscar continued to scowl.

"I'm busy."

"Well, I need to eat. And you do too. And I don't want Gemma to be mad at me. So finish up whatever it is you're doing and let's go to the pub."

Oscar looked like he was going to argue with her but then seemed to change his mind.

"The pub?"

"Yes, the pub. I assume they serve food as well as drink."

"They do. Just give me a minute."

"Okay. But if you're not downstairs in five, I'm coming back up to get you."

CHAPTER 22

Hope was about to go upstairs and drag Oscar away from his computer when she heard him coming down the stairs.

"Finally," she said. "I was about to come get you."

"I told you I needed to finish something."

"You said you'd just be a minute."

"Were you timing me?"

Hope didn't reply.

"So, the pub?" she said.

"The pub," he confirmed and headed to the front door.

Hope grabbed her jacket and followed him out.

"We're not going to drive?"

"It's not far."

"Is it safe to walk?" Hope asked him.

"You afraid of being robbed on the way to the pub?"

"No, I meant, is it safe to walk on the street?"

"There's a pavement just over there," he said, pointing down the road.

"Oh," said Hope.

They crossed the road and headed to the sidewalk.

"So, do you know who Gemma was having dinner with?" Hope asked him.

"Why do you want to know?"

"Just curious."

"It's really none of your business."

"You don't need to be rude."

He continued to walk, ignoring Hope.

"Is she married?"

"Gemma?"

"Who else would I be asking about?"

"Now who sounds rude?"

Hope gritted her teeth.

"She was," he said a minute later.

"Was?"

Oscar didn't reply.

"Does she have any children?"

Oscar acted as though he hadn't heard her.

"We're here," he said a couple of minutes later.

He held the door to the pub open for Hope, and she stepped inside.

The place looked like what you imagined an old English country pub to look like. There was a wooden bar with a handful of barstools around it, wooden beams in the ceiling and walls, wooden tables and chairs, and a half-dozen cozy-looking booths, along with a big stone fireplace with a crackling fire.

Oscar nodded at the man behind the bar who nodded back.

"Hey, Osc," said a woman with a tray.

"Nan," Oscar replied.

"Haven't seen you in a while. Everything okay?"

"All good," he said. "Just working."

"Well, take a load off and have a seat." Nan looked at Hope curiously but didn't say anything.

Oscar headed to one of the booths. A minute later, Nan came over and asked them what they wanted to drink.

"What do you have on tap?" Hope asked her.

Nan reeled off the names of a dozen or so beers and ales and a cider Hope had never heard of.

Oscar ordered a pint of ale.

"And I'll have a half-pint of that cider you mentioned,"

said Hope. "And could we get a couple of menus?"

"Coming right up," said Nan.

She returned a few minutes later with their drinks and two menus.

Hope took a sip of her cider. It was good.

"So," she said, putting it down and looking at Oscar. "What do you recommend?"

"What do I recommend?"

"I assume from the way Nan greeted you that you're a regular."

"I don't know about that."

"Well, you've been here more than I have."

"Everything's good here. Just decide what you want."

Hope picked up her menu and studied it.

"What are you going to have?" she asked him a minute later. She noticed that Oscar hadn't picked up his menu.

"The fish and chips."

"Is that what you usually get?"

"When I'm in the mood for fish and chips."

Hope told herself to ignore Oscar's snarky tone.

"You ever have the burger?"

"I have."

"Is it good?"

"I told you…"

Hope sighed.

"You know, it wouldn't kill you to not be such a grouch."

"You don't know that."

Just then Nan returned.

"You two decide?"

"Yes," said Hope. "I'll have the burger."

"How do you want it?"

"Medium?"

"Medium it is. You want chips with it?"

"Sure."

"What about you?" Nan asked Oscar.

"The fish and chips."

Hope noticed that Nan didn't have a pad or a pen.

"You're not going to write it down?" Hope asked the server, realizing right after she said it that it might sound rude. But Nan just smiled.

"Got it all in me head," she said, grinning and tapping her head. Then she left.

"Don't let her fool you," said Oscar. "There's a computer over by the bar where she enters the orders."

Hope smiled and took another sip of her cider. It was sweet and dry with just the right amount of fizz. Maybe she should have ordered a full pint as her half-pint was nearly gone.

"So, you working on a new play?"

"Hm?" said Oscar. He seemed to be distracted by something or someone across the room.

Hope looked to see what he was looking at. Just some people by the bar. Did he know them?

"I asked if you were working on a new play."

He frowned.

"It not going well?"

"You could say that."

"What's it about?"

Oscar took a healthy swig of his ale. His glass was nearly empty. He signaled to Nan to bring him another one.

Nan came over with a pint of fresh ale and a half-pint of cider.

"Thanks," said Hope.

"Your food's almost ready. Won't be a minute," Nan informed them.

"You were saying, about your play," said Hope.

Oscar took a sip of his ale and put it down.

"It's about an annoying American woman who comes to England to harass an author."

"Ha ha," said Hope. "What's it really about?"

Oscar frowned.

"I'm still figuring it out."

That at least sounded honest.

"Well, if you want someone to bounce ideas off of…"

"Thanks, but I'm good."

"Well, if you change your mind."

"I don't need your help, Ms. Halladay."

Hope was regretting asking Oscar out to dinner and thought about getting her burger to go. Then she thought of Gemma. Gemma would want her to stay.

"Fine. How about I tell you about the manuscript I'm reading? I think you'd enjoy it."

"I doubt that," said Oscar.

"How do you know?"

"Fine. Go ahead and tell me. You're going to anyway."

Hope looked at him. Was he always this grouchy?

"Well, it takes place at a horse farm, a farm not unlike the one you took me to."

Oscar didn't say anything, so Hope continued.

"The farm is in Virgina, in horse country. It belongs to a family. Been in the family for generations. Then the couple who've been running it die in a car crash."

Oscar looked down at his ale.

"The parents had always hoped their daughter, who used to love horses, would return to run the farm one day. But she'd left the farm to go to college and only rarely came back since graduating."

Hope looked over at Oscar. He looked bored, but she plowed ahead.

"So the daughter, who's been working up in New York for some hedge fund, returns to the farm to discover the farm's been losing money for years and…"

"She steps in to save it."

"Yes, but…"

"And let me guess, there's some impossibly handsome

yet emotionally distant man running the place who the daughter butts heads with. And the two wind up falling in love and saving the farm together."

Hope was scowling.

"I'm right, aren't I?" said Oscar, giving Hope a self-satisfied grin before taking another sip of his ale.

Hope hoped that he choked.

"Here you go!" said Nan, depositing their food on the table. She saw their faces. "Everything all right?"

"Fine," said Hope, still glaring at Oscar.

Nan shook her head and left.

Hope looked down at her plate.

"Something wrong?" asked Oscar.

Hope picked up her burger and took a bite. It was good. But she was no longer hungry.

"Not at all," said Hope, taking another bite of her burger. She refused to let Oscar get to her.

They ate in silence, which was fine by Hope. When they were done, Nan came back over.

"You have room for pudding?" she asked. "Everything's homemade," she told Hope.

Hope was full, but she asked what they had to be polite.

"There's banoffee pie, fruit crumble, bread pudding, and ice cream."

"They all sound delicious, but I'm full."

Nan looked at Oscar.

"What about you? Fancy a piece of banoffee pie? I know how you like it."

"I'm good," said Oscar. "Just the check."

Nan shrugged.

"Suit yourself."

She returned a minute later with the check. Oscar took it from her before Hope could grab it.

"I was going to pay," said Hope.

"I've got it," said Oscar.

"But…"

"Gemma would expect me to pay."

"Fine. But I'm paying next time."

"That's assuming there is a next time."

He put some cash down on the table and they left.

As they were walking down the cobblestone street, Hope tripped and started to flail. Oscar grabbed her just before she fell.

"I've got you," he said, holding her.

Hope looked up into his face and felt her whole body grow warm even though it was chilly out. They stood there for several seconds, Oscar holding Hope as though he was dipping her on the dance floor. Then he righted her and Hope quickly stepped away from him.

"You need to be more careful," he said.

Hope didn't reply.

She took a step and winced.

"You okay?"

"I'm fine," Hope replied. But each time she put pressure on her right foot, she felt a shooting pain.

"You're clearly not," said Oscar. "Which foot is it, your right?"

Hope nodded. Though she wasn't sure if Oscar could see as it was dark out.

"Here, let me help you," he said, putting an arm around her and instructing her to lean on him.

"I told you I was…"

"I know what you told me, but your right foot is clearly not fine. Would you rather I carried you?"

Hope suddenly had an image of Oscar picking her up and carrying her back to Gemma's and felt her face grow warm again.

"Fine," she said, leaning on him.

They made it back to Gemma's and Oscar insisted on taking a look at Hope's foot.

"It told you it's…" Hope yelped as Oscar felt her right ankle.

"It's swollen," he said. "I don't think it's broken. Probably just sprained it."

"Is that your professional opinion? You a doctor in addition to being a playwright?"

For once, Oscar didn't scowl at her.

"I didn't go to med school, but I've seen my share of sprained ankles. I'll get you some ice."

Before she could say anything, he disappeared into the kitchen, returning a minute later with a bag of ice.

"Here," he said. "Put this on it and try to keep it elevated."

"Thank you, Dr. Tennant."

"Do you need help getting to your room?"

Hope imagined him sweeping her into his arms and carrying her to her room.

"I think I can manage," she said. "I'm just going to sit here for a minute."

"Would you like some tea?"

Hope looked up at him. Why was he suddenly being so nice?

"Is there herbal tea?"

"I think so. Shall I make us some?"

"Don't go to any trouble."

"It's no trouble," he said and headed to the kitchen.

CHAPTER 23

Oscar returned a few minutes later with a tray. On it was a pot of tea, two mugs, sugar, and milk. He poured the tea into the mugs.

"What do you take in your tea?"

"What kind is it?"

"Chamomile."

"I'm fine with it as is. Thank you."

Hope took a sip. The tea was hot, but it felt good, soothing.

"I need to do some more work," said Oscar, getting up. "You going to be okay?"

"I'll be fine. Is Gemma back?"

He shrugged.

"What does that mean?"

"It means I don't know."

"What if something's happened to her?"

Oscar gave Hope an amused look.

"I'm sure she's fine."

"Do you know where she is?"

"I have a pretty good idea."

"A *pretty* good idea?"

"Gemma can take care of yourself."

You didn't seem to think so at the ball, Hope said to herself.

"Good night, Ms. Halladay."

"It's Hope."

He seemed amused again.

"Good night, *Hope.*"

"Good night, *Oscar.*"

He smiled at that, and Hope thought he had a nice smile.

She watched him as he headed up the stairs. Then she finished her tea. She went to get up, but as soon as she stepped on her right foot, she felt a shooting pain again. Maybe she should have had Oscar carry her to her room. Well, too late now.

She looked at the tea things. She hated to just leave them there. Well, hopefully, her foot would feel better in the morning, and she'd wash everything before Oscar and Gemma came down.

She carefully pushed herself up, balancing on her left leg, and hopped to the bathroom where she took two ibuprofen. Then she brushed her teeth, washed her face, and hopped to her room, changing into her nightshirt and climbing into bed. She thought about reading a manuscript but changed her mind, picking up *Villette.*

Hope winced as she got out of bed the next morning. She had forgotten about her foot. She didn't think it was broken, but it hurt, and there was a bruise on her right ankle. She made her way to the bathroom, taking two more ibuprofen and splashing cold water on her face. That done, she gingerly made her way to the kitchen to get some ice. On the way, she noticed that the tea things were no longer in the living room.

She entered the kitchen to find Gemma there, drinking a cup of tea.

"Good morning," said Gemma.

"Good morning," said Hope.

"How is your ankle?"

Had Oscar told her? Or maybe Gemma had noticed Hope limping.

"It's okay."

"Do you need to see a doctor?"

"I don't think so. I think it's just a sprain. I'm sure I'll be fine in a day or so."

"Well, if you change your mind about going to see a doctor, let me know."

"Thank you, but I'm good. I was just getting some ice."

Hope hobbled to the fridge.

"Sit," Gemma commanded. "And put your foot up on the chair. I'll get you some ice. Would you like some tea?"

"I was going to make myself some coffee." Hope glanced around the kitchen. "Where's Oscar?"

"At that horse farm of his."

"Again?"

"He goes there whenever he's feeling frustrated. Says it helps clear his head, get his mind off of things."

"Have you been there?"

"Oh yes."

"What do you think of the place?"

"I think it's a blessing. Anne and Bert provide a wonderful service."

"They do."

"You've been there?"

Hope nodded.

"Oscar took me. We mucked out stalls together and then went for a ride."

"How very interesting," said Gemma. "Here you go," she said, handing Hope a bag of ice.

Hope put the ice on her right ankle and grimaced. It was cold.

"Does it hurt?"

"It was more the shock of the cold."

Hope let the ice rest on her ankle for a minute. Then she put the bag on the table and made to get up, wincing as she did. Gemma tutted.

"Sit," said Gemma. "What do you need?"

"I was going to make myself some coffee."

"I think Oscar left some."

"No offense, but I prefer it fresh."

"No offense taken. If you tell me how much coffee to put in, I'll make it for you."

Hope was going to say she'd make it herself, but she saw the look on Gemma's face.

"Thank you," said Hope and told Gemma how much coffee and water to put in.

"Did you have a good time with your friend?" Hope asked her.

"I did," Gemma replied.

"Is this an old friend?"

"Not that old."

Hope wondered if the friend was a man or a woman. She wanted to ask Gemma, but she didn't want to seem too nosy.

"Here you go," said Gemma when the coffee was ready. "Milk and sugar?"

"Please," said Hope.

Gemma brought over a pitcher of milk and a sugar bowl.

"Help yourself."

"Thank you."

Hope stirred in a little sugar and then added a splash of milk. Then she took a sip.

"Well, I should get going," said Gemma.

"You going upstairs to work?"

"I have an appointment in town."

"An appointment?" It was rather early to have an appointment. "Is everything okay?" Hope wondered if Gemma was ill. Though she looked to be in perfect health.

"Everything's fine, dear. There's just something I need to do. I'll be back in a bit."

"To work on the manuscript."

Gemma gave her a funny look. Then it was as though a light bulb went on.

"Oh, yes, the manuscript! It's in good hands. Now I must go. I'll see you later."

Hope watched her leave. Well, that was odd. She took another sip of her coffee. She should probably eat something before getting to work. She hobbled to the pantry and took out the loaf of bread, placing two slices in the toaster. When she was done with her coffee and toast, she hobbled to the sink to wash her things. Then she hobbled back to her room.

Hope had set up shop at the dining table. It was the only place that made any sense. She had emailed Fiona the day before, asking how things were going, and Fiona had written back that everything was under control and had asked about Gemma.

Hope told her that Gemma was pretty much as she had imagined her.

Hope was typing up the report on the manuscript she had described to Oscar when he returned. He seemed to not see her.

"Everything good at the farm?" Hope called.

He stopped and looked over at her.

"Fine," he said and headed upstairs. He seemed distracted.

Gemma returned a few minutes later.

"How was your appointment?" Hope asked her. "Everything okay?"

"Everything's fine, dear," Gemma replied. "How's your ankle?"

"Better."

"Happy to hear it. Can I get you anything?"

"I'm good."

Gemma headed to the kitchen humming. She came out with a glass of water a couple of minutes later, still humming.

Well, she seems to be in a good mood, thought Hope.

"I'm heading upstairs," said Gemma. "Give a shout if you need anything."

"You do the same if you need help with the manuscript!" Hope called after her.

Ninety minutes later, Gemma came back down the stairs and pulled on her coat. Was she leaving again?

"You leaving?" Hope asked. Though, obviously, she was.

"I have a lunch date," Gemma replied. "But there's plenty of food for you and Oscar. You will make sure he eats, won't you? He gets rather grouchy when he doesn't."

"I can try," Hope replied. "Will you be here for dinner, or will you be going out again?"

"I was planning on eating here. Why?"

"Just wanted to know if I should make plans."

"Plans?" Gemma looked confused.

"For dinner, in case you and Oscar wanted some alone time."

Gemma looked amused.

"I get plenty of alone time with Oscar. Do you not want to join us?"

"I just didn't want to impose."

"You're not imposing. You're our guest. And I enjoy cooking."

"If you're sure."

"I am. So, do you have any food allergies I should be aware of? Any things you don't like to eat?"

"No food allergies. At least that I'm aware of. And I'll eat almost anything."

Gemma smiled.

"Good. I must dash, but I'll see you later."

Hope watched Gemma leave and wondered who she was seeing. Was it the same friend or a different one? And how could the manuscript possibly be finished by the end of the month when Gemma was barely at home?

Hope went back to work but was having trouble concentrating. She needed food. She was about to head to the kitchen when she remembered what Gemma said and sent a text to Oscar.

"I'm about to have lunch. Care to join me?"

No reply.

Hope waited another minute and then fired off another text.

"Gemma said to make sure you ate something."

She waited another minute. When he again didn't reply, she gingerly got up and made her way to the kitchen.

She was making herself a grilled cheese sandwich when Oscar came in.

"What are you making?"

"A grilled cheese sandwich."

He watched as Hope flipped the sandwich onto a plate.

"You want a bite?"

"No thanks," he said.

Hope shrugged.

"Suit yourself. You don't know what you're missing."

"I think I have a rather good idea."

"What are you going to have?" she asked him.

"I haven't decided."

Hope watched as he rooted around and took out bread, cheddar cheese, butter, and a cucumber, making himself a cheese and cucumber sandwich.

"And how is that any different from a grilled cheese other than not being grilled?" Hope asked him.

"It's entirely different," he said, taking a bite.

Hope watched him and then resumed eating her grilled cheese. She would never understand men, especially this one.

As they were eating, Oscar's phone rang. He glanced at the screen, frowned, and swiped to answer.

"Yes?" he said.

Hope thought he sounded rather rude and wondered who was calling.

"I'm just finishing lunch," he told the caller. "I'll call you back in a few." He ended the call and put the phone down.

Hope wanted to ask him who it was, but she doubted he'd tell her. Besides, it was none of her business.

Oscar finished the last bite of his sandwich and put his plate and glass in the sink.

"I'll wash up later," he told Hope and left the kitchen.

Hope watched him go. She doubted he would be back to wash his things anytime soon and knew she'd wind up washing them. She sighed and got up.

CHAPTER 24

Dinner with Gemma and Oscar had been surprisingly pleasant. Gemma had roasted a chicken with some vegetables, and they had shared a bottle of white wine. Technically a bottle and a half. Maybe that was why everyone seemed to be in such a good mood or so relaxed.

Gemma had been curious about Hope, asking her how she liked being an editor and who some of her favorite authors were. Then Hope asked Gemma who some of her favorite authors were. Then they veered off into a discussion about contemporary literature versus literature from the 19th century, with Oscar remaining mostly quiet.

Hope had volunteered to help clean up, but Gemma shooed her away, telling her she was a guest and to rest her ankle. Instead, she got Oscar to help her.

Hope went to bed that evening feeling a bit better about things. And the next morning, her ankle felt much better, though it was still sore. After making herself some coffee and toast, she took her laptop to the dining table and worked.

Soon, the three of them fell into a kind of routine. They would work during the day, Hope at the dining table, Gemma and Oscar upstairs. That is when Gemma was around. She seemed to have quite an active social life, having lunch or tea with this friend or that in the village. Then the three of them would typically have dinner together. Except when Gemma dined with a friend. Those nights, Oscar and Hope would dine together. It turned out, Oscar was a surprisingly good cook.

Hope had tried getting him to talk about himself, but he was reticent. So Hope wound up doing most of the talking.

That Friday, Hope was to have dinner with Edward. She hadn't seen him since he had dropped her off, though they had talked on the phone and texted. She hadn't told him about her ankle for fear of worrying him. But now that her ankle was almost all better, she welcomed the opportunity to see him and get out of the house.

The doorbell rang at seven o'clock, and Hope called out that she would get it. However, she needn't have bothered. Gemma was out, and Oscar was upstairs working.

She smiled when she saw Edward. He was nicely dressed and had a bouquet of wildflowers in his hands.

"For me?" said Hope.

"Actually, they're for Gemma," he said a bit apologetically. "I know how Lady Josephine loved wildflowers, and I thought…"

"There's very sweet of you," said Hope, smiling at him. She wondered again if Edward had a little crush on the author. "But Gemma's not here."

"Oh," said Edward, looking disappointed.

"But I'll be sure to tell her the flowers are from you. I'm sure she'll be delighted. Come in while I go find a vase to put them in."

Edward stepped inside and handed Hope the flowers.

"I'll just be a minute," she said and went to the kitchen to look for a vase.

It took a bit of searching, but Hope finally found a vase that would do. She filled it with water and placed the flowers inside. She was just coming out of the kitchen with the flowers when she saw Oscar. He was saying something to Edward, and judging by the look on Edward's face, it wasn't something good.

She hurried over, holding the vase full of flowers.

"What did Oscar say to you?" she asked Edward.

"I can't believe you didn't tell me about your ankle!"

Hope turned and glared at Oscar. Then she turned back to Edward.

"It wasn't a big deal. And as you can see, I'm fine now." However, she could tell by the look on Edward's face that he was hurt. Should she have told him? Well, too late now.

"Oscar said that he had to carry you home and that you've barely been able to walk on it."

Hope shot another scathing look at Oscar. Was it her imagination or was he enjoying this?

"He did not carry me. I merely leaned on him a bit. And I was able to get around just fine after a day or two."

"You should have called."

"And what, you'd have run over here and carried me from room to room?"

Oscar snorted at that, which earned him a dirty look from Hope.

"If you needed me to," said Edward.

Hope saw that he was serious and placed a hand on Edward's arm.

"That's very sweet of you. But as you can see, I'm fine. Now, shall we go? I'm hungry."

Oscar cleared his throat.

"Yes?" said Hope.

"You may want to put down that vase first."

Hope looked down at the vase and placed it on a nearby table. Then she went to get her jacket.

"Before you go," said Oscar, causing Hope to pause. "Remember we need to leave early tomorrow. So don't stay out too late."

Hope looked confused.

"What are you talking about?" She didn't recall making any plans with Oscar.

"You didn't forget about Farm Day, did you?"

Hope racked her brain.

"Farm Day?"

"At Ruby's Place. It's tomorrow."

"Who's Ruby?" asked Edward.

"Ruby's Place is an equestrian center that works with children and adults of differing mental and physical abilities," explained Hope. "Oscar volunteers there."

"And Farm Day is a fundraiser, an open house if you will, to raise awareness about the farm," said Oscar. "You had said you wanted to help out."

"Right." Hope had forgotten. Though, to be fair, Oscar hadn't reminded her about it. Until now. She turned to Edward. "You're more than welcome to join us. They're always looking for volunteers."

Oscar frowned at that.

"I have plans tomorrow," said Edward. "And I don't know the first thing about horses."

That seemed to cheer Oscar up.

"Hope's been a huge help," said Oscar, placing a hand on Hope's arm. "She's been getting down and dirty with me with nary a complaint."

Hope shot Oscar another dirty look. What was he playing at? Then she turned to Edward.

"I've only been there once. I helped Oscar muck out some stalls. It's rather dirty work, but I enjoyed it."

"We also went for a ride. Don't forget about that." Oscar turned to Edward. "Hope's a natural horsewoman."

"I didn't know you rode," said Edward.

"She didn't tell you?"

If looks could kill, Oscar would be dead.

"I used to ride and help take care of the horses at the stable I rode at back in Connecticut," she told Edward. "I thought I mentioned it back when we were at uni."

"I must have forgotten," said Edward.

"Anyway," said Oscar, "we need to be at the farm by eight. And it's going to be a long day. So Hope needs to get a good night's rest."

"I'll be fine," said Hope.

"If you say so. Well, enjoy your dinner. Nice seeing you again, Eddy."

He then jogged up the stairs, whistling a jaunty tune.

"What was that about?" asked Edward.

"Just ignore him," said Hope. "So, shall we go?"

"You sure you're okay? Do you need to lean on me?"

"Do I look like I need help?"

"Sorry. It's just Oscar said…"

Hope sighed.

"I'm fine, Edward. Oscar was exaggerating. Now let's go to dinner. I'm starving."

"How much farther is this place?" Hope asked Edward after they had been driving for fifteen minutes.

"Not much farther."

"And what kind of food do they serve?"

"They specialize in local, seasonal fare."

"How did you hear about it?"

"One of my clients recommended the place. He was surprised I hadn't been there. Said it was famous. Even had a Michelin star."

"Wow! You didn't have to take me someplace fancy. I'd be fine with whatever. Am I dressed all right?"

"It's not fancy, just good. And you look lovely."

Hope wasn't so sure about that, but she didn't say anything.

"Here we are!" said Edward, ten minutes later.

Edward parked the Mini, and they headed to the restaurant. It was an attractive place, simple yet elegant, with exposed brick walls on two sides, warm lighting, and tables covered with white tablecloths and a little succulent in a terra-cotta pot.

Edward gave his name to the host, and he and Hope were led to a table for two in the corner.

"Enjoy your meal," said the host, placing a wine list and two menus on the table. "A server will be over shortly."

Their server, a young woman who looked to be around their age, came over a few minutes later to take their drink order.

"Shall we get a bottle of wine?" Edward asked Hope.

"Could you give us a minute?" she asked the server.

"Of course," the woman replied.

"Is something the matter?" asked Edward.

"I was just wondering if we should maybe get just a glass of something instead of a whole bottle."

"Why? Are you worried about my driving ability? If so, I assure you, I know these roads like the back of my hand, and a couple of glasses of wine is nothing, especially with food. Or are you worried you may sleep through your alarm and miss Farm Day?"

Hope made a face.

"Fine. Go ahead and order us a bottle."

"You sure?"

"Positive."

"Red or white?"

"I suppose it depends on what we're having. We should probably take a look at the menus."

Hope picked up her menu and studied it. It was a small menu, with only five starters and the same number of main courses.

"What are you thinking of having?" Edward asked her.

"I'm torn between the lamb and one of the fish dishes. What about you?"

"I was thinking either the venison or the monkfish."

"Well, we could both get fish and get a bottle of white.

Or we could both get meat and get red. Or we could get whatever we wanted and pick a wine."

"What are you leaning toward?"

"The lamb does sound awfully good."

"Fine. You get the lamb, and I'll get the venison, and we'll get a bottle of red. Do you want to get a starter?"

"Do you want to share the vegetable terrine?"

"Sounds good to me."

They put their menus down, and Edward signaled to their server.

"Yes?" she said.

"Can you recommend a bottle of red? We're going to be having the lamb and the venison."

"May I?" she said, indicating the wine list. Edward opened it. "This Burgundy is very nice," she said, pointing to one of the Burgundies. "Or else the Pinot Noir."

"Hm," said Edward, looking quite serious.

Hope couldn't help smiling. She didn't recall Edward being into wine when they were at university. He had always drunk beer. Of course, that was years ago, and people and tastes changed.

"Let's go with the Pinot Noir. And I believe we're ready to order." He looked at Hope, who nodded. "We're going to share the vegetable terrine to start. Then the lady will have the lamb, and I'll have the venison."

"Very good, sir," said the server. "Would you like a cocktail or glass of something to start?"

"Just some water for me," said Hope.

"For me too," said Edward.

"Flat or sparkling?"

Edward looked at Hope.

"Do you have tap?" she asked the server. "If so, I'll have that."

"Me too," said Edward.

"So when did you get into wine?" Hope asked Edward after the server had gone.

"It's Lucy's fault. She had us take some wine course given by a friend of hers, and I kind of got hooked."

"Ah," said Hope.

A busboy came over with a pitcher of water and filled their water glasses. Hope thanked him and took a sip.

"Speaking of Lucy, have you heard from her since we saw her at the ball?"

"Why do you ask?"

"Just curious. If you ask me, I think she was annoyed that you showed up there with a date."

"You think so?"

"Mm," said Hope. "I'd even wager she was a bit jealous."

"Jealous? When she was there with *Gabriel?*" He pronounced it the French way.

Hope smiled.

"Gabriel can't hold a candle to you."

"I don't know about that."

"So if she phoned or texted you and said that she'd made a horrible mistake and wanted to get back together, what would you say?"

Edward took a sip of his water.

"I… uh…"

"You're not sure?"

"Look, if you don't mind, I'd rather not talk about Lucy."

"Sorry," said Hope. "I didn't mean to bring up a sore subject."

"That's all right. It's just…"

Was it Hope's imagination or did Edward seem nervous?

The server arrived with their wine. Hope watched as she uncorked it and poured a little bit into Edward's glass. He swirled it around and sniffed it. Then he took a sip while the server waited.

"It's good," he said. "Go ahead and pour."

She poured the wine into Hope's glass and then filled Edward's. When she was done and had left again, Edward turned to Hope.

"We should toast," he said.

"What should we toast to?"

"To renewing old friendships."

Hope smiled.

"To renewing old friendships."

They clinked glasses and drank. Then Edward put his glass down and looked over at Hope.

"So how's it going over there, really? Are they treating you well?"

"They are. Though…"

"Yes?"

"Gemma keeps disappearing." Edward raised an eyebrow. "Maybe that's the wrong word. She keeps going off to meet friends or to appointments, and I'm worried about the manuscript."

"Has she shared any of it with you?"

"No. But she keeps telling me that it's in good shape."

"I take it you don't believe her."

"I don't know what to believe. What about you? How's work going?"

"Good."

"You like working for yourself?"

"Best boss I've ever had," he said with a smile.

"And how's Arfur?"

"He misses you. You should come see him."

"I miss him too. Did you take him to Poppy's this evening?"

"No, he's at home. I took him for a walk before I left and will take him out again as soon as I get back."

Hope looked around the restaurant. Every table was full.

"Are you all right?" Edward asked her. "You seem a bit distracted."

"Sorry, I'm just hungry."

As if hearing her, their server arrived with their vegetable terrine and some bread.

CHAPTER 25

Dinner had been delicious, and Hope felt pleasantly full when they left the restaurant. Between the wine and the lamb and the crème brulée they had shared for dessert, Hope was feeling sleepy and nearly nodded off on the drive back to Cupid's Bow, even though it wasn't yet nine o'clock.

Edward parked in front of Gemma's and insisted on walking Hope to the door.

"Thank you for dinner," Hope said to him. "It was great."

"I enjoyed it too."

He took a step closer and placed a hand on Hope's cheek. Then he leaned in and kissed her. Hope closed her eyes and kissed him back. Edward's lips were soft and warm. But she felt nothing, no spark. He stepped back and looked at her.

"I'm sorry," he said. "I should have asked permission first. I've just been wanting to do that all night."

"It's all right," said Hope. A part of Hope had been wondering what it would feel like to kiss Edward again after all this time. Now she knew.

Suddenly, the door swung open. Hope turned to see Oscar looming in the doorway.

"What are you doing here?"

"I live here," he said. "Or had you forgotten?"

"That's not what I meant," said Hope. "I meant why are you *here* here? Were you spying on us?"

"I thought I heard a rat," he said, looking at Edward.

"Really, you thought you heard a rat, from upstairs?"

"I was in the living room, reading."

"Oh?" said Hope. "You just happened to be reading in the living room?"

"Is there a law against reading in one's living room?"

"It's Gemma's living room."

Edward's eyes went back and forth between the two of them as though watching a tennis match.

"I should go," he said as Hope and Oscar continued to glare at one another.

"You don't have to," said Hope, turning to face him. "Would you like to come in and have some herbal tea?" Though he had had a cup of coffee at the restaurant.

"Thank you. I'm good. I need to get home and take Arfur for a walk. And I know you have to be up early tomorrow."

Oscar smiled at that.

"Okay. Well, I'll see you soon, yes?"

"I'll message you," said Edward. He glanced at Oscar, then he turned and walked quickly to his car.

Hope glared at Oscar as they went inside.

"What?" he said innocently.

"You know perfectly well what. *You thought you heard a rat.* Really?"

"Was I wrong?"

"Edward is an old friend."

"Do you often kiss your old friends?"

"So you were spying on us!"

"I told you I…"

"Yes, I know what you told me. You were reading in the living room. And you just happened to see us kiss?"

"Would you care for some herbal tea?"

Hope made a face. Oscar was clearly enjoying himself. She had preferred it when he had been a silent grouch who just wanted to be left alone.

"I'm going to bed."

"Suit yourself. Just make sure you're ready by seven."

"I'll be ready."

"Shall I knock on your door, make sure you're up?"

"I'll set my alarm. Is Gemma back?"

"Not yet."

"Will you be waiting up for her too?"

"For the record, I wasn't waiting up for you."

"Could have fooled me. I'll see you in the morning."

"Pleasant dreams," he called.

Hope had set her alarm for six-fifteen. That way she could snooze for a bit before she really had to get up. Oscar had said there would be breakfast at the farm for all of the volunteers. And Hope would wait to take a shower until they got back to Gemma's. No point taking one now when she would just get sweaty and smelly at the farm. She just needed to get herself dressed and make some coffee.

She got out of bed at six-thirty and headed to the bathroom. Once she was dressed, she headed to the kitchen. Oscar was there.

"You made coffee," she said, noticing the nearly full carafe.

"I know how you enjoy your caffeine."

Hope looked over at him. Was he being snarky or nice? It was hard to tell.

She took out a mug and poured coffee into it, adding sugar and milk.

"Does it meet with your approval?"

"It's not bad."

"High praise indeed. Well, drink up. We need to get going."

"I thought we didn't need to leave until seven."

"Yes, well, I just want to make sure you'll be ready."

"I'm dressed, aren't I?"

Hope took another sip of coffee.

"Are you planning on watching me drink?"

Oscar sighed.

"Fine. I'll be in the other room. Just…"

"You don't have to say it. I'll be ready by seven. Though do you really think the horses would notice if we were a few minutes late?"

"The horses wouldn't, but Anne would."

Hope took a few more sips of coffee after Oscar left and then dumped the rest into the sink and washed her mug.

Oscar was waiting for her in the living room.

"I just need to brush my teeth and then we can go."

"So what time did Gemma get home last night?" Hope asked Oscar as they drove to Ruby's Place.

"I don't know."

"You don't know?"

"She wasn't back by the time I went up to bed."

"What time did you go up to bed?"

"Around eleven."

"Did you see her this morning?" He shook his head. "You sure she came home?"

"She's home."

"How can you tell?"

He shot her a look, one that said not to question him.

"Do you know where she was?"

"With a friend."

"Do you know this friend?"

Oscar looked over at her again.

"Why?"

"Why what?"

"Why do you care where Gemma was, or who she sees, or what time she gets home? What business is it of yours?"

"I just worry about her."

"You mean you're worried about the manuscript."

Hope felt stung. She had grown fond of Gemma and worried about her. But, okay, she was also worried about the manuscript.

"I just want to make sure she's all right."

"She's fine."

"How can you be so sure?"

"You'll just have to trust me."

They arrived at Ruby's Place to find several cars already in the lot. Oscar parked, and they made their way over to the barn.

Hope saw Anne. She was talking to a group of volunteers. At least Hope assumed that's what they were. As Oscar and Hope approached, she turned and smiled at them.

"Oscar!" she said. "Ah, and I see you brought your friend again."

"She insisted on coming," said Oscar.

Hope shot him a look. She hadn't *insisted*. He had commandeered her.

"Well, we're glad to have you," said Anne. "Hope, allow me to introduce my husband, Bert, and our older daughter, Emerald. She's down from uni for the weekend."

"Nice to meet you," Hope said to them. Though Emerald didn't look happy to meet her. Was she upset that Hope had worn her clothes?

"I didn't know you were seeing someone," Emerald said to Oscar. Was she pouting?

Ah, so that explained the look, thought Hope. Emerald had a thing for Oscar.

"I'm not," said Oscar.

"I'm just visiting," said Hope.

Emerald seemed to be deciding whether or not she believed them.

"Anyway," said Anne. "We've got lots to do before people start pouring in. We've got stables to clean, horses to groom, tack to put on…"

"Just tell us what you want us to do," said a man who Hope thought looked like a farmer out of a British period drama. "We'll do whatever needs doing."

The other volunteers, who ranged in age from teenagers to pensioners, nodded.

"Thank you, Alfred. Now, shall we get sorted?"

Hope wasn't surprised that Emerald had taken Oscar to help her groom the horses and had relegated Hope to mucking out the stalls. It was obvious Emerald fancied Oscar, even though he was at least a dozen years older than her.

Oscar had offered to switch with Hope, but Emerald wouldn't hear of it. And Hope said she didn't mind. She was there to help in whatever way she could. And she had company in the barn.

"You from America?" asked her partner in mucking out the stalls, a young man named Jimmy, who looked to be in high school.

"I am," said Hope.

"Where?" he asked.

"New York City."

"New York City, eh? You a Yankees fan?"

Hope smiled.

"You follow baseball?"

"Not really. Just know about them. So, what's it like living there? You like living in the big city?"

Hope thought about it. She never really thought of New York as a big city, though it was.

"I do."

"So what's a big city girl like you doing in Devon, mucking out stalls?"

"I grew up in the country and used to ride. Mucking out stalls was part of what one did if you had a horse."

"You have a horse?"

"Not anymore. I did, briefly, when I was much younger. What about you? Do you have a horse?"

Jimmy shook his head.

"That's why I come here. They let me ride if I help out."

"That's nice," said Hope.

They didn't speak for several minutes. Then Jimmy asked her if she and Oscar were dating.

Hope stopped what she was doing.

"Why do you ask?"

"He's never brought anyone here before."

"I see," said Hope. "Well, to answer your question, we're not dating."

"Would you like to be?"

Hope looked at him.

"I'm going to start on the next stall," she informed him. *Really*, she thought to herself. *Why did everyone here think she and Oscar were dating? Had he said something to his farm friends?*

Hope tried not to think about Oscar as she started to shovel hay. But for some reason, she kept seeing him astride Lightning, his well-formed derriere moving up and down in the saddle.

"Get a grip, Hope," she told herself, then she plunged her shovel into a pile of manure.

The volunteers were busy eating when Hope emerged from the stables. She knew she must smell from cleaning the stalls, but there was nothing she could do about it. Visitors would be arriving soon, and the volunteers would continue to be busy until the event was over that afternoon.

Hope made her way to the food table. It had been picked over, but there was still plenty to eat, which was good because Hope was starving.

"You okay?" Oscar asked her, seeing Hope scarf down her food.

"Mm," she replied, nodding her head.

"You can slow down, you know. We have a few minutes before the gates open."

Hope swallowed and took a sip of water.

"I didn't realize I was so hungry."

"Cleaning stalls is hard work. About that… I'm sorry."

Hope looked at him.

"Why are you sorry? I volunteered, remember?" Though technically Emerald had ordered her to clean the stalls.

"Yes, but you shouldn't have to spend all your time here mucking out stalls."

"I didn't mind. Besides, I had help."

Oscar was looking at her, and Hope couldn't help noticing the flecks of green in his eyes.

"Ahem."

They turned to see Emerald. She was glaring at Hope.

"Yes?" said Oscar.

Emerald turned to look at him, her scowl melting away.

"Have you tried my muffins?" she asked him. "I made them specially for you."

"Not yet," said Oscar.

"Come," she said, taking his hand and dragging him up. "You need to taste one before they're all gone."

"Sorry," Oscar mouthed to Hope as Emerald led him to the buffet table.

Anne came over.

"You must forgive Emerald," she said to Hope. "She has a crush on Oscar."

"So I noticed."

They were both looking over at Emerald, who was feeding Oscar a piece of muffin.

"We were hoping Emerald would find someone her own

age when she went off to university. But she seems set on Oscar. I know he doesn't encourage her but…"

"Does she know what a grouch he can be?"

"A grouch?" Anne seemed surprised. "He's always so wonderful with the people who visit here and the other volunteers. I'm always saying to Bert that the man has the patience of a saint, with horses and people. I've never thought of him as grouchy."

"Are we talking about the same Oscar?"

Just then Bert came over and said something to his wife. She nodded and then turned back to Hope.

"I need to go."

"Is everything all right?"

"People are queueing at the gate." She turned to the group. "Everyone! Please finish up. We're about to open the gate."

The volunteers quickly finished. Then it was showtime.

CHAPTER 26

The rest of the day went by in a blur. Hope had handed out flyers about the farm and helped out at the food and drinks table. She had offered to help lead the horses around the track and assist in other ways, but Anne and Bert had more experienced volunteers, like Oscar, and their instructors to handle the horses and riders.

Hope had been impressed watching Oscar work with first-time visitors to the farm. He was particularly good with the children, who were in awe of the big animals, wanting to touch the horses but scared to.

Oscar seemed to understand their fear and fascination and would patiently show each child who came over how and where to touch the horses. He'd even given a few of the more adventurous children carrots and apples to feed them, which would elicit giggles from the children as the horse's lips tickled their hands.

Hope remembered the first time she rode a horse, how she had been scared at first and then exhilarated. She imagined the children and even some of the adults who came to Ruby's Place must feel the same way.

She watched as Oscar helped a little girl into the saddle of a gray mare named Lady Jane. The little girl was clearly nervous, but Oscar said something to her, and she seemed to relax. Then Oscar led Lady Jane slowly around the track, the little girl waving to her parents.

Hope liked this version of Oscar much better than the grouchy one she was accustomed to. Was it the horses or the children that brought out this gentler, kinder side? She wondered. She didn't know anything about his personal life, other than that he had a sister—a half-sister. Did he have children? She was pretty sure he wasn't married. Though he could have been in the past. Perhaps he was an uncle.

They had never really discussed their personal lives, despite spending time together. Now she was curious. Perhaps she would ask him on the drive home.

Finally, the last visitors left, and Anne gathered the volunteers.

"Thank you for your hard work today," she said to the group. "Bert, Emerald, and I couldn't do what we do, provide a safe place for people of differing abilities to work with and ride horses, without all of you. And we got lots of people pledging to support Ruby's Place today.

"I only wish that Ruby could be here with us. As some of you know, she's spending the semester in Pretoria, working on her veterinary medicine degree, and couldn't make it back."

So that's where Ruby was, thought Hope. She had been surprised not to see her.

"Of course, we have more work to do now that our visitors have gone," Anne continued. "However, I understand that some of you are unable to stay."

Guilty looks were exchanged among some of the volunteers.

"Please, don't feel bad about leaving," Anne said to them. "You've done yeoman work today. And I understand you have other commitments. Go on."

At that, several of the volunteers left. Anne waited until they were far enough away to not hear her. Then she continued.

"As for the rest of you diehards, we've hired Farm to Table to organize supper for everyone, which they'll be serving after we've cleaned up the place. And there'll be wine and beer to drink as well as Alfred's Farmhouse Gin."

There was appreciative murmuring at that.

"All right. I trust you can sort yourselves. You know what needs to be done. And if you're unsure where to go or what to do, come see me or Bert or Charlie."

Charlie was the head groom, one of the few full-time employees at the farm.

"And remember, the sooner we're done, the sooner we can eat and drink," Anne said as the volunteers dispersed.

"What should I do?" Hope asked Oscar.

"You were so good at cleaning out the stalls," said Emerald, who had come over and was standing next to Oscar. "You should go back there."

"I'll do it," said Oscar.

Emerald frowned.

"I wanted you to help me with the horses."

"I don't mind cleaning the stalls again," said Hope.

"There, you see?" said Emerald. She took Oscar's arm and started to drag him away. But Oscar disengaged himself.

"Why don't you get Jimmy or Peter to help you? I'm going to help Hope."

Emerald waited a few seconds and then stalked off.

"You didn't have to do that," said Hope as they headed to the stables.

"Yes, I did."

He took a shovel and handed Hope a pitchfork, and they began to work.

"You were so good with the children today. Do you have any?" Hope casually asked.

Oscar stopped what he was doing and looked at her.

"Do I have any children? Do you think I'm hiding them somewhere?"

Hope felt her face grow warm, but she refused to be intimidated.

"I don't know. You could be."

"Well, I'm not. And I'm not married either, in case you were about to ask."

"I wasn't. I was going to ask if you had any nieces or nephews."

"Not yet."

They resumed their shoveling.

"What about you?" he asked Hope.

"What about me?"

"Any children?"

Hope stopped and looked at him.

"Do I look like I have children?"

"Don't look so offended. You did ask me."

True.

"I do not have any children."

"Any nieces or nephews?"

"Not yet. Though my brother and his wife are expecting."

Hope had just found out via a text from her mother and had been annoyed that her brother hadn't told her himself. Then again, she and her brother weren't particularly close. And since he had become a doctor, she rarely saw or heard from him.

When she had heard the news, she wondered how Hal and his wife Livy had managed to find time to even make a baby, Livy also being a doctor, a busy OB/GYN. For all she knew, the baby had been conceived in a supply closet during one of their breaks at the hospital they both worked at.

"Congratulations," he said.

"Thanks," said Hope.

They finished cleaning the stall and moved on to the next one.

"That should do it," said Oscar when they had cleaned the last stall. "Shall we go see if there's food? Though I could use a drink."

"And I could use a shower."

"There's one just over there," said Oscar.

"I know, but I didn't bring a change of clothes. And I'd feel weird taking a shower with everyone here. I can wait until we get back. I'll just wash my hands and face. You might want to do the same."

"That bad, eh?"

She looked at his face. It was a rather handsome face, even with some dirt on it.

"You just have a smudge right there," she said, touching his cheek.

Hope froze as he looked at her, her face starting to flush.

"Sorry, I…"

"Don't be," said Oscar.

The next thing Hope knew, they were kissing. And unlike the kiss she had received from Edward, Oscar's kiss made Hope feel as though she would combust.

Oscar pulled her closer, his tongue seeking hers as his hands explored her body. Hope could feel his desire as she pressed against him. He pushed her up against the wall and darted his tongue into her ear, then worked his way down her neck.

He reached under her shirt and teased her nipple as he continued to kiss her, and Hope let out a low moan. She reached for the fly to his jeans, moving her hand over him.

They were so lost in each other that they didn't hear someone calling Oscar's name.

"Oscar?"

It was Emerald.

They froze. Hope quickly straightened her shirt and smoothed her hair as Oscar adjusted himself.

Oscar told Hope to stay put while he dealt with Emerald. Hope made a face but didn't say anything. The last thing she needed was Emerald suspecting something.

"Were you looking for me?" said Oscar, stepping out of the stall. "I was just finishing up."

Emerald glanced around.

"Where's Hope?"

"She went to freshen up."

"Come have a drink with me."

"Let me go wash up. I'll meet you over there."

Emerald pouted.

"Okay. Just don't be long."

"I won't."

"You can come out now," said Oscar after Emerald had left.

Hope emerged from the stall.

"You think she bought it?"

"Why wouldn't she?"

"Well, I should go wash up. I must look a fright."

"I think you look beautiful."

Hope looked at him. Was he teasing her? It was hard to tell.

"You may want to wash up too."

"I was planning on it. See you over at the drinks table?"

"See you there."

Hope stood looking at herself in the bathroom mirror. She looked a bit wild. She washed her hands and face and then dried them. Then she combed her fingers through her hair. She still looked a bit wild, but at least her hands and face were clean. She would take a shower as soon as she got back to Gemma's.

She left the bathroom and followed the noise. Several tables, some covered in food, others for sitting, had been set out in a nearby field, along with a bar of sorts. The other volunteers were busy drinking and eating. Hope looked for Oscar and saw him talking to Bert.

"Help yourself to a drink." It was Anne. Hope hadn't noticed her. She had been watching Oscar. How did he manage to look so calm? "There's gin, wine, and beer—as well as ginger beer, Dandelion & Burdock, and mineral water."

"Thanks," said Hope.

"You all right?" Anne asked her.

"I'm fine. It's just been a long day, and I'm a bit knackered."

Anne smiled.

"Already talking like an Englishwoman. Well, go get yourself something to eat and drink. That'll fix you up."

Hope headed over to the bar. One of the volunteers—Hope was pretty sure his name was Laurence—was there fixing himself a drink.

"Do we just help ourselves?" she asked him. She didn't see a bartender.

"That's the idea," he said.

She looked at his drink.

"Gin and tonic?"

"Indeed." He took a sip and smacked his lips. "You can't beat Alfred's gin. Best in the county."

"Oh?"

"You ever had it?"

Hope shook her head.

"Then you must try some! Alfred's Farmhouse Gin is famous in these parts. He makes it himself. Well, he used to. Now he has someone else making it."

"Alfred as in that Alfred?" she said, pointing to a volunteer named Alfred, the one she thought looked like a farmer from an English period drama, who was chatting with Charlie.

"The very same," said Laurence. "He used to make it in his barn and give it to friends and neighbors as gifts. They told him he should sell it, and one of his neighbors helped him get a loan. Next thing you know, the stuff is flying off the shelves."

"Wow," said Hope.

"Only problem is, the stuff's become so popular, it's hard to find. Alfred insists on producing small batches, even though he has someone making it for him, and it sells out quickly. Anne and Bert are lucky to have a case. Come, you must try some."

Laurence proceeded to fix Hope a gin and tonic.

"Here you go," he said, handing it to her. He watched as she took a sip, waiting for her reaction.

"It's good," she said.

"Told ya. I'm afraid I don't remember your name."

"It's Hope," said Hope.

"Laurence," said Laurence.

"You a regular?"

"I am. My little girl likes to come here and ride the ponies. We don't have a lot of extra spending money, so I help out in return."

Hope smiled.

"It's a special place Anne and Bert've got here," Laurence continued. "It's made a world of difference to my Evie."

"Was Evie here today?"

Laurence nodded.

"Her mother had to practically drag her away. She loves this place."

They took a sip of their drinks.

"We should get some food before it's gone," Laurence said, and Hope followed him over to where the food tables were set up.

She helped herself to some food and took a seat with some of the other volunteers. They immediately began asking her questions: What brought her to Devon and what did she think of it?

She told them that she had come to Devon for work and although she hadn't seen much of the county, she loved what she had seen. They were clearly pleased with her answer and asked her what she did. She told them she was an editor for a publishing house based in New York, and they wanted to know what authors she worked with.

Hope named a few, but most of the volunteers hadn't heard of them. Hope deliberately didn't mention Gemma.

"So which author brought you to Devon?" asked one of the volunteers.

"I'm not at liberty to say," replied Hope.

"Aw, come on. You can tell us," said another. "We won't tell."

There was some chuckling at that.

Just then, Hope saw Oscar looking over at her.

"Sorry, but I really can't say."

"Can you at least give us a hint?" asked one of the other volunteers.

Hope had opened her mouth to reply to the man, but Oscar had come over.

"We should go," he said.

"Okay," she replied.

"Must you?" It was Emerald, who had once again appeared without Hope noticing her creep up.

"I'm afraid we must," said Oscar. Emerald was pouting. "But I'll see you soon."

"No, you won't. I'm going back to uni tomorrow."

"Well, I'm sure I'll see you the next time you're home."

Anne came over and told her daughter to leave Oscar alone, which only made Emerald pout more.

"You two leaving?" she asked Oscar.

"We are."

"Well, thanks for coming," Anne said to the two of them. Then she turned to Hope. "You're welcome here anytime. And I promise, we won't make you clean out the stalls the next time."

Hope smiled.

"Thank you," she said. "But I really didn't mind."

"Let's go," said Oscar, "before Anne ropes us into helping her clean up."

Anne smiled, and Oscar led Hope to the car park.

CHAPTER 27

"Thank you for taking me to the farm today," Hope said as they drove back to Gemma's.

Oscar didn't reply. He looked preoccupied. Hope wondered what he was thinking. Was he thinking about what had happened at the stable? Hope was pretty sure that if Emerald hadn't interrupted them, things would have gone a lot further. The thought made Hope squirm in her seat.

"You all right?" Oscar asked, glancing over at her.

"I'm fine. Why?"

"You seem a bit antsy."

"I just want to get these smelly clothes off and get a shower."

Oscar looked over at her again, and Hope immediately felt her face grow warm. Was he thinking about her without her clothes on? Or maybe he was envisioning her in the shower.

Stop it! Hope told herself and looked out the window.

They arrived at Gemma's a short time later. There was a car parked in front, and Hope thought she recognized it.

Oscar was frowning.

"Is something wrong?" she asked him.

He didn't reply. Just got out of the car and headed to the house, not bothering to wait for Hope. As soon as he reached the front door, it swung open.

"It's about time," said Felicity. "Where have you been?"

Oscar glared at her.

Hope knew she was staring but couldn't help it. She had done a search for *Felicity Rogers* after Edward had told her who she was. She was a model/actress, just like Edward had said. So how did she know Oscar? Were they dating? But wasn't Felicity supposed to be seeing some tech billionaire?

"What are you doing here?" Oscar asked her.

"I missed you," said Felicity. "Aren't you happy to see me?"

"Not especially."

Felicity pouted. Then she noticed Hope.

"Oh my," she said. "What on earth have you done to her, Oscar?"

Hope suddenly felt self-conscious. She knew she looked a bit rough, but the way Felicity was looking at her…

"Are you going to let us in?" Oscar asked Felicity.

"Sorry," she said, opening the door wider. "Won't you come in?"

Oscar gave her a dirty look.

"Where's Gemma?"

"Out with you-know-who."

Hope wondered who *you-know-who* was.

"I'm going to take a shower," she said.

"Wait," said Felicity. Hope stopped. "We haven't been formally introduced. I'm Felicity, Oscar's…" Oscar was subtly shaking his head. "An old friend," she finally said.

Hope looked over at Oscar, but he had on his poker face.

"Nice to meet you," said Hope. "Now if you don't mind? It's been a long day."

"Go right ahead," said Felicity.

She watched as Hope made her way to the bathroom. When she was gone, she turned to Oscar.

"What's going on?"

"What do you mean?"

"You two take a tumble in the hay?"

Oscar frowned.

"Hope and I were at the farm."

"You took her to the farm?"

"So?"

"You've never taken me to the farm."

"I didn't think you were interested."

"Not especially. So, what were the two of you doing there, other than taking a roll in the hay?"

Oscar glared at her.

"We were helping out. It was Farm Day."

"You dragged Hope to Farm Day?"

"She volunteered."

"I'm sure."

"What are you doing here, Fe?"

"I told you. I missed you."

"You'll excuse me if I don't believe you."

"If you must know, Graham and I had a row."

"Another one?"

Felicity scowled.

"Anyway, I felt it best to get away for a couple of days."

"Well, you can't stay here."

"Why not?"

"Hope's using your room."

"So?"

He gave her a look.

"I could always sleep in your room."

"No."

"We have shared a room before."

"Not in a long time."

"Fine. I'll sleep in Gemma's room. I doubt she'll be home tonight."

"Did you see her?"

"I did. She was humming."

"Humming?"

"You know what it means when she hums."

Oscar did.

"So she's been seeing him?"

"I assume so."

"You didn't ask?"

"I didn't think it was my place."

"You really are hopeless. Speaking of hope, have you told her?"

"Told her what?"

Felicity sighed.

"You know perfectly well what."

"No."

"What about Gemma? Is she okay with all of this?"

"Gemma understands."

"If you say so. I just hope you know what you're doing."

"I do. You should have told me you were coming down."

"I would have, but it was a bit last minute. You want to go to the pub for a drink? You look like you could use one."

"I need to work."

"It's Saturday night, Oscar. No one works on Saturday night."

"I do. And so have you. And now, if you don't mind, I'd appreciate it if you would leave."

"But I just got here. And I'm too tired to drive all the way back to London."

"In the morning then."

"Fine. And here I thought you'd be happy to see me."

Oscar sighed.

"I am happy to see you, Fe. I'm just tired. And I have work to do. I promise, as soon as I'm done, I'll come back to London, and you can drag me around."

Felicity smiled.

"So you'll let me take you to Soho House, and you'll be nice to my friends?"

"If I agree, will you leave as soon as you're up tomorrow?"

"If you want me to leave before noon, you'll need to sweeten the deal."

"Name your price."

Felicity did, and Oscar begrudgingly agreed.

"Now will you go?"

"In the morning. In the meantime, I'm off to the pub. You sure you won't join me?"

"I'm sure. I need to work."

"You know what they say, all work and no play…"

"Good night, Fe," said Oscar. "And try not to get into any trouble."

Hope waited for the water to warm up. It was taking forever. Or so it seemed. When it finally did, she got into the shower and let the hot water cascade over her. She closed her eyes and immediately thought of Oscar, how his fingers and mouth had felt. She stood under the warm water imagining him there and then told herself to forget him. She'd be going home soon. And besides, Oscar wasn't good boyfriend material.

Hope finished showering and toweled off. She went to put on her pajamas and realized she had left them in her room. And no way was she putting back on her smelly clothes. She wrapped her damp towel around her torso and left the bathroom. The house seemed very quiet. Had Oscar and Felicity gone out? She again wondered if they were dating or had dated in the past. They made a handsome couple.

She went to her room and put on her big concert tee instead of her pajamas and got on her bed, planning to read. Then she realized she was thirsty. She got up and headed to the kitchen. She stopped by the stairs but didn't hear anything, and there didn't appear to be a light on. No doubt Oscar, Felicity, and Gemma were all out.

Hope got to the kitchen and flipped on the light switch. She was leaning against a counter, taking a sip of water, when Oscar walked in. Hope felt his eyes on her and realized she wasn't wearing a bra and that her concert tee barely covered her thighs. But she refused to be embarrassed. What was he doing in the kitchen anyway?

"Yes?" she said. "Is there a problem?"

"You're not cold?" he asked her.

"I'm fine. Why?"

He glanced at her chest, and Hope realized that her nipples were hard. She moved her arm to cover them. Oscar grinned.

"What are *you* doing here?" she asked him.

"I might ask you the same thing."

"I went to get a glass of water. I thought you had gone out with Felicity. Where is she?"

"At the pub."

"You didn't go with her?"

"I had work to do."

"But it's Saturday."

"You've never worked on a Saturday?"

Hope didn't answer.

"You didn't answer my question. Why are you here?"

"Same as you."

Hope looked confused. Then Oscar went to get a glass and filled it with water. He took a sip.

"You've got your water. You can go now."

Oscar didn't move.

"Go on," she said. "Didn't you say you had work to do?"

"I'm just admiring the view." Hope frowned. "You look quite fetching in that."

"Is that supposed to be a compliment?"

"It is," he said and moved towards her. Hope froze. "Do you always walk around strange houses nearly naked?" he whispered in her ear.

Hope felt her face heat. The rest of her body was also becoming quite warm. She wanted to run, but she couldn't move.

"You smell good too," he said, nuzzling her neck.

"It's my body lotion."

"Mm…" he said, caressing her thigh. Then he kissed her neck.

Hope moaned.

"What about Felicity?"

"She won't be home for a while."

"And Gemma? What if she walks in?"

"She won't."

Hope extricated herself, though she didn't want to. She liked how Oscar's body felt. But she had a job to do, and fooling around with Oscar could jeopardize it.

"I'm going back to my room."

"Would you like company?"

A little voice was screaming *YES!* But Hope told him no. Then she grabbed her water and scurried to her room, the sound of Oscar's laughter following her.

Hope read for a while and then turned off the light. But she couldn't fall asleep. She had too many thoughts zinging around her brain, many of them having to do with Oscar. What was he playing at? Was he trying to distract her? She had to admit, he was doing a very good job. But if he thought that flirting with her would get her to forget about the deadline, he had another thing coming.

CHAPTER 28

Despite not being able to fall asleep right away, Hope slept well that evening. Though she was troubled by her dreams, all of which featured Oscar, or rather Oscar as Lord Dashingly, with Hope as Lady Emily. *Great*, she thought, *now I've become a character in one of Gemma's books.*

She went to the bathroom and then threw on a pair of jeans and a sweatshirt. No way was she leaving her room in her concert tee again anytime soon. She headed to the kitchen to make herself coffee. However, when she got there, she saw there was coffee in the pot. And seated at the table was Oscar.

"You make coffee?"

"Has anyone told you you're very observant?"

Hope scowled.

"Is it fresh?"

"What do you consider fresh? I made it less than twenty minutes ago. It should still be warm."

Hope went over and poured some coffee into a mug. It was warm, not hot. She would make a fresh pot as soon as Oscar left.

"Where's Felicity, having a lie-in?" She wondered where Felicity had slept—and with whom.

"She just left."

"So early?" It was just after nine.

"She was eager to get back to London."

Hope didn't believe him.

"What about Gemma?"

As if hearing her name, Gemma waltzed into the kitchen.

"Good morning, children!" She seemed awfully cheerful.

Oscar shot her a look.

"Don't be such a grouch, Oscar."

Hope couldn't help smiling.

"Did you enjoy your day at the farm, Hope? Sorry I wasn't around when you got back."

"Very much," said Hope. "Where were you?"

"Spending time with an old friend."

There was a twinkle in her eye as she said it.

At the mention of an *old friend*, Hope thought of Oscar and Felicity.

"Is something wrong, dear?"

"Hm?" said Hope.

"You're frowning. Very bad for the forehead. Gives you wrinkles."

"I didn't realize I was frowning."

"Anyway, I'm glad you're both here," said Gemma. "I need to go up to London for a few days."

Oscar raised an eyebrow.

"No need for you to come with me," Gemma told him. "You stay here and work on the..." Hope saw Oscar giving Gemma a look. "On your play."

"When will you be back?" Hope asked her. "Is everything okay?"

"Everything's fine. I just need to take care of a few things."

"But what about the..." Hope stopped herself.

"The manuscript is in good hands," Gemma reassured her. But Hope didn't feel reassured.

"When are you leaving?"

"I'm planning on taking the afternoon train."

"Today?" said Hope.

"Yes. Is there a problem?"

Hope opened her mouth and then closed it. She couldn't forbid Gemma from going to London. And maybe Gemma planned on working on the manuscript there.

"Good," said Gemma. Then she asked Oscar if there was hot water in the kettle. He said that she'd need to boil some, which Gemma proceeded to do.

"Did you have a good time with your friend?" Hope asked as Gemma waited for the water to boil.

"I did," she replied. She rummaged in a cabinet. "Oscar, where's that tea that I like?"

Oscar got up and retrieved it, placing the container next to Gemma.

"Thank you." She hummed as she placed some tea leaves in a metal ball, which she then placed in a little pot. As soon as the water had boiled, she poured some over the tea leaves. "Right," she said after she had poured some tea into a mug. "I'm heading upstairs. I have things to do before I go. Oscar, would you drive me to the station later?"

Oscar said that he would.

"Wonderful. Now if you both would excuse me?"

Hope watched her go.

"Any idea why she needs to go to London?" Hope asked Oscar. Could she be ill? Oscar had said Gemma was fine. And Gemma certainly seemed fine. But Hope remembered how her mother had hidden her cancer diagnosis for weeks.

"No," he replied.

"Is she ill? You can tell me if she is. My mother didn't tell anyone at first when she had cancer. We thought she was just seeing a friend when she was actually meeting with doctors."

"She's fine, Hope."

"How can you be sure? You said she'd been under the weather for months, so ill she couldn't write."

"Gemma doesn't have cancer."

"Are you sure?"

"I am. She would have told me."

Hope was dubious, but she didn't argue with him.

"Will she be working in London?"

"Ah, now the truth comes out. You're still worried about the manuscript."

"I won't deny it, but I'm more worried about Gemma." It was the truth.

"She fine. Trust me."

Again, he asked her to trust him, but why should she? He and Gemma were hiding something. Hope was sure of it.

"Can I see what she's written?"

"Not yet."

"Why not?"

"I told you, she'll share it with you when she's finished."

"Yet she allowed you to show me those early chapters."

"Which were dreadful."

"They weren't dreadful. They just needed a bit of work."

"Well, she's reworked them, and they're much better now."

"I'd love to see them."

"You will. When…"

"I don't want to wait, Oscar. The pages are due by the end of the month. That's a week away. I need to see the manuscript. Now."

Oscar got up.

"Where are you going?"

"Back upstairs to work."

"But it's Sunday."

"You know what they say, no rest for the weary."

"I thought it was no rest for the wicked."

The way he was looking at her made Hope's toes curl. No rest for the wicked, indeed.

"So how's the play coming?"

"It's coming. And now I must be going."

He left the kitchen, Hope staring after him. When he had gone, Hope emptied her mug and the coffee pot and brewed a fresh pot.

Hope had started to work and then stopped. She wasn't really in the mood to work. It was Sunday after all. Instead, she took herself for a walk around Cupid's Bow. All of the shops around the green were closed, except for the bakery. Hope wasn't planning on going in, but as the door to the bakery opened, the smell of freshly baked bread wafted out, and Hope found herself entering. Was this the bakery Gemma used to own?

"Can I help you?" asked a cheerful-looking woman. She was standing behind a glass case filled with delicious-looking baked goods.

Hope examined the buns and pastries.

"Could I get a cinnamon bun, please?" She hadn't eaten anything and discovered she was hungry.

"For here or to go?"

Hope looked around. There was a counter with a couple of stools by the large plate glass window, and the bakery was empty, except for Hope and the woman behind the display case.

"For here," said Hope.

"Have a seat," said the woman. "I'll bring it over."

Hope pulled out one of the stools and sat. A minute later, the bakery woman came over with Hope's cinnamon bun.

"Here's a fork and knife to eat it with," she said. "It can be a bit messy."

"Thanks," said Hope. She cut off a piece of the cinnamon bun and popped it into her mouth. The frosting melted on her tongue. "Wow!" she said. "This may be the best cinnamon bun I've ever had."

The bakery woman looked pleased.

"Where are you visiting from?"

"New York."

"Ooh, New York. I've always wanted to go there. Got a cousin who lives in Queens, but I've never been."

"You should go," said Hope. She took another bite of the cinnamon bun. It was warm and gooey with just the right amount of spice.

"If you don't mind my asking, what brings you to Cupid's Bow?"

"I'm here for work."

"And what kind of work might that be?"

Hope wondered if the woman was lonely. Or maybe she was naturally chatty.

"Sorry. You don't have to tell me. My husband's always telling me not to stick my nose in other people's business."

"That's all right," said Hope. "I'm an editor."

"Ooh, an editor. What sort of things do you edit?"

"Books."

"What kinds of books? I love to read, especially romance novels. Though I don't have much time for it. The bakery keeps me too busy. I try to read at night before I go to bed, but I'm always falling asleep before I'm two pages in."

Hope smiled. She liked the woman. She reminded Hope of some of the middle-aged contestants she'd seen competing on the *Great British Baking Show*.

"I know the feeling," said Hope. "I often fall asleep reading."

"That makes me feel better," said the woman.

"Have you always owned this bakery?" Hope asked her.

"No, my husband and I bought it just a couple of years ago, not long after we moved here."

"Did you know the previous owner?"

"No. The agent said she hadn't owned it very long, barely a year."

"What about the owner before that? Was it always a bakery?"

"Why do you want to know?" said the woman, looking at Hope a bit suspiciously.

"Just curious. The shop seems like it's been here forever."

Just then the door opened and a couple walked in. They were soon followed by a family. Within seconds, the little place was full. Church must have let out, Hope thought.

Hope took another bite of her cinnamon bun and then wrapped the rest in a paper napkin. She thought about asking for a box, but with all the people waiting to be helped, Hope didn't want to disturb the bakery owner.

She left the bakery with the bun in her bag and walked around the green. Then she explored some of the side streets. She came across a dog park and thought of Edward. She hadn't heard from him since their dinner.

She pulled out her phone and started to compose a text to him. Then she erased what she had written. She started typing again and frowned. Finally, she settled on a single word, *Hey.*

She was putting her phone away when she felt it vibrating in her hand. Edward had texted her back.

"Hey yourself. How was the farm?"

"Good," she replied. "How was your day?"

"Good."

"You want to get together this week?"

"I'm going to London for a few days."

"Oh? When are you going?"

"Tomorrow."

"Work trip?"

"Yes."

Odd. Edward hadn't mentioned a work trip when she'd seen him Friday.

"When will you be back?"

"Not sure yet."

"OK," Hope typed. "Let me know when you're back?"

"Of course. Everything good at Gemma's? Oscar behaving?"

Hope felt herself start to blush at the mention of Oscar. "Mostly."

"I need to go," Edward wrote. "I'll text you when I'm back."

"OK. Have a good trip!"

Hope stared at her screen for several more seconds, waiting to see if Edward was going to add anything. When he didn't, she pocketed her phone. A couple of dogs were chasing each other around the dog park. Hope watched them for a couple of minutes, then she headed back to Gemma's.

CHAPTER 29

The house was quiet when Hope returned. And Oscar's car was gone. He must have driven Gemma to the train station. Which meant he would be gone for a while. Hope looked over at the staircase. She hadn't been upstairs since she had moved in.

"Oscar?" she called, standing at the foot of the stairway. "Gemma?"

No answer.

She climbed several steps and then paused, seeing if she heard anything. But all was quiet. She finished climbing the stairs and stood outside Gemma's office. She knocked.

"Oscar? Gemma?"

No answer.

She tried the door. It was locked. She rattled the doorknob. Of course, Oscar would lock it. He didn't trust her. But why? She was going to read the manuscript eventually. Why not let her get a jump on things? Unless Gemma and Oscar had lied about the manuscript being in good shape.

Hope looked down at the doorknob. She could always try to pick the lock. Though she had never picked a lock before. But how hard could it be? There wasn't a deadbolt. She stood there for several seconds, thinking about it.

"No," she said. "I just have to trust them."

She looked down the hall. The doors to Gemma's and

Oscar's rooms were closed. Were they locked as well? She took a step in their direction and stopped. She wasn't a snoop. She tried the door to Gemma's office again. Still locked. She sighed and headed back down the stairs.

Oscar returned a little before two. Hope was in an armchair reading.

"Gemma get off okay?"

"Hm?" He seemed preoccupied.

"I asked if Gemma got off okay."

"Oh yes, fine."

"Is everything all right?"

"Why?"

"You seem a bit preoccupied."

He frowned.

"Everything's fine." He started to head upstairs.

"You know, you don't have to work so hard," Hope called.

Oscar stopped and turned.

"Says the woman who demanded Gemma produce eighty thousand words by the end of the month or else."

"Hey," said Hope. "She's had plenty of time to work on the book. Over a year, in fact. She knew the deadline. Or you certainly did. Which, by the way, Ashley extended, twice. But Gemma chose to ignore it."

Oscar was scowling now.

"She didn't choose to ignore it. She just…" He stopped himself.

"She just what?"

"Nothing. I have work to do, and taking Gemma to Exeter took longer than expected."

"You working on your play, the one about the annoying editor who moves in with her author and nags him to death?"

Oscar smiled.

"Exactly."

"What's it really about?"

"I told you."

Hope rolled her eyes.

"Fine. Be that way. Though I don't know why it's such a big secret. What is it with the two of you? You can trust me, you know."

"Can I?" said Oscar.

The way he was looking at her made Hope's insides feel a bit fluttery. But she didn't want him to know how he made her feel, so she sat up straighter and looked him in the eye.

"Yes, you can."

He walked over to where Hope was seated, and Hope felt her heart hammering inside her chest.

"I'd like to trust you," he said, leaning over her.

The way he was looking at her... He reached out and touched her face, caressing it. Hope closed her eyes.

Then Oscar's phone began to ring.

Hope wasn't sure if she was disappointed or relieved.

He hesitated before answering.

"Hold on," he told the caller. He gave Hope a last lingering look and then turned and headed up the stairs.

Hope watched him go. Then she picked up the manuscript she'd been reading. But she was having trouble focusing. Curse Oscar. Though it wasn't entirely his fault. It was probably her blood sugar. She'd only eaten half a cinnamon bun.

She put down the manuscript and went to the kitchen. But she didn't know what she wanted. After poking her head in the refrigerator and the pantry, she decided to make herself a vegetable omelet. She took out the ingredients and began chopping up the vegetables.

She was about to start sautéing them when she heard Gemma in her head, telling her to make sure Oscar ate. Hope tried to ignore the voice, but it was useless. She sighed and put down the bowl of vegetables and headed upstairs.

The door to the office was closed, so Hope knocked.

"Oscar, you in there?" Though she knew that he was. She knocked again, louder this time, and practically shouted his name.

A few seconds later, the door flew open.

"Yes?" said Oscar. He looked annoyed. "Is the house on fire? I'm trying to work."

"No, the house is not on fire. I'm making myself a veggie omelet and wanted to know if you wanted some. There's more than enough for two."

"Thank you, but I'm not hungry."

"Have you eaten today?"

"You sound like Gemma."

"And Gemma would want to know that you'd eaten something."

"I had coffee this morning."

"Coffee isn't a meal." Though it often was for Hope.

"I'll eat something later."

"When?"

"What do you mean, *when*?"

"I mean when were you planning on eating?"

They stared at one another.

"If I eat, will you leave me alone the rest of the afternoon?"

"Yes."

"Fine."

"You just need to come downstairs."

Oscar scowled.

"Fine. Just give me a few minutes."

"Fine," said Hope. "But don't take too long."

"I said I'd be down in a few. Now if you wouldn't mind?"

Hope stepped away from the door as Oscar closed it.

"Okay, but if you're not down in five minutes, I'm coming back up and dragging you downstairs!" she called.

"Here you go," said Hope, placing a plate in front of Oscar.

"Thank you," he replied. "Though you really don't have to feed me."

"I know I don't have to. I just didn't want the food to go to waste. Can I get you something to drink?"

Oscar sighed.

"I'll have a glass of water."

Hope filled two glasses with water and brought them over to the table.

"Are you going to sit?" he asked her.

"I was about to."

She sat down across from him.

"*Bon appetit!*" she said and dug into her omelet.

She watched as Oscar took a bite and began to chew.

"Yes?" he said.

Hope quickly turned back to her own plate.

They were silent as they ate, Hope glancing at Oscar occasionally, wanting to say something and then changing her mind. They had eaten several meals together since Hope had moved in, and none of those meals had felt as awkward as this one. However, those meals had been eaten with Gemma or were before *the kiss*, as Hope thought of it.

Oscar put down his fork and got up.

"You done?" she said. Though it was obvious from his empty plate that he was.

"I am." He turned to go and then stopped and turned around. "Thank you for the omelet."

"You're welcome."

Then he left.

Hope finished her omelet and then cleared the table and washed up. When she was done, she headed to her computer. But she wasn't in the mood to work. Instead, she texted Dani.

"What are you up to today?"

Dani replied a minute later.

"I'm having brunch with Rachel and Levi." Rachel was Dani's roommate from college and one of her best friends. Levi was Rachel's boyfriend.

"Where are you guys going?"

"Banter."

Hope sighed. It was one of her favorite brunch spots.

"What's up over there in Jolly Old England?"

"Not much."

"How's the manuscript coming? Gemma almost done?"

"I think so? She said it was in good shape and that I'd have it by the end of the month, but she keeps disappearing."

"Disappearing? Where does she go?"

"London this time."

"Did Oscar go with her?"

"No, he's still here."

"Bummer."

"He's not so bad."

"Oh? Are we talking about the same Oscar?"

Hope hadn't told Dani about what had happened at the farm.

"You still there?" typed Dani when Hope didn't reply right away.

"He kissed me."

"He kissed you? I'm calling."

Hope was typing a reply when her phone rang. She thought about not answering, but Dani knew she was there.

"He kissed you?!" said Dani. "I hope you slapped him and told Gemma."

"Um… It was sort of mutual."

"You kissed him?! What was it like? Is he a good kisser? Though jerks like him usually are."

Hope thought about how to answer.

"It was good."

"How good? On a scale of one to ten with ten being the best…"

"Definitely a ten."

"Wow! And how exactly did this kiss happen?"

Hope told her all about Farm Day.

"That Emerald sounds like a bitch."

"Yes, well, I sort of understand."

"I would have told her off."

"Her parents run the farm."

"So what? So, you and Oscar. And here I thought you hated him."

"I never said that. And since I've been here, I've seen a whole other side of him."

"His backside? I bet he has a cute derriere."

"Get your mind out of the gutter." Though, of course, Hope immediately pictured Oscar's bottom. It looked pretty good in a pair of jeans.

"So, you going to sleep with him?"

"Please. I'm going to be heading back to the States next week, as soon as Gemma finishes the manuscript, and I barely know him."

"Which is why you need to sleep with him! You don't need to marry the guy. Just have a little fun while you're over there."

"Not a good idea. Besides, I don't think it would be ethical."

"He's not your professor, Hope."

"I know, but… It just seems wrong."

Hope could hear Dani sigh.

"What about Edward?"

"What about him?"

"You two… you know."

"No. We're just friends, Dani."

"Bummer. I thought for sure the two of you would hook up. You did date when you went to school over there."

"That was a long time ago, and things change."

"So you didn't sleep with him?"

"No. I think he's still getting over his girlfriend. They were pretty serious."

Dani sighed.

"I had such high hopes for you."

"I told you, I'm here to work, not to hook up with someone with a British accent."

Time to change the subject.

"How's Morris?"

"He's good. He misses you."

"I miss him too. Give him some scritches for me."

"I will. And Hope?"

"Yes?"

"Try to have some fun while you're over there."

"I'll try. Say hi to Rachel and Levi for me."

"Will do."

Then they ended the call.

CHAPTER 30

Hope didn't see Oscar the rest of the afternoon. No doubt he was working on his play. It was after seven now, and Hope was starting to think about dinner. She glanced up at the stairs. She had promised not to disturb him the rest of the afternoon. But it was technically evening now.

Hope went to the kitchen to poke around. But she wasn't in the mood to cook. She had noticed a fish and chips place in town. Would it be open? If not, there was always the pub. Though were pubs allowed to be open on Sundays? She couldn't remember. Well, she could always look it up. Though Oscar would know.

She went back to the living room and glanced up the stairs. It was awfully quiet.

Go on, Hope, she told herself.

She started up the stairs and then stopped.

"I should just go on my own," she said aloud. Then she heard Gemma's voice again. Hope sighed and continued up the stairs. She stood outside the office, took a deep breath, and knocked. No response. Oscar probably had his headphones on and couldn't hear her. She knocked again, louder this time, and called his name. Still no answer.

She turned to go and then changed her mind.

"Oscar?" she called. Still nothing.

She tried the door. It was unlocked. She slowly opened it. Oscar was seated in front of his computer. Or rather slumped in front of it, his head resting on his hands. Was he asleep?

She went over to him.

"Oscar?" she said, softly.

His eyes were closed. She checked to see if he was breathing. He was.

"Oscar?" she said, gently laying a hand on his shoulder.

His eyes flew open, and he reared back.

"What are you doing in here?" he said. He looked a bit wild.

Hope held her right hand over her heart, trying to stop it from racing. He had given her quite a scare.

"I came to see if you wanted to grab something to eat in town. I knocked and called your name, but you didn't answer. And I... was worried."

"As you can see, I'm perfectly fine. And what happened to you not disturbing me?"

"I promised not to bother you the rest of the afternoon. But it's evening now."

Oscar looked out the window and frowned.

"You want to get something to eat with me in town?"

He turned back to Hope.

"Are you asking me out?"

"No, I just... I was heading into town to get something to eat, and I thought maybe..."

Why was she so nervous? Maybe it was the way Oscar was looking at her, as though he might snack on her.

"Now that you mention it, I could use a pint. Let's go to the pub."

"Is it open?"

Oscar gave her a look.

"Why wouldn't it be?"

"Because it's Sunday?"

"It's open."

"Okay. So, the pub?"

"I just need a minute."

Hope made a face, and Oscar sighed.

"I need to save what I was working on. I'll be down shortly. Now shoo."

Hope glanced at Oscar's laptop, but it was asleep.

"Go," he said.

Reluctantly, Hope left and headed downstairs.

They sat in the same booth they had sat in the last time.

"Is this your usual table?" Hope asked him.

Before he could answer, Nan had come over, asking what they wanted to drink. Oscar ordered a pint of the local ale, and Hope ordered a glass of white wine.

"No cider today, luv?"

"Maybe later. Just a glass of white wine for now, thanks." Then she turned to Oscar. "So, how's the playing going?"

"It's going," he said. He looked to be reading something on his phone.

"Everything okay?"

"Yes, fine. Why?"

"You're staring quite intently at your phone."

He frowned and put it away as Nan came over with their drinks.

"Could we get a couple of menus?" Hope asked her.

Nan looked at Oscar, who nodded. Then she went to get menus. She deposited them on the table a minute later and said she'd be back in a few to take their order.

"Is she the only server here?" Hope asked Oscar, watching as Nan went from table to table.

"Mostly. They have someone else who helps out on Fridays and Saturdays."

Hope took a sip of her wine. She should have ordered cider... or beer.

"Do you know what you're going to have?" she asked

him. Oscar hadn't picked up a menu.

He nodded as he took a sip of his ale.

"What?"

"The Sunday roast."

"Is that roast beef?" Edward's mother had served a Sunday roast. But Hope wasn't sure if all Sunday roasts were the same.

"It is, with potatoes, veg, and Yorkshire pudding."

"Is the one here any good?"

"Try it and find out."

"You haven't had it?"

"I have."

"So, is it any good?"

"Would I order it if it wasn't?"

Hope made a face.

"Everything all right here?" said Nan. "You ready?"

"I'll have the Sunday roast," said Hope.

Nan looked over at Oscar.

"Make that two."

"And another pint?"

Oscar nodded, and Nan started to move away.

"Could I get a half-pint of Otter Ale?" Hope asked her.

Nan looked over at Hope's wine glass but didn't say anything.

"So, how's the play going?" Hope asked Oscar after Nan had left. "You making good progress?"

"Not really."

"What's the problem? You seem to be spending an awful lot of time on it."

Oscar frowned.

Nan brought over their drinks, and Hope thanked her.

"Fine. If you don't want to talk about the play, we can talk about something else. What do you want to talk about?"

"Who says we need to talk?"

Hope made a face. She didn't like this version of Oscar.

"How did you meet Gemma?"

"How did I meet her?"

"Yes. How did you meet her?"

He looked thoughtful.

"I guess you could say, I've known her forever."

"So you met her when you were little? Was she a friend of your mom's?"

"You could say that." He smiled as he took a sip of his ale.

"And what about you?"

"What about me?"

"Why'd you become an editor?"

"I guess it's because I love books."

"That's it?"

"What do you mean? Isn't that enough?"

"I mean, lots of people like to read, but most don't become editors."

"True. Some open book shops or go work in libraries."

"You ever try to write a book?"

"A couple of times."

"And?"

"I prefer editing them. It's easier."

Oscar smiled at that.

Hope took a sip of her ale. It wasn't bad.

"So, why did you decide to become a playwright?"

"Just sort of fell into it."

"How does one fall into writing plays?"

"How does one become an editor? I liked watching plays and fancied writing one myself."

"I saw that you had one performed in Edinburgh. What was that like?"

Oscar took a sip of his ale before answering.

"Wonderful and awful."

"Why awful?"

"It raised expectations."

"And that's bad?"

"It is when you're worried your next play won't be good enough."

Hope could actually understand the feeling.

"Have you written any plays since then?"

"A couple."

"Have they been produced anywhere?"

"Not yet."

"Why not?"

He shrugged and drank his ale.

"You have a good feeling about the new one?"

"Why do you care?"

"I don't know. I just do. Is that why you're in Devon, to work on the new play?"

"Something like that."

"And Gemma's okay with you crashing at her place?"

"She hasn't complained yet."

Again, Hope wondered what their relationship was.

"But you have a place in London."

"I do."

"Do you live alone or share it with someone?" Hope didn't know why she asked. Actually, she did.

"I share it," said Oscar. He saw Hope's look of disappointment, though Hope had tried to hide it. "With my sister," he added.

"You share it with your sister?"

He nodded as he took a sip of his ale.

"She's not there most of the time. Though if she breaks up with her latest beau, which seems likely, she'll be back."

"You two get along?"

"Well enough."

"Here you go!" Nan had arrived with their food.

Hope looked down at her plate. It was a lot of food. She looked over at Oscar. He was already digging in. Hope picked up her fork and knife and cut off a piece of the roast beef. She popped it into her mouth and began to chew.

"Mm," she said. It was good. Next she tried a piece of the roasted potato. It was also good.

Oscar smiled.

"Told you it was good."

Though, in fact, he hadn't.

They didn't speak until Oscar had finished what was on his plate.

"You done?" he asked her.

There was a bit of roast beef, potato, and veg left on her plate. But Hope was too full to finish it.

"I am. It was a lot of food."

"No room for pudding?"

"How can you even think of dessert?" Hope asked him.

He shrugged.

"I guess I was hungrier than I thought."

Nan came over and asked Hope if she was done.

"I am," Hope replied. "It was delicious."

"You save room for pudding? We've got spotted dick tonight."

"Spotted dick?"

She saw Oscar grinning.

"It's a steamed pudding made with dried fruit," he explained.

"Right," said Hope. "I knew that. I'm too full for dessert, but you go ahead."

Nan looked over at him.

"No pudding tonight, Nan. Just the check."

"Your loss," she said. Then she took their plates.

"You could have gotten something," said Hope.

"That's all right. I should get back."

"You're going to work on your play some more?"

"I was thinking about it."

Nan had returned with the check. Hope went to get it, but Oscar was faster, handing Nan his credit card.

"Can I pay for half?"

"You can pay next time."

"You said that the last time."

Oscar got up and headed to the door, holding it open for Hope.

"You think you can make it back without twisting your ankle?" he asked her as they stepped outside.

"Very funny," said Hope. "I'll be fine."

"I don't know. Otter Ale is pretty strong."

Hope made a face.

"If you want, you can ride on my back." He leaned over and patted his back.

Was he drunk?

"Thanks, but I think I can make it back on my own," Hope replied. Then she headed off down the road, not waiting for Oscar.

CHAPTER 31

Hope tripped on a cobblestone on the way back, but she quickly righted herself.

"You okay?" said Oscar.

"Perfectly fine," Hope said, brushing him off.

They got back to Gemma's, and Oscar let them in.

"You want some tea or coffee?" he asked her.

"You going to have some?"

"I was thinking about it."

"Which?"

He looked thoughtful.

"I'm tempted to make some coffee."

"I don't think I'd be able to sleep if I had coffee. I'll just have some herbal tea."

"I'll join you. I should probably back off the coffee."

He boiled some water and got down two mugs.

"Hope you don't mind if I use the tea bags."

"That's fine," said Hope.

She watched as he poured water into the mugs.

"Well, I should head up."

"You're really going to work?" said Hope.

"Is that a problem?"

"No, I just… Don't stay up too late."

"Thank you for your concern. I'll be fine."

Hope frowned. Why did he have to be so snarky? As if sensing Hope's displeasure, he paused.

"What are you planning on doing?"

"I'll probably read in bed when I'm done with my tea."

"Another manuscript?"

"No, a book, one published a long time ago."

"What are you reading?"

Hope regarded him. Did he really want to know what she was reading?

"*Villette* by Charlotte Brontë. I found it in the bookcase. I hadn't read it in years."

"Any good?"

"You've never read it?"

"Not really my thing."

"Charlotte Brontë or Victorian novels in general?"

"The latter."

"Huh. I would think with Gemma…" She paused. "Don't tell me you've never read Gemma's books."

"Of course I've read Gemma's books."

Hope felt stupid. Of course he had.

"Yet you don't like Victorian literature."

"You think Gemma's books are literature?"

"You don't? They're very well written. And just as enjoyable as Brontë's work. In fact, I would say they're more enjoyable."

"Really?"

"What?" said Hope. "You don't think romance novels can be well written?"

"I didn't say that. I just find it amusing that you'd put Gemma's work in the same category as Charlotte Brontë's."

"That's not what I…" Hope sighed. The man was infuriating, always twisting what she said.

"So tell me an author you like."

"Neil Gaiman."

"Neil Gaiman?"

"You've never heard of him?"

Hope shook her head.

"*Good Omens? Stardust? Coraline? American Gods?*"

"*Good Omens* is a series, isn't it, on Amazon Prime? And wasn't *Coraline* a movie?"

Oscar sighed and mumbled something.

"So, why do you like him?"

"Why do you like Charlotte Brontë?"

"She's a good writer, and I can relate to some of her characters. Is that why you like Gaiman?"

"Something like that."

Hope got up.

"I think I'll finish my tea in my room." Oscar didn't move. "I thought you had to work."

"So now you're saying I should work?"

Hope glared at him.

"Do whatever you like. I don't care." Then she huffed out of the kitchen.

Hope had fallen asleep while reading *Villette*, but she was awakened by the sound of floorboards creaking. Was there an intruder in the house? She waited in bed, not turning on her light, silently listening. There it was again. Someone was in the living room. She looked to see what time it was, but she had turned off her phone. She fumbled for it on the nightstand and switched it on. It was 2 a.m.

She heard the creaking again. It must be Oscar. But what was he doing downstairs at 2 a.m.?

Hope turned on her lamp and got out of bed. It was dark in the living room, and she had left her phone on her nightstand. She stood still, waiting to see if she heard anything. But the creaking had stopped. She told herself it must have been Oscar, probably gone to the kitchen to get something, and then gone back upstairs. Then she noticed that there was a light on in the kitchen. Maybe he was still in there.

Hope told herself she should go back to bed. Instead, she

found herself heading to the kitchen.

She slowly opened the door. Oscar was standing next to the sink, his back to her. He was dressed in a pair of loose-fitting pajama bottoms and nothing else. Hope swallowed.

"Oscar?"

"Jesus!" he said, whipping around. "You scared me. What are you doing here?"

"I could ask you the same thing," she said, trying not to stare at his bare chest. "I heard creaking and thought it could be an intruder." Then she spotted the plate. "Is that a cheese sandwich?"

Hope saw Oscar looking at her and realized she was only wearing her old concert tee. Suddenly, she felt naked.

"What are you smiling at?" she said, resisting the urge to cover herself. "And why are you eating?"

"I was hungry."

"And where's your top?"

"My top?"

"To your pajamas."

Again, Hope tried not to stare at his torso. How did a man who spent all day in front of a computer have abs that toned?

"Like what you see?" he said, continuing to smile.

Hope could feel her face growing warm, but she refused to be intimidated.

"I could ask you the same thing."

"Very much," he replied.

Cocky bastard.

Hope looked over at the plate.

"You want some?" he asked her.

"No. I'm still full from dinner." He shrugged. "I'm going back to bed," she announced. "Next time you need a midnight snack, do try to be a little quieter."

"And next time you decide to surprise an intruder, do wear something a little less enticing."

"Enticing?" said Hope.

"Mm," said Oscar, eyeing her. "I doubt an intruder would leave if he saw you looking like that."

"Oh?" said Hope, swallowing. Oscar had taken a couple of steps towards her. And the way he was looking at her… It made her pulse race. The sensible voice in her head said that she should turn around and hurry back to her room. But she just stood there.

Oscar was now directly in front of her. And she could feel the heat from his body. A part of her wanted to reach out and touch his chest.

"Go on," he said.

"Excuse me?" said Hope.

"I saw the way you were looking at my chest. Go ahead and touch it."

Hope scowled.

"Are you afraid?"

"Afraid of touching your chest? Hardly." Though she could feel herself tremble as he took another step towards her.

He reached out and placed a stray lock of hair behind Hope's ear. Hope shivered at his touch.

"You should go back to bed," he said, his eyes locked on hers.

"I should?" said Hope. He had such lovely eyes, like a storm-tossed sea.

"Uh-hm," he said as his finger was tracing a path down her neck. Hope was finding it hard to think.

Hope closed her eyes even as that little voice inside her head told her to turn around and go to her room.

"Look at me, Hope."

Hope opened her eyes. It was a mistake.

"Would you like me to kiss you?"

Hope swallowed. Then she found herself nodding. Oscar smiled. Then he leaned over and kissed her.

Hope closed her eyes as Oscar's lips softly pressed against hers. The kiss was gentle at first, then, as she opened her mouth to him, it became more passionate.

Hope lost track of time as they continued to kiss, Oscar's hands exploring her body, finding all of her sensitive spots. Hope ran her right hand along the top of his pajamas. Oscar's chest wasn't the only hard thing. She began to move her hand, slowly stroking him, when he stopped her.

"You don't want me to?" she asked him, confused.

His gaze was smoldering, and Hope felt she might burst into flames.

"Quite the opposite," he replied. "But if you continue to do that then…"

"Then what?" she said, running her hand over his length.

He closed his eyes, and Hope smiled. Then he stopped her again.

"What?" she said.

He grabbed her hand and held it up to his mouth. Then he began sucking on her fingers as his right hand found its way between her legs. Hope moaned as she closed her eyes. His fingers continued to rub her most sensitive spot, and Hope thought her knees might give way.

"Yes," he said. "Let yourself go."

Hope braced herself against the hutch as Oscar continued to explore her.

"Let's go to your room," he whispered in her ear.

"My room?"

"It's closer than mine."

There was that voice again, telling Hope this was wrong. But Hope ignored it and led Oscar to her room.

It was light out when Hope woke up, and she was alone. She hadn't really expected Oscar to be there. A part of her was relieved that he wasn't. She didn't know what had come over her. Or Oscar for that matter. Not that she regretted what had happened. It had been some of the best sex she'd ever had.

They had spent the morning exploring and pleasuring each other, eventually falling asleep, exhausted.

Hope reached over to the night table and turned on her phone. It was nearly nine-thirty.

She stayed in bed for a few more minutes, replaying everything she had done with Oscar. Had he enjoyed it as much as she had? She had thought so at the time. But if he had enjoyed himself, why hadn't he stayed?

Hope got up and went to the bathroom. The house felt quiet. Was Oscar asleep? She went into the kitchen. The coffee maker was on the counter, the carafe nearly full. There was a note next to it. *Went to the farm*, it read. *Help yourself.* It was signed with an *x*.

Hope stared at the note. Oscar hadn't said anything about going to the farm. Or maybe she hadn't heard him.

She poured herself a cup of coffee, adding sugar and milk. She wondered when Oscar had left. The note didn't say. And she hadn't heard him. She thought about texting him but decided not to.

She finished her coffee and then went to take a shower.

Hope spent the rest of the morning working, but she was distracted. Should she text him? It was nearly noon, and she hadn't heard from him. Well, other than the note. Was he still at the farm? What was he doing there? Her phone began to ring. Hope swiped to answer without looking at the caller ID.

"Oscar?"

"It's Ashley."

Hope winced. Then she composed herself.

"Hey, Ash. You're up early. Everything okay?"

"You tell me. I haven't heard from you in days."

Those days were known as the weekend. But Hope kept that thought to herself.

"I sent you an update on Friday."

"So?"

Hope rolled her eyes.

"Aren't you supposed to be on maternity leave?"

"Just tell me about the manuscript. Have you read it?"

"Not yet."

"Why not?"

"She hasn't finished it yet."

"Tell her you need to see it, that I order her to show it to you."

Yeah, like that's going to make a difference, Hope thought. Though Ashley had managed to convince Oscar to let Hope stay there.

"She's in London right now so…"

"What is she doing in London? Is she working on the manuscript there?"

"I don't know. She's supposed to be back in a couple of days."

"And did she say anything about the manuscript before she left?"

"Just that it was in good hands."

"What's that supposed to mean?"

"I think it means that it's in good shape. She and Oscar have been locked away in their office since I got here." She didn't mention Gemma's forays to see her friends, or one old friend in particular.

"Yes, well, I'd feel a lot better if you'd seen it. It's nearly the end of the month. And we can't afford to miss another deadline."

"I know. I actually tried to sneak a peek the other day, but the door to the office was locked."

"Why was it locked?"

"To keep nosy editors out."

"Well, try again."

"I don't know, Ashley. Gemma and Oscar aren't here and…"

"Perfect. Go up there now and find the manuscript."

"I don't think that's a good idea. Besides, Oscar could be back any minute."

"Where is he?"

"At Ruby's Place. He went there early this morning."

"Well, while he's at Ruby's, you should go take a look at the manuscript."

"I told you, I…"

"Look, Hope, you want that promotion, yes?"

Hope made a face. Ashley wasn't playing fair.

"I'm not breaking into their office."

"Who said anything about breaking in? Just go see if it's unlocked."

"And if it isn't?"

Ashley sighed.

"Then you can wait for Oscar or Gemma to get back and tell them I insisted they show you the manuscript. If they object, tell them to call me."

Hope sighed.

"Fine. I'll go check."

"Good girl. Now run along and call me back."

Hope made another face but told Ashley that she would. Then she ended the call. Hope walked over to the staircase and looked up. While she had gone up there before in hopes of sneaking a peek at the manuscript, this time felt different.

She hesitated. Then she told herself that the door was probably locked. Having convinced herself it was, she headed up the stairs. She stood outside the office, staring at the door. It was closed. Was it also locked? She nervously reached out her right hand, placing it on the doorknob.

CHAPTER 32

Hope turned the knob. The door swung open. Hope hadn't expected it to be unlocked and just stood there. She saw Oscar's desk with his laptop on it. It was open, though the screen was blank. He must have been in a hurry not to have closed his laptop and locked the door. Or maybe he thought he could trust her now. That thought made what Hope was about to do that much harder.

For a minute, she thought about turning around and leaving. She could always tell Ashley that the door had been locked. But she was a terrible liar, and, to be honest, she wanted to see the manuscript. If, indeed, there was a manuscript.

She walked over to Gemma's desk. The typewriter looked the same as it did the last time she had seen it. In fact, it had dust on it. As though it hadn't been used. And the stack of paper next to it looked to be untouched. Hope frowned. It sure didn't look as though Gemma had been busy. Quite the opposite.

She went over to Oscar's computer. Maybe Gemma had given Oscar the pages to input and then thrown them out or burned them. Though would she really do that?

Hope pressed a key, expecting nothing to happen, and was surprised when the screen sprang to life. She peered at it. Was that Oscar's play? But it didn't look like a play. Hope began to read and then stopped. She scanned his desk for typewritten pages, but there were none. She went over to the wastebasket. It was empty. Where had Gemma's pages gone? There was a fireplace downstairs, but they hadn't used it since she'd been there. She made a face and went back over to Oscar's laptop.

She started to read again and then stopped, thinking she heard something. Or rather someone. But it was just the wind. She pulled out Oscar's chair and sat. If Oscar came home and caught her… Well, she didn't want to think about that.

She stared at the screen. Was she really going to do this? *It's not like you're doing anything illegal,* she told herself. Though she knew that Oscar and Gemma would consider it an invasion of privacy. Still, she had a job to do.

She took a deep breath and scrolled to the beginning of the manuscript. She was a third of the way through it when she heard him. She hadn't heard the creak of the stairs or him entering the room. But she knew he was there.

"Hope."

She turned to see Oscar looking at her. Or maybe he was looking at the laptop. Hope tried to make out the look on his face. Was it anger? Fear?

"What are you doing in here?"

"The door was open, and I… Ashley wanted to know about the manuscript, if I had read it. And I told her I hadn't. And she insisted…"

He cut her off.

"I told you…"

"I know what you told me, but we're running out of time, and Ashley's nervous."

"How much did you read?"

"Enough."

"What does that mean?"

"Where are Gemma's pages?"

"What do you mean?"

"That typewriter hasn't been used in months. And there are no typewritten pages. Where are they, Oscar? There's nothing in the wastebasket. And I know she didn't burn them."

Oscar seemed amused.

"What's so funny?"

"Nothing, actually," he said, turning serious. "I just didn't take you for a snoop."

"I'm not. At least, not usually. But I have a job to do, which you and Gemma have been preventing me from doing." Hope was getting angry now. "And Ashley, the person who paid Gemma a sizable advance for a third book, which she has yet to deliver, insisted that I find out what was up, even if it meant breaking into your office."

"So Ashley made you do it? That's your excuse?"

"It doesn't matter. What matters is that you tell me the truth."

"The truth?"

"About who wrote this," she said, indicating the laptop.

"Gemma wrote it."

"I don't believe you. Where are the pages?"

"The pages?"

"You told Ashley that Gemma typed everything. So where are the typewritten pages, Oscar?"

"Right," said Oscar, running a hand through his hair.

"You want to know what my theory is?"

Oscar didn't answer.

"I don't think Gemma wrote this."

"You don't?"

"No, I don't. I think you did."

She was looking at him, trying to read his expression.

"You think I wrote that? But you know how I feel about romance and Victorian novels."

"I know what you told me. But you're the only one who could have written this. Gemma's barely been here. And much of this was written when she was out." Hope had checked the date and time stamps on the file. "Did you write the first two also?"

Oscar didn't speak. And Hope knew she was right.

"What I don't understand is, why the subterfuge?"

Oscar sighed.

"Could we discuss this in the kitchen?"

"Why not here?"

"Because I'm hungry. It's been a long morning, and I haven't eaten."

"You haven't? Why not?"

"There wasn't time. I had to go to the farm."

"Were you supposed to volunteer this morning? You didn't say anything."

"There was a bit of an emergency. Several of the volunteers and instructors called in sick. Some bug going around. We're lucky we didn't catch it."

Hope studied him. He didn't seem like he was lying.

"Fine. We'll continue this conversation downstairs. But I want answers."

He waited for her to get up. Then they made their way down the stairs.

Hope watched as Oscar made himself a sandwich and grabbed a beer.

"So?" she said, watching as he took a bite of the sandwich and washed it down with a sip of beer. "Explain."

"Explain what?"

"About the manuscript! That you're Gemma Lovegood!" Hope didn't mean to raise her voice, but she was angry. She didn't like being deceived.

Oscar took another sip of his beer.

"You thought you could just keep it from me?"

"We had hoped to."

"Who is she?"

"Who?"

"Gemma! Or the woman who's been pretending to be her. Is this even her house?" Though Gemma's name had been stamped into that copy of *Villette*. Had that stamp been put there to fool Hope? Though how could they have known she'd read *Villette*? Had they stamped all of the books in the house?

"It is," said Oscar. Hope was annoyed by how calm he was. "If you must know, she's my mother."

Hope stared at him. She hadn't been expecting that. Though as she looked at Oscar, she could see the resemblance.

"Your mother? I don't understand. But your last name is Tennant."

"Tennant was my father's name."

"Was?"

"He died when I was little."

"Oh, I'm sorry. And Lovegood? Where did that come from? Did you make it up?"

"Lovegood is Mum's maiden name."

"Oh. But I still don't understand. Why the subterfuge? Why not just say you wrote it?"

Oscar gave her a look.

"I doubt people would be interested in reading a Victorian romance by Oscar Tennant. But Gemma Lovegood has a certain ring to it, don't you think?" He smiled and took another sip of beer.

"I thought you hated Victorian novels. Yet you went and wrote one. Make that two, no three. Why?"

"First of all, I never said I *hated* them. They're just not my cup of tea, so to speak."

"So why did you write them?"

Oscar sighed.

"If you must know, I did it on a dare."

"You wrote *Belle of the Ball* on a dare? Who dared you?"

"Felicity."

"Felicity as in Felicity Rogers, the supermodel?"

Oscar nodded as he chewed a bite of his sandwich.

"What's the deal with you two anyway? Are you dating?"

Oscar nearly choked.

"Me date Felicity?" He said it as though it was an absurd idea.

"Don't look at me like that. She's a very attractive woman, and you're…" She waved her hand around. "Single."

Oscar smiled, knowing full well what Hope really meant.

"Thank you. I'm sure Felicity would be most amused to know you thought we were dating."

"Why?"

"Because she's my sister."

"What?" said Hope. "Felicity Rogers is your sister? I don't understand."

"Well, technically, she's my half-sister. As I told you…"

"Why didn't you tell me she was your half-sister?"

"I did tell you I had a half-sister."

"Yes, but you didn't say it was Felicity."

He shrugged.

"And Felicity's father… are he and Gemma still…?" Hope hadn't noticed a wedding ring on Gemma's finger. Not that that meant anything. But she suspected that Gemma had been seeing someone in the village. Was her husband in London, and she had come to Devon for a tryst? It would explain a few things.

"No, she divorced Jim a long time ago. Caught him cheating on her when Felicity was still in the cradle."

"Sorry."

"Don't be. Jim Rogers was a cad. She was right to leave him."

"Still, it must have been hard, raising two kids on her own."

"It was. But Mum's a trooper."

"And you said your father died when you were little? How old were you?"

"I was three."

"That must have been rough."

"Honestly, I don't remember him. Though I know Mum loved him."

"When did she meet Jim Rogers?"

"She'd known Jim for years. He was one of my father's best mates. Bit of a ladies' man. Probably had his eye on Mum when Dad was alive. As soon as Dad was buried, he swooped in. Gemma was quite broken up by my father's death, and, well, Jim could be quite charming. She said she resisted his advances at first, but she was lonely, and, well, next thing she knew, she was pregnant with Felicity."

"And she decided to go through with the pregnancy?"

"It wasn't a choice to her. To his credit, Jim offered to marry her when he found out."

"So they got married."

Oscar nodded.

"It was a mistake. Jim was a player. Once he got Mum, he needed a new challenge."

"That's awful."

Oscar shrugged.

"I never liked him."

"When did they divorce?"

"When Felicity was little."

"Does Felicity ever see him?"

"All the time."

"Really?"

He nodded.

"She likes his money. He's loaded and can deny her nothing."

"Huh. So Felicity dared you to write a book?"

"Not just a book, a romance novel."

"Why a romance novel?"

"Felicity has a thing for romance novels. Always has one on her. She takes them to all her modeling jobs. Apparently, models have to wait around a lot. I would make fun of her, or rather the books, and one day she had enough. She said that if I thought the books were such throwaways, why didn't I try writing one and see how easy it was. We were at a pub, and I may have imbibed a bit too much, and I told her, piece of cake. We even made a bet on it. The loser was to treat the winner to dinner at the restaurant of their choice."

"That doesn't seem like much of a bet."

"You don't know Felicity. If I had lost, she would have made me take her to some Michelin-starred restaurant in Paris."

Hope stared at him. Was he serious? Judging by his expression, he was.

"So you really thought you could write a romance novel? Had you ever written one before?"

"No, of course not. But I thought, how hard could it be?"

"It's harder than you think."

He looked at her.

"Have you ever written one?"

Hope hesitated.

"I tried."

"What happened?"

"I… This isn't about me. It's about you and Gemma. So, what happened? Obviously, you wrote the book. How long did it take you?"

"Felicity said she'd give me a year, but I told her I could do it in half the time."

"Very sure of yourself."

"As I said, I had been drinking."

"So that was the bet: You had to write a romance novel in six months or treat Felicity to dinner at the restaurant of her choice?"

"Pretty much."

"And did she say what sort of romance novel it had to be?"

"She didn't specify."

"So you chose Victorian?"

"It seemed as good a choice as any."

"What I don't understand is, how did the book wind up at Herstory?"

"Ah, that," said Oscar. "I never intended for the book to be published."

"You didn't?"

"No. It was a silly bet. I just wanted to prove to Felicity that I could do it."

"And you did."

"Yes, but then Felicity got it into her head that the book should be published."

"She thought it was that good?"

Oscar didn't comment.

"You didn't think it was good?"

"I thought it was adequate."

"But why didn't you want it published?"

"Because I'm a serious playwright, not a romance novelist."

He said *romance novelist* as though it was something unpleasant.

"You can't be both?"

Oscar made a face.

"So, what happened? How did it get to Herstory?"

"Felicity sent the manuscript to a few people she knew, asking for their opinion."

"And?"

"They loved it."

"Did she tell them that you had written it?"

"No. She deliberately kept that a secret."

"So, how did the manuscript wind up at Herstory?" Hope asked again.

"One of the women Felicity showed it to knew Ashley."

"She didn't know any editors or agents over here?"

"She may have, but… she asked Felicity if she could send the manuscript to Ashley."

"Did Felicity's friend know that Herstory only published books by women authors?"

"She did."

"Did she tell Felicity that?"

"Of course."

"And knowing that, Felicity told her friend to send Ashley the manuscript?" Oscar nodded. "So whose idea was it to attribute the book to Gemma Lovegood?"

"Felicity's."

"Did she check with you and Gemma first?"

"No."

"When did you find out what she had done?"

"After Ashley said that she wanted to purchase the book."

"Were you and Gemma angry?"

"At first. Then Felicity told me about the advance."

"And you changed your mind."

"I needed the money. Writing plays doesn't pay very well. And I was in a bit of a rut. But I wasn't happy about taking the money."

"What about Gemma? She was willing to go along with it?"

"She wanted to help her children."

"Yet she refused to meet with or even speak with Ashley or do public appearances."

"Correct. She was willing to have her name on the books, even though she didn't like deceiving people. But she drew the line at pretending to be Gemma Lovegood, romance novelist."

"So you became her beard. Or rather she was your beard."

He nodded.

"What about Felicity? Why didn't she play Gemma's agent? She is an actress."

"She was too busy. Besides, it made more sense for me to be Gemma's agent. After all, I had written the books."

"So you say Gemma refused to do appearances, yet she agreed to be the guest of honor at the benefit in London."

"That was an exception. Patsy's an old friend of Mum's, and it was for a good cause. And we didn't think anyone from Herstory would be there. Mum was terrified when she learned you were there."

That explained Gemma's odd behavior that evening.

"Still, if you hated doing it, why did you agree to write two more books?"

"Herstory offered me a ridiculous amount of money."

"So it was solely about the money?"

"I told you, writing plays…"

"But you had a play performed at the Edinburgh festival. It won some sort of award, as I recall."

"Yes, but that was years ago. And my next play went nowhere. I figured writing another romance was easy money. I'd whip off the next book and then get back to writing plays."

"So what happened with book three?"

"I lost interest."

"You lost interest?"

"How many times can you make two people fall in love?"

Was he serious?

"So, you, what, just blew it off?"

"I was hoping you'd just go away. Forget about the book."

"You clearly don't know Ashley."

"Clearly. I didn't think she'd threaten to sue. I offered to pay her back the advance, over time. But she wasn't having it."

"I'm confused. You say you lost interest, but the manuscript I just read was pretty good. Much better than those first pages you showed me. What changed? Was it Ashley's threat?"

"It wasn't Ashley's threat."

"Then what was it?"

Oscar looked at her.

"You."

"Me? What did I do, other than annoy you?"

Oscar smiled.

"What did you think of Hattie, the young American heiress who's engaged against her will to the impoverished British lord?"

"I liked her. Why?"

"Anything about her feel... familiar?"

Hope went over what she had read. Suddenly, her face grew warm.

"Hattie's supposed to be me?"

"Well, not exactly you. Obviously."

"And Lord Stanhope?"

Oscar's smile grew broader. Hope was definitely blushing now.

"I... So, how does it end?" The manuscript had stopped short at around sixty thousand words.

"I'm not sure. Maybe you could help me?"

Hope looked at him suspiciously.

"Why do you suddenly want my help?"

"That's why you're here, isn't it? To help me?"

"I thought you didn't want my help."

"I changed my mind."

"What made you change it?"

"I want to work on my new play."

"You can't do both?"

"No."

"So what do you want me to do?"

"I want you to finish writing the book."

CHAPTER 33

"Excuse me?" said Hope.

"You heard me," said Oscar. "I'd like you to finish the book for me."

"Hold up. Twenty-four hours ago, I wasn't allowed to read the manuscript. Now you want me to finish it for you?"

"Correct."

This made no sense.

"I don't understand."

"It's simple. I want to work on my play, and you have a book to deliver."

"A book that you—as Gemma—were supposed to have written."

"I've written most of it."

"So why not just finish it?"

"I told you, I want to focus on my play."

"And you can't wait until you've finished *Balls and Chains*? Also, is that really the title?"

"You don't like it?"

"I…" Hope wasn't sure. It was kind of amusing. "I haven't decided."

"In any case, to answer your question, it can't wait. What's the saying, strike while the iron is hot?"

"Okay. But why me?"

"Why not you? You are a Victorian scholar, as you have

often reminded me. And you've edited dozens of books. Surely, you can…"

"It's not the same!" said Hope, interrupting him.

"What isn't?"

"Editing and writing."

"They're not that different. Editors often rewrite manuscripts. Surely, you've done it."

"I've never rewritten someone else's work."

"But you've suggested revisions?"

"Of course. That's my job."

"Well, then, think of it as revising."

Hope made a face.

"And why should I finish the manuscript for you?"

"I seem to recall something about a promotion for getting Ashley the manuscript by the end of the month. And time is ticking."

"That's not fair."

Oscar got up.

"Life isn't fair."

"Where are you going?"

"Upstairs to work on my play."

He started to leave.

"Wait," said Hope.

He stopped.

"Let's say I agree to work on the book." Oscar waited. "Would you help me?"

"Of course. Though I'll be a bit busy."

"And I can work upstairs in the office?"

"I told you, I don't like company when I'm working."

"You said Gemma didn't like company."

"Well, as you now know, we are one and the same."

"Not exactly. Speaking of Gemma, what was she doing up there while you were busy writing?"

"Reading mostly or playing games on her phone."

"Huh. And how will she feel about all of this?"

"You mean about you finishing the book?"

Hope nodded.

"I'm sure she'll be delighted. She likes you."

"She does?"

"She thinks you're feisty."

"Feisty?"

Hope didn't think of herself as feisty.

"She likes how you stood up to me."

"Yes, well," said Hope.

"So, are you going to tell Ashley?"

Hope thought about it.

"No." Oscar looked relieved. "But you should tell Gemma."

"I was planning on it."

"And you really don't think she'll mind?"

"Not at all. Especially when I tell her I'm working on a new play."

"What's it about?"

"I told you."

Hope rolled her eyes.

"So will you let me work in the office?"

"No. I told you…"

"What if I have a question?"

"You can message me."

"That's ridiculous. There are two perfectly good desks up there, and it's not as though we'd be next to each other."

"You planning on using Gemma's old typewriter?"

"I was thinking I'd move it, with your permission, of course."

"Fine," said Oscar. "But I warn you, I require absolute silence."

"You listen to music, don't you?"

"That's different. I meant, no talking."

"What if I have a question?"

"Message me."

Hope realized he was serious.

"Fine."

Oscar got up.

"And now if you would excuse me?"

"Wait," said Hope. He paused. "Send me the manuscript."

"Consider it done." Then he turned and left the kitchen.

Hope waited until Oscar was gone and then fixed herself some lunch. What had she just gotten herself into? A part of her was excited by the challenge, another part dreading it. She had tried to write books before, including a romance novel. But each time she abandoned the project less than halfway in, unable to finish it. This time, however, would be different. Or so she told herself. She wasn't actually writing the book, just editing it. And, okay, coming up with an ending.

Should Hattie and Lord Stanhope have a happily ever after? That's what people would expect. Though at the beginning of the novel, Hattie had been miserable about being married off to a British lord she had never met. She was a romantic who believed in true love.

As for Lord Stanhope, he was a bit of a misanthrope, who had been burdened and burned by his father's debts and women who just wanted him for his title. And now his mother had arranged for him to be married to this American heiress to save the estate.

True, it wasn't the most original plot. But Oscar was a good writer, and Hope felt she knew these two characters. No doubt because they reminded her a bit of herself and Oscar. As soon as she had finished lunch, she would go back to the beginning and reread what Oscar had written.

She had just taken a bite of her sandwich when her phone began to ring. She looked down at the caller ID. It was Ashley. She thought about letting the call go to voicemail, but then she'd just have to call her back later.

"Hey, Ash. What's up?"

"Well?" said her boss. "Were you able to find the manuscript?"

Hope thought quickly. Should she tell her the truth?

"I did."

"And? Did you read it?"

"I did."

"And? Is it any good?"

"It's very good."

"Thank God. You want to send it to me?"

"Not yet. It's not finished."

"How much has she written?"

"Maybe sixty thousand words?"

"Good enough. Send it to me."

"I'd rather wait until it's finished."

"And when will that be?"

"Soon." Hope mentally crossed her fingers.

"Fine. But if there's a problem, you're to let me know right away. We need that manuscript, Hope."

"I know. And I promise."

Hope thought she heard a baby crying in the background.

"How's the baby?"

"Still not sleeping."

"What about Derek?"

"He's sleeping just fine."

"I meant, is he helping with the baby?"

"When he can. He's been away."

"What about the nanny?"

"I had to fire her."

No wonder Ashley sounded grumpy.

Hope thought she heard another wail.

"I need to go," said Ashley. "Just get me that manuscript as soon as you can."

"I will," said Hope, but Ashley had already hung up.

Hope looked down at her phone and saw that she had an email from Fiona, asking her to call. Hope finished her sandwich and then called her.

"Hey," she said. "What's up?"

"Did you speak to Ashley?"

"I just did. Why?"

"She's been on the warpath. Another author missed her deadline."

"Which one?"

"Candy Floss."

"The erotica writer?"

"Yup."

"What's her excuse?"

"Sick mother."

"What does Ashley expect me to do about it? I don't even work with Candy."

"I know. She's just pissed about all of these writers missing deadlines."

"There are other writers?"

"No, just those two. But Ashley's worried that if word gets out, other writers will think it's okay to miss their deadlines."

"I doubt that. And how would they find out?"

"I'm just letting you know that Ashley really needs Gemma to deliver."

"I know. And as I told her, she'll have the manuscript by the end of the month."

"Have you read it?"

"I have."

"And?"

"It's good."

"Just good?"

"Okay, it's very good."

"I can't wait to read it. What's the title?"

"*Balls and Chains.* But I'm thinking we should change it."

"Why? I like it. It's kind of kinky."

Leave it to Fiona.

"How's England?" she asked. "You having fun over there?"

"I'm here to work, Fiona."

"That ball you went to was work?"

Hope should have never told her about the ball.

"It was."

"I'd like to have that kind of work. Tell me you've at least been to a pub."

"I have."

"Good. Well, I should go. Been a bit busy around here what with you and Ashley gone."

"You holding up?"

"I am, but I may need a day off or two when you get back."

Hope understood.

"Anything else?" she asked Fiona.

"No, I just wanted to make sure you talked to Ashley."

"I did. We're good."

"So, when will you be back?"

"Next week, I hope."

"Good. I've got to run. And please, Hope, try to have a little fun, for me, before you come back."

"I'll try," said Hope.

It was time to go upstairs and deal with the manuscript. Hope grabbed her laptop and headed up. The door to the office was closed. Hope thought about just opening it, but she knocked first. No answer. She knocked again and announced that she was coming in. Well, assuming the door was unlocked. She wouldn't be surprised if Oscar had locked it.

She turned the knob, and the door opened.

Oscar was at his desk, his fingers flying over his keyboard. He had his headphones on. He was probably listening to music. Hope wondered what kind of music he listened to. She would ask him later.

She went over and stood next to him, waiting for him to notice her. When he didn't, she cleared her throat. Nothing.

He was so intent on his work that he didn't seem to see her. She waved a hand in front of his face. He turned and looked up at her.

"Yes?" he said, clearly irritated by the disruption.

"Did you send me the manuscript?" Hope hadn't seen it in her email.

Oscar frowned and opened his email.

"I forgot." He moved his hand over his mouse and clicked. "You should have it now."

Hope heard her phone ping. She pulled it out and saw that she had an email from Oscar.

"Thank you." She glanced around. The typewriter was still on Gemma's desk. "Okay if I move the typewriter?"

"Do whatever you want," said Oscar, looking at his computer.

Hope leaned over, to see what he had written. He immediately shut the lid.

"Do you mind?"

Oscar the grouch had returned.

"Fine," said Hope. "I'm going."

She went over to Gemma's desk and picked up the typewriter, placing it on an empty shelf. She put the ream of paper next to it. The desk was dusty.

"Do you mind if I clean Gemma's desk?" she asked him. He didn't reply. He was too busy typing. "I'm just going to get a rag," she informed him. Again, he ignored her.

Hope went downstairs to look for some dust remover and a rag and found a dishcloth. It would have to do. She went back upstairs and wiped off the desk. Better. Then she put her laptop on it. She sat down in the chair and opened her laptop. It felt weird to be sitting at Gemma's desk. Though Oscar had said Gemma rarely used it.

Hope glanced over at him. He was entirely focused on the screen in front of him. She wondered what the play was about. She turned back to her computer and opened her email. Then she downloaded the manuscript.

CHAPTER 34

Hope got up and stretched. She didn't know how Oscar could just sit there like that, for hours, without getting up. She went over to him.

"Yes?" he said, noticing her looming over him.

"You should get up and stretch, take a walk."

"Why?"

"You've been sitting there for hours. Sitting that long isn't good for you."

"I'll take my chances."

"The play's that important?"

He looked up at her. Clearly, it was.

"Well, I'm going to take a walk."

"Do that."

"Sure you don't want to join me?"

"I told you, I… Fine," he said, seeing the look on Hope's face. "If it will get you to leave me alone the rest of the day."

"There's not much day left. It's technically evening."

"Is it?" He seemed surprised.

"You didn't know? There's a window right there."

He glanced out.

"It appears you are right. Well, in that case, shall we go grab a pint?"

"I thought you needed to work."

"Beer helps me think."

"Hm."

"You said you wanted me to take a walk."

"I wasn't thinking to the pub."

"Suit yourself."

"Fine," she said. "We'll walk to the pub."

Oscar smiled.

"So, any thoughts on the manuscript?"

"Several," said Hope.

"Care to share them?"

"Not yet."

They had almost reached the pub when Hope suggested they walk around the village green first.

"Why?" he asked her.

"Because it's a lovely evening, and you've been hunched over your computer all day."

"For the record, I do not hunch." But he followed Hope around the green.

"I shall now get myself a pint of the White Horse's finest ale," he announced and headed to the pub, Hope following him.

Ned, the barman, greeted them with a nod.

"You mind sitting at the bar?" Oscar asked Hope.

"That's fine," said Hope.

"What'll it be?" Ned asked them.

Oscar ordered a pint of ale, and Hope a half-pint of cider, which Ned brought over a minute later. Hope would miss going to the pub and having cider when she got back to the States. Not that you couldn't find cider there. But it wasn't the same.

"So, how's the play going?" Hope asked him.

"Good, I think."

"You're not sure?"

"I think it's going well, but I will wait until I'm done to pass judgment."

"Are you going to tell me what it's about?"

"I told you. It's about an annoying editor who goes to

live with an author who's behind on his manuscript."

Hope made a face.

"Fine. Be that way. Though I don't know why you won't tell me what it's really about."

Oscar shrugged and finished his ale.

"I should get back."

"So soon? Don't you want something to eat?"

"I'm not hungry. And I have work to do. But feel free to stay."

"That's all right," said Hope. "I should go back and finish reading the manuscript."

Oscar left some money on the bar, and the two of them left.

It was dark by the time Hope had finished reading *Balls and Chains*. She liked the book, but she was unsure how to end it. She looked over at Oscar. He had barely moved since they had returned, busily typing away. She wondered what his play was really about.

She turned back to her laptop. Ashley had emailed her, asking for a report on the manuscript. Hope thought about what to tell her.

Hope liked the main female character, Henrietta "Hattie" Hollingsworth. She was the only daughter of a steel baron from the Midwest, who had been sent away to a finishing school in Switzerland to tame her more wild ways. Though it hadn't done much good. Hattie returned to the States as feisty as ever, much to her mother's dismay.

As for Lord Oliver Stanhope, the man Hattie was to marry, he was clearly a version of Oscar. However, as far as Hope knew, Oscar wasn't heavily in debt, and his mother wasn't insisting he marry.

In the novel, neither Hattie nor Stanhope, a friend of Lord Dashingly's—the link between *Balls and Chains* and the previous book—are thrilled about the arranged marriage, to put it mildly. Both consider marriage a kind of chain. And neither is excited about attending balls, especially the one announcing their engagement. Hence the title of the book.

However, it is at one of these balls—one prior to the one announcing their betrothal—that Hattie meets the dashing Sir Edward Mountebank, who, Hope thought, bore a physical resemblance to her Edward.

Hattie had gone to school in Switzerland with Edward's sister, Georgina, but she had never met Edward until now.

Hattie is thrilled to see Georgina and is immediately attracted to the charming Edward, especially after being given a chilly reception by most of the *ton*, London's fashionable set. No doubt they knew or suspected that Lord Stanhope, one of England's most eligible and most handsome bachelors, was only marrying Hattie for her father's money.

Edward, however, is anything but chilly to Hattie and immediately seeks her favor. He is also an excellent dancer and makes her laugh with his witty barbs about the *ton*. Adding to his appeal is how Lord Stanhope reacts to seeing him and Hattie together.

Even though he knows Hattie is engaged to Lord Stanhope, Edward asks Hattie if he may call on her—with his sister. And Hattie says of course. The three are soon inseparable, and Hattie finds herself wishing she was engaged to Edward instead of the sulky Lord Stanhope.

Lord Stanhope, seeing the growing closeness between his intended and Edward, warns Hattie not to trust Edward, telling her that Edward isn't what he appears to be. But Hattie believes that Lord Stanhope is just saying that because he doesn't want her to be happy. And she continues to welcome Edward's attention.

As her wedding day draws closer, Hattie frets that she will never be able to see Edward again and confesses her fears to him. Edward then confesses that he is in love with her and suggests that they elope.

Hattie is initially shocked. She could never do something so rash. Yet a part of her is excited by the idea. And she tells Edward she will think upon it.

That evening, while she is dining with Lord Stanhope, he again warns her about Edward, saying he has heard rumors.

"What sort of rumors?" Hattie asks.

Lord Stanhope informs her that Edward is an inveterate gambler who has gambled away his inheritance and has been looking for a rich wife to refill his coffers.

Hattie doesn't believe him. She tells him that Georgina would have said something if that were true. Stanhope tells her that Georgina doesn't know.

As soon as they are finished with dinner, Hattie excuses herself. She is angry with Stanhope for besmirching Edward's good name. Who was he to talk about debt when he had debts of his own?

The next day, Edward calls upon Hattie with Georgina and renews his proposal. This time, Hattie, still angry with Lord Stanhope, accepts. She will elope with him, and Georgina will be the witness. Edward kisses her then, taking Hattie by surprise.

Hattie has imagined being kissed by Edward several times, how it would feel. But this was not at all how she had imagined it. And she wonders if kissing is overrated.

Edward asks her if anything is wrong, and Hattie demurs. However, the more she thinks about things, the less she is inclined to run away with him.

Edward, on the other hand, insists that they must elope right away. To which Hattie says that she needs a few days to get ready. Edward tries to convince her that they should not delay. But the more he tries to persuade her, the firmer Hattie is in her resolve.

The next day, while at a dress fitting, Hattie overhears two matrons discussing some cad. Hattie tries not to listen, but it is impossible not to. And she is shocked when she hears Edward's name.

Per the two women, Edward had tried to elope with Lord Chesterfield's daughter, Eliza, Lady Eugenia and Lady Emily's younger sister. And the only thing that had stopped him from ruining Lady Eliza was Lord Stanhope, who had somehow gotten wind of the elopement and intercepted their carriage. The two women went on to coo about how Lord Stanhope had saved the day.

"Such a noble man," one of the women had sighed.

"And him being married off to that ungrateful American," said the other.

Hattie frowned at that. Clearly, the two women didn't know who she was and that she could hear them. Or maybe they didn't care.

At first, Hattie refuses to believe what she has just heard. It's just gossip, she tells herself. Still, didn't gossip usually contain a grain of truth? And the two women were members of the *ton*.

As she heads home in the carriage, Hattie decides to tell Edward that she has changed her mind and sends him a note. Edward, however, is not to be deterred. He shows up at the townhome her parents had rented for the season unannounced, while her parents are at the theater, Hattie having claimed a headache and stayed home. He insists that she come away with him that very instant, but Hattie refuses.

Edward then grabs Hattie and tries to force her into his carriage. Fortunately, Lord Stanhope arrives in the nick of time and… And that was where the manuscript ended.

Hope looked over at Oscar. How could he have ended it there? He must have had some idea how he wanted the book to end. Clearly, Lord Stanhope was there to rescue Hattie from Edward's clutches. Would the two of them then fall in love? That would be the logical conclusion. But if so, why hadn't Oscar written that?

He had told Hope to message him with any questions, but he was right over there.

Hope got up and walked over to his desk, waiting for him to notice her. But he continued to type, having eyes only for the screen in front of him. Tired of waiting, Hope tapped him on the shoulder. Finally, he turned his head and looked up at her.

"Yes?"

"How could you end the book like that?"

"I told you, I…"

Hope cut him off.

"What happens to Hattie and Lord Stanhope? Do they get a happily ever after?"

"That's up to you to decide."

"On, come on, Oscar! You must have some idea how the book should end."

"The ball's in your court," he said, grinning.

"Ha ha. Very funny. Look, I need to send a report to Ashley, and I need to know how the book's supposed to end."

"And I told you, you decide."

"But…" Hope collected herself. "You don't really think Hattie should wind up with Edward, do you?"

"You didn't like him?"

"No, he's a cad."

Oscar smiled at that.

"So you want her to wind up with Lord Stanhope."

"Do *you* think they should wind up together?"

"I think readers would expect them to wind up together."

"That's not what I asked you. What I want to know is, what do you think? Do Hattie and Lord Stanhope belong together?"

CHAPTER 35

Oscar waited for Hope to reply, but Hope found she was unable to. She had a feeling Oscar wasn't just talking about Hattie and Lord Stanhope but about the two of them, and she didn't have an answer to that question. Did the two of them belong together? Hope couldn't deny being attracted to him. And the sex was pretty great. But her life was in the States, and his life was here. Still, as she looked at him, a part of her could imagine a future with him.

"We're just talking about the book, right?" she finally said.

"What else?" he replied.

"Then yes, I think they belong together. But I think they have some work to do, some obstacles to overcome."

"Sounds like you have your ending." Then he turned back to his computer.

Hope watched him for a few seconds and then went back to her desk.

Oscar was still at his computer when Hope decided to call it a night. She had written down some ideas of how the book could end and had finished the first draft of her report for Ashley. She would review it in the morning and then send it off.

"I'm going to bed," she announced.

Oscar continued to type, either unaware Hope had said anything or else ignoring her. She thought about going over to him, but judging by the look on his face, she thought it best to let him be.

She went downstairs and got ready for bed. She was reading *Villette* when she found herself nodding off. So she put the book down and turned off the light.

That night, she dreamed she was Hattie, and that Oscar was Lord Stanhope. They were attending a ball, one similar to the Historical Romance Society Ball. Lord Stanhope had asked Hattie for a dance, and as they whirled around the dance floor, Hattie/Hope felt a frisson of desire as Lord Stanhope/Oscar held her.

The scene then shifted to the balcony. It was a cool evening, and Lord Stanhope/Oscar asked her if she was cold. "A little," she replied. Then Oscar/Lord Stanhope said he would warm her.

The next thing Hope/Hattie knew, Oscar/Lord Stanhope was kissing her, and she didn't want him to stop.

"Hattie, there's something I need to tell you," Lord Stanhope/Oscar whispered in her ear.

"Yes?" Hope/Hattie said, looking up at him.

"I…" began Lord Stanhope/Oscar.

Then Hope woke up.

"No!" she said, furious at herself for waking up at the good part. What was Lord Stanhope/Oscar about to tell her?

Hope tried to go back to sleep, but she was unable to. Finally, at around six-thirty, she gave up and went to the kitchen to make herself some coffee, throwing on a pair of jeans and a sweatshirt over her nightshirt. She half expected to see Oscar there, but there was no sign of him. No doubt he had been up half the night working on his play and was asleep.

She took out the coffee maker and made enough coffee

for the two of them. When it was ready, she poured herself a mug and took it upstairs to the office.

The door to the office was unlocked, and there was no sign of Oscar. Hope silently closed the door and went over to her desk. She opened her laptop and read over her report on *Balls and Chains*, making a few edits. Then she sent it to Ashley.

Hope was still unsure how the book should end. She knew people would expect Hattie and Lord Stanhope to get married and live happily ever after. But a part of her wanted something different for the plucky heroine. She didn't want Hattie to be just another woman who, upon finding love, subjugated herself to the man she married.

Hope was staring at her screen when Oscar came in. He looked tired and held a mug in his hands.

"Thanks for the coffee," he said.

"You're welcome. How late were you up last night?"

"You don't want to know."

"That late, eh?"

He looked over at her computer.

"How's the manuscript coming along?"

"I'm still trying to figure out the ending. You sure you don't want to help?"

He smiled.

"I told you. It's up to you how their story ends."

Hope looked up at him, wondering again if he meant Hattie and Stanhope or her and him.

"Do you believe in happily ever afters?"

He looked thoughtful.

"I think they're true for some people."

"But not for you?"

"I didn't say that."

"But you were thinking it."

"So now you read minds?"

Hope frowned.

"So what's your story, Oscar? Were you never in love? Or were you and you got dumped?"

Hope knew very little about Oscar's personal life. When she would ask him about it, he'd deflect. But she couldn't help wondering if he had based any of the male characters in the books on himself. And, if so, which ones?

"I should get to work," he said.

"You got dumped, didn't you?"

Oscar ignored her.

"Fine. Be that way. I'm going to take a shower. Care to join me?"

Hope had no idea why she had said that. Though it may have had to do with how sexy Oscar looked right now, with his wrinkled t-shirt and his hair tousled. And the way he was looking at her right now made her toes curl.

"My shower or yours?"

"Which is closer?"

Oscar grinned.

"Come," he said and led her down the hall.

They wound up in Oscar's bed after they had showered. Hope didn't want to leave, but she had work to do, as did Oscar. Oscar got out of bed first, Hope watching him get dressed.

"You going to spend the morning in my bed?" he asked her. "You're more than welcome to."

"As tempting as that sounds," said Hope, "I should throw on some clothes and get to work."

"Suit yourself."

He finished dressing and headed to the office. Reluctantly, Hope got up and went downstairs to change. When she got to the office, Oscar was seated in front of his computer with his headphones on.

Hope admired his ability to focus. She watched him for

a few seconds, then she went to her desk. She was working on the manuscript, but she kept thinking about Oscar, glancing over at him periodically.

Around noon, she received an email from Ashley. She seemed happy with the book report, but she was worried about getting the manuscript on time. Hope reassured her that she would have a first draft of the manuscript by the end of the month, though it would need editing. Ashley quickly wrote back that she was fine with that. She just needed to get the ball rolling.

At one, Hope announced she was getting something to eat and dragged Oscar downstairs. They ate quickly and went back upstairs to work.

At six, after spending all afternoon typing, Hope needed a break. She sent a text to Oscar. "Fancy a pint at the pub?"

She waited for him to reply, but he didn't take his eyes off his laptop. Finally, she got up and went over to him, tapping him on the shoulder. He stopped typing and looked up at her.

"Yes?"

"I'm taking a break. You want to grab a pint at the pub?"

"Can you give me a minute? I need to finish this scene."

"Okay, but don't take too long."

"I won't. I'm almost done."

Hope didn't move.

"Do you mind waiting for me downstairs?"

Hope sighed but complied, warning him that she'd be back up if he didn't come down in the next ten minutes.

As she waited, she checked her messages. Dani had written to her, letting her know that all was well and that she was going out again with Hope's new neighbor, Gary. Hope smiled at that and told her friend that she needed details.

She had also received a text from Edward, letting her know he was back and asking if she was free for dinner that weekend.

That weekend. It would be her last in England as it was almost the end of the month and time for her to go home. She had been meaning to send Peter at Good Vibes an email, but she had kept putting it off. She would reach out to him as soon as she got back from the pub.

There was no sign of Oscar, so Hope headed back up the stairs. She didn't bother to knock, just went straight over to him.

"Ahem," she said, tapping his shoulder.

He stopped what he was doing and looked up at her.

"I'm here to drag you to the pub."

"I'm almost done."

"You said that fifteen minutes ago."

"Well, I need a few more minutes."

"No," said Hope. "Save what you're doing. We're going to the pub and getting some dinner."

"Is that an order?"

"It is," said Hope. "I'm hungry."

Oscar saved his work and rose.

"Well, I wouldn't want you to starve."

Nan greeted them as they came through the door and told them to take a seat. Hope led Oscar to a booth, and a minute later Nan came over with menus, asking what they wanted to drink. As had become their custom, Oscar ordered a pint of ale, and Hope ordered a half-pint of cider.

"How's the play coming?" Hope asked him.

"Good. How's the book?"

"Good."

Nan came over with their drinks and said she'd be back to take their order.

"Have you heard from Gemma?" Hope asked Oscar after she'd taken a sip of cider.

"A bit."

"What does that mean?"

"It means she let me know that she got to London safely, but I haven't really heard from her since. Though I know she had lunch with Felicity yesterday."

"You didn't tell her?"

"Tell her what?"

Hope looked at him.

"That I know about you and the books?"

"Not yet."

Hope heard a phone ringing.

"Is that yours?" she asked Oscar.

"It is."

"Are you going to answer it?"

"I wasn't planning to."

"What if it's Gemma?"

"She'll leave a message."

The phone stopped ringing, then it began to ring again.

"You should probably get it," said Hope. "It could be important."

Oscar took out his phone, looked at the screen, and frowned.

"What's up?" Hope asked him. "Is it Gemma?"

"No," he said, putting the phone face down on the table.

It started to ring again. Oscar picked it up and silenced it.

"Same caller?" asked Hope, curious now.

Oscar took a sip of ale. Then he asked Hope if she had decided on an ending for the book.

"To be honest, I'm still struggling with it."

"Now you know how I feel."

"You sure you don't want to finish it?"

"Can't. I need to finish the play."

"How long do you think it will take you?"

"If I keep up the current pace, I should have a first draft in a month or so."

"Wow. That's fast."

"Yes, well, that's being optimistic. It'll probably take much longer. And then I'll need to go back in and review it."

Hope was going to ask him again what it was about, but she knew what he would say. Instead she announced she was going to the loo.

As she headed back to the table a few minutes later, she saw Oscar was on his phone. However, as soon as he saw her, he ended the call and put his phone away.

"Who were you talking to? Was it the person who kept phoning you?"

"It's not important."

Hope wondered why he was being cagey. Then she had a troubling thought.

"Was it your girlfriend?"

Oscar gave her a funny look.

"My girlfriend?"

"I'd understand," she said. Though, really, she wouldn't.

"You think I have a girlfriend?"

"Do you?"

"Do you really think I would sleep with you if I had a girlfriend?"

Hope studied his face. He seemed angry. But he could be a good actor.

"I don't know. Every time I ask you about your personal life, you deflect."

Oscar frowned.

"Fine. What is it you want to know?"

"Well, for starters, do you have a girlfriend?"

"I told you, I…"

"What you said or implied was that you wouldn't sleep with me if you had a girlfriend."

"Which any normal person would understand meant that I hadn't a girlfriend."

"Fine. So you're single?"

"I am."

"Good."

"What about you? You have a beau waiting for you back in the States?"

"No. To be honest, I'd kind of sworn off men after my last relationship."

"Oh? What happened?"

"He invited me to live with him, and then I caught him sleeping with one of his coworkers."

"Ouch."

"Yeah."

"I take it you didn't move in with him."

"I did not."

"And you decided to swear off men after one bad relationship?"

"It wasn't just one. I had a couple guys I thought were serious cheat on me. So I decided to focus on my career. What about you? Any serious relationships in your past?"

"Does being engaged count?"

Hope stared at him.

"You were engaged?"

Oscar nodded.

"What happened?"

"She broke it off, left me for another guy."

"No! Really?"

He nodded.

"What happened? Who was she?"

"You really want to know?"

"I do."

"If you're sure…"

"Tell me!" said Hope.

"Her name was Lana." Hope didn't like her already. "I met her at the Edinburgh festival. She had gone to see my play, and attended a talk I gave about it. After the talk, she told me how much the play had meant to her and asked me out for a drink.

"She was gorgeous, and I was flattered. So I said yes. We had a bit too much to drink, and I wound up going to her flat.

"I saw her again the next night, and the night after that. I was crazy about Lana. She was different from any of the other women I had dated. She worked at a bar and had a bunch of side hustles. And the sex was amazing."

Hope dug her nails into the palm of her hand.

"When the festival ended, Lana asked me to stay, but I said I needed to go back to London, to work on my new play. She said she understood and would visit me there.

"She came down a couple of weeks later, and I barely got any work done. But I didn't care. All I could think about was Lana. Eventually, she said that she needed to go back to Scotland. That's when I proposed to her."

"You proposed after knowing her for only, what, a month?"

"In retrospect, it seems insane. But Lana had bewitched me. I couldn't think when she wasn't with me. Or when she was with me," he added, smiling to himself.

Hope frowned.

"So, what happened? I assume she said yes as you said you'd been engaged."

"She did. At first she seemed excited. Then she went back to Scotland."

"What happened when she went back to Scotland?"

"At first we talked or texted every day. Then she stopped returning my calls and texts."

"Had she met someone there?"

"In a way. She got back together with her ex. Apparently, when he heard about me, that I had proposed to Lana, he got jealous and told Lana he wanted her back."

"So she dumped you for her ex?"

Oscar nodded as he took a sip of his ale.

"Ouch. That sucks. Are they still together?"

"I have no idea. I blocked her after I found out."

"How did you find out?"

"She told me. Said it wasn't personal, just that she and Rory had a history, and she needed to give him another shot."

"And you haven't dated anyone since?"

"I didn't say that. I just haven't been serious about anyone until…"

Hope saw him looking at her and felt her face grow warm. However, just then Nan came over and asked them if they were ready to order.

"Give us a minute," Oscar told her.

After Nan left, Oscar asked Hope what she wanted. *You,* she said to herself. Instead, she picked up her menu.

CHAPTER 36

Hope woke up the next morning to find Oscar still in her bed. She smiled. They had had quite an evening, the two of them tearing each other's clothes off as soon as they got back to Gemma's.

Hope quietly got out of bed and went to the bathroom. When she returned, Oscar was up.

"Good morning," she said. She loved how he looked first thing.

"Good morning," he replied. He seemed relaxed.

"I'm surprised you're still here."

"Oh?"

"I thought you were eager to work on your play."

"The play can wait."

"It can?"

"Uh-hm," he said, looking at her.

"What?" said Hope.

"Come here."

"Why?"

"Do I need a reason?"

Hope went over to him, and he pulled her onto the bed. She squealed as he nuzzled her neck.

"What about the play?" she said.

"The play can wait," he repeated. "There's something I need to do first."

"What's that?" said Hope, though she had a pretty good idea. "Let me show you."

Hope was both exhausted and exhilarated when Oscar finally left. The man was insatiable. Though she hadn't minded one little bit. It had been nearly a year since she had been with someone. And she considered it making up for lost time.

She dragged herself out of bed and went to make coffee. Oscar was in the kitchen, standing by the coffee maker.

"It's almost ready," he informed her.

As soon as it was, he poured himself a mugful and took the mug upstairs. Hope watched him leave, staring at his backside. Then she fixed herself a cup. She took a sip and tried to decide if she should go upstairs to the office or take a shower first. The shower won.

When she got to the office, Oscar was dressed and seated in front of his computer, his headphones in place. Hope didn't disturb him, but she had an urge to go over and nuzzle his neck. Instead, she went to her desk.

She had decided that Hattie and Stanhope would wind up together, but she didn't want the traditional happy ending, where they got married, had several children, and that was that. Hope wanted more for Hattie. But what?

Hattie needed something, something of her own, a cause or... maybe a career? Though women in Victorian times rarely had careers. Still, an idea had begun to percolate in Hope's head. And the more Hope thought about it, the more she liked it. Of course, it would mean revising the manuscript. But Hope was quite good at that.

She scrolled to the beginning of the book and began to read.

"You want some lunch?"

It was Oscar.

"Hm?" said Hope, looking up at him. She had been too busy working on the manuscript to think about food.

"I asked if you wanted some lunch. I'm going to go eat something."

Hope looked at the time. It was after one.

"I could probably use some food," she said and followed Oscar downstairs.

"I heard from Gemma," he said as he made them an omelet.

"Oh? What did she have to say?"

"She'll be back tomorrow."

"Do you need to go pick her up?"

"No, she said she has a ride."

"Her old friend?"

"Mm," said Oscar, concentrating on the omelet. He slid it onto a plate and divided it in two. Then he removed two pieces of toast from the toaster. "Here you go," he said, placing one of the plates in front of Hope.

"Thank you."

"Did you tell Gemma about the book?"

"Not yet."

"Why not?"

"It's not like we've actually spoken."

"But you'll tell her when she gets back?"

"Are you worried she won't approve? I told you, she'll probably be delighted."

Hope wasn't so sure about that, but she didn't say anything. Instead, she took a bite of her omelet.

"You figure out the ending to the book?"

"I have," said Hope, taking another bite.

"You going to tell me?"

"No, you can read it when it's published."

Oscar frowned.

"Now you know what it feels like."

Hope quickly finished her omelet and got up.

"You're leaving?" said Oscar.

"I need to get back to work. You don't mind doing the washing up, do you?" Without waiting for an answer, she left the kitchen and went upstairs.

Hope felt a tad bad about leaving Oscar to do the washing up. However, there wasn't that much to clean, and she had done the dishes plenty of times. Also, time was ticking. She had a lot to do and not much time to do it as she would be flying back to New York on Monday after she and Oscar spent the weekend in London. It had been his idea to spend the weekend there, and Hope had been thrilled when he had suggested it.

That night, Hope slept in Oscar's room. They hadn't planned it. It had just happened. They had both been working late, and Hope had joked that she was too tired to make it down the stairs. Then Oscar had suggested she sleep in his room. And, well…

As Hope lay in bed, she wondered if she and Oscar would continue to sleep together once Gemma got back. She rolled over to ask him, but he had fallen asleep.

Gemma returned the following afternoon. Hope had been nervous all day, even though Oscar had reassured her that Gemma would be fine with Hope taking over as Gemma Lovegood. And he had been correct. Gemma had been more than fine with the idea. She thought it brilliant, especially as it meant that Oscar could get back to writing plays. To celebrate, Gemma said she would make them a special dinner that evening.

"But you just got back," said Hope. "Don't you want to relax?"

"I've got plenty of time to relax. Besides, I enjoy cooking. I find it relaxing. I'll just pop out to the market and get a few things. Any requests?"

Hope and Oscar both said she could make whatever she liked.

That evening, the three of them sat down to a dinner of duck à l'orange with roasted vegetables and champagne. Gemma said that she had been saving the bottle for a special occasion. She poured some of the bubbly liquid into everyone's glass, then she raised hers.

"To Hope and Oscar!" she said.

"What about you?" said Hope.

"Oh, I haven't done anything," said Gemma.

"You let Oscar use your name and kept his secret."

"That was nothing. Well, if you won't let me drink to the two of you, how about we drink to good health?"

"I'll drink to that," said Hope.

"To good health!" they said in unison and drank.

"And to making new friends," added Hope, smiling at Oscar and Gemma. They smiled back at her and drank.

"So how are you finding being Gemma Lovegood?" Gemma asked Hope.

"I was a bit intimidated at first, but… I think I'm getting the hang of it. Though Oscar's a tough act to follow."

"You think you'll keep at it?"

"You mean write another one?"

Gemma nodded.

"Oh no," said Hope. "I'm one and done."

"Why?"

"I'm happy being an editor."

"What if Ms. Wallingford wants another novel?"

"Let's cross that bridge when we come to it. So, how was your trip?"

"It was very nice. I suppose Oscar told you about Felicity."

"He did. Is she all right?"

"She's fine. She's just had a bit of a rough go of it lately."

"I'm sorry to hear that," said Hope. She was curious

about Gemma's daughter, the supermodel, but she didn't want to pry.

"She finally break up with Graham?" Oscar asked his mother.

"She did. To which I say, good riddance. I never liked that man."

"So she's back at the flat?"

"She is, though she's off to Milan for some show."

"Poor baby."

They finished up, and Oscar announced that he should go get some work done. Hope said she'd help Gemma clean up, even though Gemma said she was fine.

"So, you and Oscar…" said Gemma as she washed the dishes.

"What about me and Oscar?" Hope replied, keeping her eyes on the dish she was drying.

"He likes you, you know."

Hope didn't know what to say.

"Did he say something to you?"

"He didn't have to. I saw the way he looked at you. I gather you like him too."

"I do," said Hope. Why bother to deny it?

"I'm glad," said Gemma.

"I've been working at your desk," said Hope, not wanting to discuss her relationship with Oscar. "I hope you don't mind."

"Not at all."

They were silent as they finished the washing up.

"I should probably go up to the office and do a bit of work," Hope said as she finished drying the last plate. "Did Oscar tell you that we're going to London for the weekend, before I fly home Monday?"

"He mentioned it. I'll be sorry to see you go."

"I'll be sorry too, but it's time."

She helped Gemma put away the things and then said she was going upstairs.

Oscar was on his laptop, but he stopped working when Hope came over.

"Yes?" he said.

"Gemma knows."

"What does she know?"

"About us. Or she suspects something."

"So? Did she say something to you?"

"Not really."

"Then what's the problem?"

"It just feels weird with her being here and us, you know…"

"Sleeping together?"

Hope nodded.

"I'm sure she won't care."

"Really?"

"She's not a prude, you know."

"I know but… I don't think I'm comfortable sleeping together with her here."

Oscar frowned.

"I'm sure she won't mind."

"Sorry, but I don't think I can have sex with you with your mother across the hall."

"Fine. I'll sleep in your room."

"What I meant was, I think we should wait until we get to London."

"Why?"

"I told you. I don't feel comfortable shagging you with your mother here."

"Suit yourself," he said. Then he turned back to his computer.

"Don't be angry," said Hope.

Oscar sighed.

"I'm not angry. I'm just tired. I haven't been getting a lot of sleep lately. A certain person's been keeping me up."

Hope felt her face turning pink.

"So we both could use some rest." She leaned over and

gave him a kiss. "I think I'm going to skip working tonight and go read in my room. I'll see you in the morning."

It took Hope a while to fall asleep. When she did, she dreamed of Hattie and Stanhope again.

The next morning, Hope found Gemma and Oscar in the kitchen when she got there.

"Oh, good, you're up," said Gemma. "How do you feel about pancakes? I thought it would be fun to make some. I know how you Americans like them."

"You don't need to make me pancakes," said Hope.

"It's no bother," said Gemma. "Consider it my going away present."

"But you made duck—and we had that champagne."

"I, for one, would love some pancakes," said Oscar.

"That settles it," said Gemma. "I'm making some."

The pancakes were delicious. A bit different than the ones Hope was used to, more like crepes, but Hope didn't say anything.

After breakfast, Hope and Oscar went upstairs to work while Gemma met up with a friend. Hope had been busy revising *Balls and Chains*, working in the new plot. Hattie, she had decided, was a writer who had been secretly publishing short stories under her pen name, H.H. Hollings. And part of the reason she hadn't wanted to get married was that she feared a husband would put an end to her career when he found out. After all, no respectable Victorian gentleman wanted his wife to work, especially to be writing the kind of bawdy tales H.H. Hollings penned.

However, at a quarter to one Hope had to stop. She was having a farewell lunch with Edward at one.

"Where are you going?" Oscar asked her.

"I need to get changed for my lunch with Edward."

Oscar frowned.

"Are you jealous?"

"Me? Of course not." But Hope could tell that he was.

"Well, you have nothing to worry about. Edward and I are just friends."

"Mm."

Hope leaned over and gave him a kiss.

"I'll see you later."

CHAPTER 37

Gemma had answered the door when Edward rang, and Hope came downstairs to find the two of them chatting amiably.

"I hope I'm not interrupting," said Hope.

"Not at all," said Gemma.

"You ready?" asked Edward.

"I am," said Hope.

"It was nice chatting with you, Ms. Lovegood," said Edward.

"Please, call me Gemma."

Edward smiled at that.

"Let's go," said Hope.

They walked to Edward's car, and Hope asked him where they were having lunch.

"I was thinking we could try this new gastro pub. It's not far from Cupid's Bow, and it's gotten good reviews."

"Sounds good! Let's go!"

They got in the Mini. Was it Hope's imagination or did Edward seem nervous?

"Is everything all right?" she asked him.

"Why?" he said, glancing over at her.

"You seem a bit preoccupied."

"I just have some things on my mind."

They arrived at the gastro pub a few minutes later and were seated at a table for two. Edward ordered a beer, and

Hope wondered what was up. He didn't usually drink at lunch.

"I have a confession to make," he said after taking a sip of his beer. Hope waited for him to go on. "I saw Lucy."

Hope hadn't been expecting that.

"You saw Lucy? Is that why you went to London?"

"Partly. She'd been messaging me since we saw her at the ball, telling me she'd made a mistake and wanted to give it another go."

"What about Gabriel?"

"She broke up with him."

Hope wondered if it was the other way around.

"So, what happened? Are you two back together?" Hope hadn't liked Lucy, but if she was who Edward wanted…

"No. It was a mistake thinking we could just pick up as though nothing had happened, as though we wanted the same things."

"What happened?"

"Lucy insisted we go to this party hosted by one of her posh friends. I didn't want to go. I had just got there. But Lucy said it would be rude not to."

"Did something happen at the party?"

"Nothing in particular. I just felt like a wallflower. It wasn't really my crowd."

"Did you say something to Lucy?"

"I told her I wanted to leave, and she got annoyed."

"So, what happened? Did you leave?"

"I stayed, but the next morning, I told Lucy it was over between us. For good this time."

"How did she react?"

"Not well. She screamed at me. Told me that I had led her on, which was rich as she was the one who'd been hounding me to get back together."

Hope quietly sipped her water.

"I felt bad, but…"

"I'm so sorry, Edward."

"Don't be. I'm fine with it."

"Are you?"

"I am. Actually, I'm better than fine. I took your advice, and I asked Poppy out."

"You did? When? Was this before or after Lucy said she wanted you back?"

"Before, actually. I ran into Poppy at the pub after you moved out, and I asked her if she'd like to have dinner sometime."

"I gather she said yes."

"She did. We went out the next night and had a really good time. Then Lucy phoned, and… I needed to know, you know? Before I got involved with someone."

Hope understood.

"Did you tell Poppy about Lucy?"

Edward shook his head.

"But I knew when I saw Lucy again that it was all wrong. And when I got back home and got Arfur, I told Poppy about her."

"How did she react?"

"She said she understood."

"So, you two are good?"

Edward smiled.

"Yeah, we are. I'm seeing her later, actually."

"I'm very happy for you."

"Are you really?"

"Of course I am! I'm the one who told you to ask her out!"

"Right. And what about you?"

"What about me?"

"What's going on with you and Oscar?"

"What do you mean?"

"Come on, Hope. I'm not blind. I'll admit, when I heard you were coming here, I had sort of hoped we might reconnect. But when I saw the way you and Oscar looked at each other, I knew I didn't have a chance."

"You did? How did we look at each other? I couldn't stand Oscar when I first met him."

Edward smiled.

"It's the old enemies-to-lovers trope."

Hope stared at him.

"I told you, I read romance novels."

Just then their server came over, asking if they were ready to order.

"Thank you for lunch," said Edward as they drove back to Cupid's Bow. "Though you didn't have to do that."

"It was my pleasure," said Hope. She had insisted on paying, to thank Edward for letting her stay with him.

"So, where are you taking Poppy to dinner?"

"To this little French bistro."

"I'm sure she'll love it."

"And what about you and Oscar? Will you two see each other after you go back to the States?"

"I don't know. We haven't really discussed it."

"You should talk to him."

"Mm," said Hope, noncommittally. She wasn't prepared to have that talk with Oscar, even though she'd thought about it.

"Don't wait too long."

They had arrived back at Gemma's.

"Do you want to come in?" Hope asked him.

"I better not. I don't want Oscar growling at me."

"He won't growl at you."

Edward gave her a look.

"So, I guess this is it," she said.

"I guess so."

Hope leaned over and gave him a kiss on the cheek.

"Thanks for being such a good friend."

"It was my pleasure."

Hope got out and headed down the walkway.

Edward rolled down his window.

"If you ever need a place to crash in Devon again, let me know!"

Hope smiled and waved goodbye.

She entered Gemma's cottage and was relieved to not find Oscar waiting for her. She went upstairs to the office. He was at his desk working. Hope went over to him.

"You're back," he said.

"Very observant of you."

"How was your lunch?"

"Good. Edward's seeing Poppy."

"Who's Poppy?"

"His neighbor. She looks after Arfur."

"Who's Arfur?"

"His dog."

"He has a dog named Arfur?"

"Technically, it's King Arfur."

Oscar shook his head.

"You packed?" he asked Hope.

"I just got back. I was planning on doing it later."

"Don't forget, we're driving to London later."

"I didn't forget. I just want to get a little work in, then I'll pack. I don't have that much to pack. Are you packed?"

"I don't need to pack. I have stuff at the flat."

"Right. Well, I'll just do a bit of work and then…" But Oscar's attention was already back on his laptop.

"Ahem," said Oscar, standing beside Hope.

"Yes?" she said.

"Time for you to go downstairs and pack."

"What time is it?" She had been so eager to finish the

manuscript, she had lost track of the time.

"It's four-thirty. We should go soon."

"Just give me a few more minutes."

"Five more minutes, then I'm dragging you downstairs."

It felt weird to be driving to London with Oscar, weird but exciting. Oscar had gotten them tickets to see a show in the West End the following evening, and he had made other plans for them. Though Hope would have been happy to hole up at his flat for the next two days.

On the drive, she thought about broaching the topic of what would happen after she left. Would they try to see each other? Though Hope only got two weeks' vacation. Would Oscar come see her in New York?

"You okay?" he asked her.

"I'm fine," Hope replied.

"Are you sure? You seem a bit preoccupied."

Hope thought about bringing up what would happen to them once she got back to the States. But she wasn't ready to have that conversation. Instead, she told him she was excited about being back in London.

"I'm warning you, the flat could be a mess," he told Hope as he took out his keys. "Felicity's not the best housekeeper under normal circumstances, and considering she just broke up with Graham and had to go to Milan…"

"I consider myself warned."

Oscar opened the door and let Hope in. The flat didn't look messy.

"She must have had the cleaners in," Oscar said.

There was a note with Oscar's name on it on a little table in the living room. Oscar picked it up.

"It's from Felicity."

"What does she say?"

"To have a good time."

"That was nice of her."

"Mm. Are you hungry?"

"I could eat. Is there someplace nearby?"

"Take your pick."

"I don't care as long as I don't have to change."

"I know just the place. Do you like pizza?"

"Is that a trick question?"

Oscar smiled.

"Come. It's just around the corner."

Dinner had been yummy. Though spending the weekend in London with Oscar had been more so. They had gone horseback riding in Hyde Park Saturday afternoon, and then to the theater Saturday evening. On Sunday they slept in and then went for a long walk. That afternoon, Oscar took Hope to see a play written by a friend. Then they had dinner at a little bistro and spent the rest of the evening in bed.

Hope felt as though she was living inside a romance novel. But she didn't know how this one would end.

Monday came too quickly, and a part of Hope—a big part—didn't want to leave. Oscar had offered to drive her to Heathrow, but Hope said that she was fine taking the train. It would be easier and faster. And she didn't want one of those tearful, cliché airport goodbye scenes. Oscar had smiled at that.

"I'll miss you," she said over breakfast. They still hadn't talked about what would happen after she left.

"I know," he replied. Hope swatted his arm, and he grinned. "I'll miss you too."

"You could always visit me. There's lots to do and see in New York."

"I know. But I need to work on my play."

"You seem in a hurry to finish it."

"I am."

"Why put so much pressure on yourself?"

"I want to enter it into a couple of festivals."

"Which ones?"

"I'd rather not say. I don't want to jinx things."

Hope looked at her phone.

"I should finish getting ready. I need to go soon."

"Must you go?"

She looked at Oscar. At that moment, she wished she could stay. But she missed her apartment and Morris and her friends. She'd never been away this long.

"I must."

She returned a few minutes later with her suitcase and backpack.

"Are you sure I can't help you with those?" Oscar asked her.

"I'm good," said Hope. "But thank you."

"You'll let me know when you touch down?"

"I will."

She went over and kissed him.

"I'll miss you, Hope Halladay," he whispered in her ear.

"I'll miss you too."

Then she placed her backpack on her back, picked up her suitcase, and left.

CHAPTER 38

Hope arrived home to find Morris waiting for her, along with a Welcome Home banner. She was tired. It was after eleven in London. But she knew she should try to stay up, at least until nine.

She had texted Oscar as soon as she had landed. He had replied with a thumbs-up emoji. She was a bit disappointed that was all he had texted, but she told herself he was probably too busy to write. And an emoji was better than nothing.

To stay awake, Hope started a load of laundry and ordered Chinese food. Then she turned on Netflix. A little after nine, she realized she had fallen asleep on the couch, Morris having fallen asleep beside her. She got up and went to the bathroom. Then she changed and climbed into bed. Soon she was fast asleep.

It was dark when Hope woke up. She looked over at her alarm clock. It was a little after five. She groaned and tried to go back to sleep, but it was useless. And Morris was meowing for food. Hope went to the kitchen to feed him and made herself some coffee.

She turned on her phone and found a message from Ashley reminding her that she was expecting Gemma's manuscript TODAY in uppercase letters. Hope rolled her eyes. Type A indeed.

It was too early to go to the office, so Hope went to get her computer. She had read through *Balls and Chains* on the plane, reminding herself that it was just a first draft. She could edit it after Ashley read through it. A part of Hope wanted to tell Ashley the truth about the book. But that would lead to a lot of questions. Best to let her think Gemma Lovegood wrote it. Unless she hated it. Then she would probably have to come clean.

She typed a cover note to go with the manuscript but decided to take a shower before sending the email to Ashley. When she was dressed, she read over what she had written, attached the manuscript, and hit *send*. It was a little after seven-thirty. Dani had left Hope some food, but Hope decided she would pick up something at her favorite bakery on her way to work.

She arrived at the office a little after eight and found the place nearly empty, most of the editors not usually getting in until eight-thirty or nine. That was fine by Hope. It gave her time to see what Fiona had left for her.

Hope entered her cubicle, immediately noticed the large pile of folders on her desk, and frowned. She started to pick one up and then stopped. She would wait to go over everything with Fiona. She had other things to do in the meantime.

Fiona arrived a half hour later.

"You're back," she said.

"I am," said Hope.

"Good. Ashley's been driving me crazy."

"Sorry. I guess maternity leave doesn't agree with her."

"Tell me about it. Oh, and FYI, she says she's planning on coming back next week."

"To the office?"

"Yep! Says she's losing her mind being home twenty-four-seven with the baby."

"I heard about the nanny. So she hasn't found a new one?"

"Not yet. She's still interviewing people. But I gather she's close to hiring a new one if she's planning on coming back next week."

"Maybe it will take longer."

"We can hope," said Fiona.

Hope couldn't help smiling.

"So, you want to go over all of these folders you left on my desk?"

"Give me a few," said Fiona. "I just got here."

Hope said that was fine, and Fiona went to put her things away.

It amazed Hope how quickly she had fallen back into her old routine despite being away for several weeks. She had a few long days at the office playing catch up, but by Friday evening, she felt she was almost there.

The next week, Ashley returned.

Hope hadn't heard anything from her about *Balls and Chains* and had been nervous. Did Ashley not like it? It was unusual for her boss not to say anything. Should Hope say something?

Ashley was too busy to meet with Hope the first morning she was back. But she called Hope into her office that afternoon. Ashley's door was closed, so Hope knocked.

"Come in!" called her boss.

Hope entered.

"Take a seat," Ashley instructed.

Hope hadn't seen Ashley in nearly six weeks and hadn't known what to expect. Yet her boss looked exactly the same. Correction: She looked exactly the same as before her pregnancy began to show. Indeed, if you hadn't known Ashley had been pregnant, you wouldn't. Clearly, Ashley had been working out. Or maybe it was stress.

"Thank you for handling things in my absence," Ashley began.

"You should really thank Fiona," Hope said.

"Whatever. Anyway, the reason I wanted to see you is, I want to discuss Gemma's latest."

Here it comes, thought Hope. *She hated it.*

"It's different from her first two books."

"Different good or different bad?"

"What do you think?"

Hope looked at her boss, but she couldn't read her expression.

"Different good?"

Ashley smiled.

"Different very good."

Hope mentally breathed a sigh of relief.

"The style's a bit different. But I'm okay with that. And I liked the plot twist. Very clever. Reminded me a bit of that *Bridgerton* book."

"Which one? There are, like, eight of them."

"You know the one. Anyway, I've already spoken to Marketing about the book. They're planning a whole campaign around it. And we're going to hold the launch party right before Valentine's Day. Speaking of which, I want you to get in touch with Oscar. Tell him I want him and Gemma to be here for it."

Hope opened her mouth to remind Ashley about Gemma not liking to attend events, but it seemed Ashley already knew what Hope was going to say.

"Tell them I insist," said Ashley. "She attended that ball in London. She can attend her own book launch. We'll fly them over and put them up for a few days."

Hope didn't say anything. She had too many thoughts pinging through her brain.

"Is there a problem, Hope?"

"Hm?"

"You didn't answer me."

"Sorry, was there a question?"

"I was expecting you to say you'd get on it."

"I'll get on it."

"Excellent."

"Is there anything else you wanted to discuss?" *Like my promotion?* Hope thought.

"I," Ashley began. However, her cell phone was buzzing. She looked down at it. "I need to get this," she told Hope.

Hope remained seated. Ashley threw her a look, and Hope got up. She was nearly at the door when Ashley called out to her.

"By the way, I haven't forgotten about that promotion."

Hope turned around and was going to say something, but Ashley was speaking to whoever had called her, so Hope left.

The next nine months were a blur. Hope had received her promotion, which had resulted in more work. But Hope didn't mind. She enjoyed working with authors. She was even trying to become one herself. It had been hard finding time to write, but she had forced herself to do it. She'd had an idea in her head for a book since she got back from England, and this time she was determined to see it through. Now she was almost done with the first draft.

She planned on showing it to Ashley after the book launch, which was in a week.

She and Oscar had been texting, talking, and video chatting regularly. Hope had hoped he would visit her, but he claimed to be too busy to make it across the pond. However, soon they would see each other in person. And Hope wasn't sure if the butterflies she was feeling were due to excitement or nervousness.

Hope still couldn't believe Oscar and Gemma were actually coming to the book launch. Oscar hadn't wanted Gemma to go, fearing she'd be overwhelmed. But Gemma surprised them both by insisting they attend.

They had arrived the day before the big event, and Hope would be having dinner with them at their hotel that evening. There was something they wanted to discuss with her before the party.

Hope had been nervous all day and had asked Oscar, via text, to just tell her what was up, but he had refused. He and Gemma would tell her when they saw her.

Hope had spent way too much time getting ready for their dinner. But she wanted to look perfect for Oscar. Or, if not perfect, make him see what he'd been missing. She needn't have worried. As soon as she walked into the hotel bar, Oscar's face lit up.

He kissed her and whispered in her ear that she looked beautiful, and Hope felt her face (and other parts of her body) grow warm.

"You don't look so bad yourself," she said.

Frankly, if Gemma hadn't been sitting there, she'd have dragged Oscar up to his room and torn his clothes off. And judging by the way he was looking at her, he was thinking the same thing.

"Shall we go to our table?" Hope suggested.

Once they were seated and had ordered drinks, Hope asked them about their flight. But what she really wanted to know was, why had they wanted to meet with her?

She waited until they'd been served their drinks, then she asked.

"I've decided to retire," said Gemma.

Hope was confused.

"I don't understand. I thought you were retired."

"What Gemma means," said Oscar, "is that she no longer wants her name attached to the books."

Hope stared at them.

"But what about *Balls and Chains*? It's already been printed with Gemma's name on it."

"Sorry. What she means is that there will be no more Gemma Lovegoods after the new one comes out."

"Does Ashley know?" Hope was ninety-nine percent

certain Ashley didn't. Otherwise, Hope would have heard about it.

"Not yet," said Oscar. "We're planning on telling her tomorrow when we meet with her."

"I need some water," said Hope. She signaled to a nearby busboy, who came over with a pitcher and poured some water into her glass. Hope immediately took a sip.

"Are you okay?" asked Gemma.

"Not really," said Hope. "When did you decide this?"

"We've been discussing it for a while," said Gemma. "Then Ms. Wallingford forced the issue."

"She did? What did she say?"

"She told Oscar that she wanted two more books."

Hope looked at Oscar.

"She did?" He nodded. "She didn't say anything to me." Hope couldn't help feeling a bit offended.

"When did she ask you to write two more books?"

"A while ago."

"A while ago? How long ago are we talking about? Why didn't you tell me?" *And why didn't Ashley tell her that she wanted more Gemma Lovegoods?*

"We thought you knew," said Gemma.

"Well, I didn't. So what did you tell her when she asked you—or rather Gemma—to write two more books?"

"I told her no," said Oscar. "But your boss clearly doesn't understand the meaning of the word."

"Tell me about it," said Hope. "I told you, once Ashley has her mind set on something… So where did you leave it?"

"As I said, we're meeting with her tomorrow, where we shall make it quite clear that Gemma is done."

"Look, I know you want to be done but could you do me a favor and wait until after the launch party to tell Ashley? She's been on edge all week, and this could put her over it."

Gemma looked at her son.

"I suppose it couldn't hurt to wait a day."

Oscar frowned but didn't say anything.

"Thank you," said Hope, relieved. "Just out of curiosity, how much did she offer you to write two more books?"

Oscar told her, and Hope whistled.

"Wow. And you turned that down?"

"Some things are more important than money."

"Oscar's very excited about his new play," Gemma said.

"Did you finish it?" Hope knew he'd been revising it.

He nodded.

"I'd love to see it."

Oscar took a sip of his drink.

"I'm not ready to share it yet."

Hope was disappointed.

"Speaking of books," said Gemma, "Oscar tells me you've been busy writing one of your own and that's it's very good."

"You read it already?" Hope had just sent it to him.

"I started reading it on the plane. And I didn't think it was a secret."

"Ashley doesn't know about it, and I'd like to keep it that way until I'm ready to share it with her."

"What are you waiting for?" asked Gemma.

"I'm just not ready to share it with her yet," said Hope.

Fortunately, she was saved from having to explain more by their server. He wanted to know if they were ready to order. Oscar asked him to give them a few minutes. And Hope, grateful for the distraction, suggested they decide what they would get.

Oscar and Gemma showed up at Herstory the next morning. The whole office had been buzzing about Gemma Lovegood being there, and people were lining the hallway to get a look at the famously reclusive author. Hope wondered if they should have hired a bodyguard for Gemma. But Oscar protected his mother from the crowd of gawkers, ushering her into Ashley's office.

Hope had wanted to be there, but Ashley told her that her presence wasn't necessary. Hope had been miffed, but she didn't say anything. Instead, she busied herself in her cubicle, nervously glancing over at Ashley's office from time to time.

Finally, the door to Ashley's office opened, and Hope saw Oscar and Gemma leave. She hurried over to intercept them, but Ashley intercepted her first, telling Hope she wanted to see her in her office *now*.

Hope glanced over at Oscar and Gemma. They were nearly at the elevator bank.

"I'm waiting," said Ashley.

Hope sighed and turned around.

"Close the door," Ashley instructed her, taking a seat behind her desk.

Hope closed the door and turned to face her boss.

"Have a seat."

Hope sat.

"So, when were you planning on telling me?"

Hope tried to read Ashley's expression but was unable to.

"Tell you what?"

Ashley didn't appear to be angry, but you never knew with her.

"About you and Gemma."

"What about me and Gemma?" she said, starting to perspire.

"That you helped her write her latest book. I believe her exact words were, 'I'd have never been able to finish it without Hope.'"

"She said that?"

"She did. That wasn't all." Hope swallowed. "She also informed me that she was done."

"Done?" Hope asked nervously.

"As in she wasn't interested in writing more books."

What happened to them not saying anything until after the launch party?

"Did you know?"

"I…" Hope was a terrible liar. "She may have mentioned something during dinner last night."

"And you didn't bother to inform me that our bestselling author was thinking about retiring?"

Hope felt sick.

"We have other bestselling authors."

"No one who's sold as many books as Gemma Lovegood, which is why I called you in here. I know Gemma trusts you and…"

"I can't make Gemma write more books," said Hope, interrupting her boss.

Ashley looked annoyed.

"If you would let me finish. I wasn't going to ask you to pressure her. Oscar made it very clear that Gemma would not be writing any more books."

"So, what is it you want me to do?"

"I want you to write them."

"Excuse me?" said Hope.

"It's the perfect solution. You're already familiar with Gemma's books and have a degree in Victorian Literature. And, according to Gemma, you practically wrote the last one."

"I don't know, Ashley. Did you run this by Gemma and Oscar?" She couldn't see Oscar agreeing to it.

"I wanted to talk to you first. What do you say?"

"I…" Hope didn't like the way her boss was looking at her. "Actually, I've been working on my own book."

"Not on company time, I hope."

"Of course not," said Hope. "But I was hoping to show it to you when I've finished editing it."

"That's fine. I'd be happy to take a look. But your first priority is Gemma, or rather making sure there are more Gemmas."

"I… Writing a book is a lot of work. And I don't see how I could do that and my regular job."

"We'd figure something out. And we'd pay you a fee for doing it."

"You would?"

"Of course."

Hope stopped herself. What was she thinking? She knew how Gemma and Oscar felt. And frankly, she had no interest in becoming the new Gemma Lovegood. She wanted to focus on her own work.

"I think you should speak to Gemma and Oscar."

"I'll run it by them at the party later. I'm sure they'll be fine with it. Especially when I reassure them that Gemma would still be entitled to a royalty."

Hope wasn't so sure about that.

Ashley's cell phone was ringing. She picked it up and told the caller to hold on. Then she covered the phone and turned to Hope. "Think about my offer."

Hope left the office a bit dazed. She was flattered by Ashley's offer, but she didn't want to be the next Gemma Lovegood, even if it meant getting paid more money. But if she turned down the job, would Ashley then not consider Hope's book? It was a quandary, and Hope wished she could talk to someone about it. But no one else knew the truth about Gemma. Well, except for Oscar.

She took out her phone and sent him a text, asking if he could meet her for lunch. He replied a few minutes later, asking her what time and where. Hope asked if he was free at twelve-thirty and gave him the name of a nearby sandwich shop.

He was waiting for Hope when she got there.

"What's up?" he asked her after they had ordered. Hope told him what had transpired. "Just tell her no," he said when Hope had finished.

"I want to, but I'm worried then she won't read my book or, worse, that she'll fire me."

"Seriously, she'd fire you for saying no?"

"You don't know Ashley."

"Actually, I think I do. And I don't think she would fire you. Would she be annoyed? Yes. But fire her best editor? Absolutely not."

"I wouldn't say I'm her best editor."

"Anyway, if she's stupid enough to let you go, I'm sure you could find another job. Or maybe your book will get published and you won't need to work at Herstory."

"But I like working at Herstory, and I'd like them to publish my book."

They picked up their food and took a seat at a table.

"So is Gemma having lunch with her friend?" Hope asked. Gemma had mentioned she was meeting an old friend over dinner.

"She is."

"But she'll be at the party later."

"She will. Don't worry."

They made small talk as they ate. Then Oscar said he had to go. He had an appointment.

"Oh?" said Hope. "Where are you off to?" He hadn't mentioned an appointment at dinner.

"I'll tell you about it later." He then gave her a kiss and told her to wish him luck.

"Good luck," she called as he headed down the street.

CHAPTER 39

Hope stood near the entrance to the venue where the book launch party was being held. She was waiting for Oscar and Gemma to arrive. Despite what Oscar had said, Hope worried that Gemma would be a no-show. But a little after six, they arrived.

"You made it!" said Hope.

"Did you really think we'd miss your big debut?" said Oscar.

"Sh!" said Hope, looking around.

Oscar seemed amused.

"I don't know about the two of you," said Gemma, "but I could use a drink."

"Come," said Hope. "The bar's just over there."

However, they had only gone a few feet before Ashley intercepted them.

"Gemma! You made it!" Oscar cleared his throat. "Oscar," she said, less enthusiastically. Then she turned her attention back to Gemma. "Come," she said, taking Gemma's arm. "There are some people I want you to meet." And before Oscar could protest, Ashley had led Gemma away.

"Will she be all right?" Hope asked Oscar.

"She'll be fine. We've been practicing."

"Practicing?"

"Preparing her for any questions people might ask about the new book."

"Has she read it?"

"Of course."

They watched as Ashley led Gemma over to two women who seemed delighted to meet the famous author. Then Hope turned back to Oscar.

"How did your appointment go?"

"Good," he said, still looking at Gemma.

"Are you going to tell me what it was about?"

"Later." Something, or someone, had caught his eye. "Is that Gretchen Millhaus?" he asked.

Hope saw where he was looking.

"It is. Why?"

Gretchen Millhaus was one of their authors. She had written a memoir about hitchhiking across America as a sixty-something woman and it had become a bestseller.

"I read her book. She sounds fascinating."

"She is. Would you like me to introduce you?"

"If you wouldn't mind."

Hope had lost track of Gemma and Oscar. She had been doing the rounds, chatting with guests, including Bellamy Bradley, one of her favorite literary agents. She had even let slip to Bellamy, after she'd had a glass of wine, that she'd written a book, a rom-com set in England, and Bellamy had told her to send her the manuscript when it was ready. Hope thought that Bellamy was probably just being polite, but she said that she would.

She had just spotted Oscar and Gemma across the room when Ashley called for everyone's attention. She was standing at the podium that had been set up, speaking into a microphone.

"Everyone, if I could have your attention, please," she repeated. The room quieted. "We are here tonight to celebrate the launch of Gemma Lovegood's latest masterpiece, *Balls and*

Chains." Someone in the crowd whooped at that, and Ashley smiled. "Yes, we're all very excited. And tonight we have a very special guest with us.

"As many of you know, Gemma Lovegood doesn't normally do public appearances. In fact, she rarely leaves her little village of Cupid's Bow in Southwest England. However, she has made an exception for us, crossing the pond to be with us this evening."

Hope thought Ashley was laying it on a bit thick and wondered what Gemma and Oscar thought of her speech. Well, she would soon find out.

Ashley looked over to where Gemma and Oscar were standing.

"Gemma, would you come up here?"

There was murmuring in the crowd as Oscar escorted Gemma to the stage.

Ashley beamed at the author. Then she turned to the guests.

"Ladies and gentlemen, I give you Gemma Lovegood!"

There was hearty applause and more whooping from the audience. Gemma smiled at them.

"Thank you," she said. "This is all a bit overwhelming."

"We love you, Gemma!" someone in the audience shouted, which made Gemma smile.

"I love you too," Gemma replied, which earned some laughs. Then she continued. "I am so pleased to know that you all enjoy my books. I enjoy them too." More laughter. "And I have a feeling you will enjoy the new one just as much. I know I did." Again, there was polite laughter.

Gemma paused and looked over at Oscar, who nodded at her.

"There is an expression, it takes a village," Gemma continued. "I don't know about a village, but I know there wouldn't be a Gemma Lovegood without my wonderful agent, Oscar Tennant..." Several people looked over at Oscar, whose gaze was fixed on Gemma. "Thank you, Oscar. For everything." She then sought out Hope. "I also need to thank my new editor, Hope Halladay. I think it's fair to say, without Hope, there wouldn't be a third book."

Hope hadn't been expecting that and felt herself blushing.

"However," said Gemma. "Much as I have enjoyed the books, I regret to inform you that *Balls and Chains* will be the last Gemma Lovegood. I've decided to put the cover back on my typewriter and retire. At least from writing. Thank you." Then she stepped off the stage, where Oscar was waiting for her.

Hope stared at them. What had Gemma and Oscar done? There was loud murmuring from the crowd. Then Hope spotted Ashley. Her boss looked apoplectic. Hope made a beeline for her, to try to stop her from going after Gemma.

"Did you know she would do this?" said Ashley.

"No!" said Hope. But she sensed that Ashley didn't believe her.

Ashley spun around, no doubt looking for Gemma and Oscar.

"Where are they?"

"I don't know," said Hope.

"Well, go find them. I want an explanation, and I want it now."

Hope scurried away. She had never seen her boss so angry. Where had Gemma and Oscar gone? Then she spotted them. They were headed to the exit.

"Stop!" she called. They paused. "I can't believe you did that."

"Shall we talk someplace a little more private?" Oscar calmly suggested. People were looking at them.

"Fine," said Hope. "Follow me." She led them to a small room and closed the door. "Now, tell me, what did you two think you were doing? You could have at least warned me. What happened to waiting?"

"Oscar told me about your meeting with Ashley," said Gemma. "How she wanted you to be the next Gemma Lovegood. And we just thought…"

"We thought we should nip it in the bud," said Oscar.

"I appreciate you wanting to help," said Hope. "But I would have thought of something, something that wouldn't cause a near riot."

"We're sorry," said Gemma. "We were just trying to help."

Hope looked at her. It was hard to be mad at Gemma.

"I know you were, and I'll think of something."

"We should probably go," said Oscar.

"You can't," said Hope. "Gemma has to sign books."

Gemma looked at Oscar. He was frowning.

"You can stand next to Gemma, make sure no one bothers her. But if she sneaks out, there will be a riot."

Gemma was still looking at Oscar, who continued to frown.

"I did tell you not to announce your retirement at the party."

"I guess I need to face the music," Gemma sighed.

"I'll be right next to you," said Oscar.

"As will I," said Hope. "Now, shall we go? The sooner you finish signing books, the sooner you can leave."

Gemma nodded, and Hope escorted them to the book table.

The book signing had gone relatively smoothly. Everyone had been eager to have the last Gemma Lovegood signed by Gemma Lovegood. It would be a collector's item. And Ashley seemed to have calmed down. Though she told Hope she wanted to speak with her in her office first thing the next morning.

Hope had nodded, her attention focused on keeping

people from asking Gemma too many questions. Though Oscar was doing an excellent job of that.

After signing countless books, Oscar announced that Gemma was tired and that he was taking her back to the hotel. There were some disappointed partygoers, but Ashley assured them that everyone who wanted a signed copy would get one.

Hope went to tell Ashley that she was leaving too. But Ashley, who was speaking with an agent, waved her away.

"Are you okay?" Hope asked Gemma as they stepped outside.

"I have a cramp in my hand, but I'm okay," she replied.

"I appreciate you signing all of those books. They'll be collector's items."

"You really think so?"

Hope nodded.

"Come," said Oscar, laying a hand on his mother's arm. "I'll take you back to the hotel."

"Why don't you spend a little time with Hope?" Gemma suggested. "I can get to the hotel on my own."

"Are you sure?"

"Positive. You two young people need some time alone. I'll be fine."

"At least let me get you a cab."

"Very well."

Oscar hailed a cab and waited as it pulled away.

"You want to come to my place?" Hope asked him.

He smiled.

"I thought you'd never ask."

"Welcome," said Hope, opening the door to her apartment.

Morris was there to greet them and went to sniff Oscar.

"I hope you like cats."

Oscar knelt and scratched Morris's head. Morris purred.

Then Oscar stood up.

"I'm sorry about tonight," he said.

"I know you and Gemma were just trying to help."

"We were, but we didn't think it through. Are you going to be all right?"

"I don't know. To be honest, I'm a little stressed out."

"Well, I know just the thing to help you get rid of some of that stress."

"Oh?" said Hope. "And what's that?"

Oscar grinned.

"Where's the bedroom?"

Oscar left a little before midnight, saying he had an early meeting. Hope asked him what the meeting was about, but he wouldn't tell her. Where did he keep running off to?

She slept for a little while, but she kept waking up, nervous about her meeting with Ashley.

When she finally got out of bed and turned on her phone the next morning, she found a message from her boss. She had a migraine and needed to reschedule their meeting. Hope breathed a sigh of relief. Though she knew she wasn't out of the woods.

Even though Ashley wouldn't be in, Hope knew that she needed to go to work. But she was dreading it. Everyone there likely knew or had heard about what had happened at the launch party. She thought about calling in sick. However, she knew she'd have to face everyone at some point.

She got to the office and headed straight to her cubicle. Again, she wished she had a door. She made herself look busy, so people would avoid asking questions. It mostly worked. Around eleven, she received a text from Oscar, asking if she could meet him for lunch.

Hope was happy to have an excuse to get out of the office and asked him when and where.

Oscar suggested a café near Hope's office and was waiting for her when she got there. He kissed her on the cheek, and they were shown to a table for two.

"You look happy," she said.

"I am," he said.

"Your meeting go well?"

"Very well."

Hope waited for him to say more. When he didn't, she asked him what he was so happy about.

"My play is to be produced!"

"It is? That's wonderful! At Edinburgh again?"

"No."

"Where?"

"Here."

"Here?" said Hope. "As in New York City?"

Oscar nodded.

"That's amazing! How? When? Is that what your meeting was about?"

He nodded again.

"A good friend sent my play to a producer he knows here in the States. He liked what he read and was interested in producing it Off Broadway. Well, more Off Off Broadway, but still."

"That's amazing," Hope said again. "When will it be staged?"

"Late spring."

"This spring?" Spring was just over a month away.

Oscar nodded.

"Why didn't you tell me?"

"I wanted to wait until all of the details had been worked out. But I signed the paperwork this morning."

Hope was stunned.

"Where will it be performed?"

"At a little theater in the West Village. It's to be a limited run, just a few weeks. But if it does well, they may extend it."

"I'm sure it will do well. When does it open?"

"In May. Rehearsals are to start a couple of weeks before."

"Will you be here for rehearsals?"

"I was planning on it."

"If you need a place to stay…"

"Thank you, but the producer said he'd put me up. Apparently, he has an apartment where he puts up visiting artists."

"Oh," said Hope, disappointed.

"But I was hoping…"

"Yes?"

"That I could see you while I'm here."

"Of course!" said Hope. "As much as you like."

He grinned at that.

They finished lunch, and Hope said that she needed to get back to the office.

"You want to have dinner at my place tonight?" she asked him. "That is if you and Gemma don't have plans."

"Gemma's busy, but I'm free. What time?"

"Say seven?"

"I'll see you then."

Hope found it difficult to concentrate at work that afternoon. She kept thinking about Oscar and what it would mean for him to be in New York for at least a month.

Finally, it was time to leave. Hope stopped at the supermarket on her way home to pick up food for dinner. She would slow-roast a steak and roast some sweet potatoes to go with it.

Oscar arrived promptly at seven. He was carrying a large paper bag.

"What's in there?" she asked.

He removed a six-pack of cider.

"I know how much you like it."

Hope smiled and took his coat.

"Hello, Morris," he said, looking down.

Morris was rubbing himself against Oscar's legs. Oscar leaned down and petted him.

"Something smells good."

"I made chocolate chip cookies."

"For dinner?"

"For afterward. We're having steak and sweet potatoes first."

"Everything sounds delicious. Though not as delicious as you."

The way Oscar was looking at her made Hope want to forget about dinner. But the steak and sweet potatoes were almost ready.

"Dinner will be in just a few minutes."

"Anything I can do?"

"Yes. Stop looking at me like that."

"Like what?"

"Like you want to devour me."

Oscar grinned.

"So, can I read your play now that it's going to be produced?" Hope asked Oscar as they lay in bed.

"I'd rather you wait and go see it."

Hope sighed.

"A play's not the same as a book. It's better if you see it."

"Fine. Will you at least tell me what it's about?"

"It's about an editor who…"

"That again? I don't know why you won't just tell me what it's really about."

"I don't know why you don't believe me."

"Because I know you're just teasing me."

"Suit yourself. By the way, I finished reading your book."

"And?"

"I enjoyed it. Are you going to send it to that agent you mentioned, Bellamy something or other?"

"Bellamy Bradley? Maybe. Look, can we talk about something else? I don't really want to discuss my book right now."

"Fine," said Oscar. "We don't need to talk." Then he rolled over and began kissing her.

He left around midnight again. Hope had wanted him to stay, but he said that he had a meeting with his producers the next morning, and he didn't want to look like he had just rolled out of bed. However, he promised to call Hope before he and Gemma headed to the airport.

Hope arrived at the office to find Ashley already there, her door open. Hope wasn't in the mood for a tongue-lashing from her boss, so she quickly walked past Ashley's office, hoping Ashley wouldn't see her. She had made it to her cubicle unseen when Fiona stopped by.

"Are you okay?" she asked Hope. "I heard about what happened at the book launch." Fiona had been sick.

"You're lucky you were sick," said Hope. Fiona looked at her. "You know what I mean. Are you feeling better?"

"I am. I think it was one of those twenty-four-hour things. So, is it true? There won't be any more Gemma Lovegoods?"

"It's true," said Hope. "So, have you spoken to Ashley this morning?"

"No, I've been avoiding her."

"Probably wise."

"I need to go," said Fiona. "Lots to do."

Hope spent the morning focusing on work, or trying to. She had been reading a new manuscript when she sensed someone standing in her doorway. She turned and saw Ashley.

"Do you have a minute?" Ashley asked her.

She seemed tired, and she had circles under her eyes. Hope wondered if she still had a headache.

"Of course," said Hope.

"Would you mind coming to my office?"

Hope followed Ashley to her office.

"Close the door and take a seat."

Hope closed the door and sat.

"I received a call from Gemma a little while ago."

"Oh?" said Hope.

"She wanted to apologize about the other night before she left."

"That was nice of her," said Hope.

"It would have been nicer if she hadn't announced her retirement in front of a room full of her fans and the press. But I've discussed it with Marketing, and we've come up with a new plan to market the book."

"A new plan?" Hope hadn't heard anything about a new plan.

"We're planning on marketing it as the last Gemma Lovegood. Readers will go crazy, especially when we offer a limited number of signed copies. We're even thinking of running a contest."

"Wow," said Hope.

Ashley was smiling.

"I know. Gemma also mentioned you."

"She did? What did she say about me?"

"She said that she'd read your book and that it was one of the best pieces of contemporary fiction she'd read in a long time."

"She said that?"

"She did. And I must say, I'm a bit hurt, Hope."

"You are? Why?"

"I thought you were going to show it to me first. And now I hear that you've shared it with Gemma and Bellamy Bradley. Knowing Bellamy, she's probably sent it to half a dozen editors already."

Hope doubted that. Mainly because she hadn't sent her manuscript to Bellamy yet. *Wait. Had Oscar sent it to her?*

"I'm going to have a word with Bellamy."

"Please don't," said Hope. "At least, not until I've spoken with her."

"I don't know. What if another editor wants it?"

"I… uh…"

"Look, I need you to promise me you won't sign with anyone until I've read your manuscript. Will you send it to me?"

"You really want to read it?"

Ashley rarely read spec manuscripts.

"I wouldn't ask if I didn't want to."

"I'll email it to you when I get back to my office."

"Do that." Then she dismissed Hope.

Hope walked back to her office wondering what had just happened.

CHAPTER 40

It was the opening night of Oscar's play. He had left two tickets for Hope. Hope had brought Dani, who loved the theater and had been dying to meet Oscar. After the show, they would go to the after-party.

Hope hadn't told Oscar her big news yet. They had both been so busy lately that they had barely seen each other. But she planned on telling him later.

"I'm so excited!" said Dani as they took their seats.

"Me too," said Hope, looking around. The theater was packed. Though it wasn't a large venue. Still, there must have been over a hundred people there. She saw Gemma and Felicity seated on the other side of the theater and waved to them, but they didn't see her.

The lights went out a few minutes later, and Hope and Dani waited for the curtain to go up.

"Did you know?" Dani asked Hope at intermission.

To be fair, Oscar had told her what the play was about, several times. But Hope hadn't believed him. Clearly, she should have.

"Not really," Hope replied.

"So, is the well-meaning but annoying editor supposed to be you? She doesn't look like you but…"

"It's a play, Dani. Fiction."

Hope didn't mean to snap at her friend, but she wasn't thrilled with the fictional version of herself.

"Well, I can't wait to see what happens in the second act!"

"Neither can I," said Hope.

When the play was over, Dani sighed.

"I love a happy ending. So, are you planning on moving to England to be with Oscar?"

In the play, the editor (who seemed a lot like Hope) and the author (who seemed a lot like Oscar) fall in love, and the editor winds up moving to London to be with the author.

"No," said Hope. "The play's not real, Dani."

"I just thought…"

Hope was scanning the room for Oscar. She wanted to have a word with him. There he was, talking to some people. She started to head towards him, Dani trailing her, when she was intercepted by Felicity.

"Hope!" said Felicity, looking happy to see her. "What did you think of the play?"

"It was interesting."

"Just interesting?"

"You're Felicity Rogers," said Dani, staring up at the supermodel, who looked as though she'd just come from a fashion shoot.

Felicity smiled at her.

"I am. And you are?"

"Daniella O'Reilly. I'm a friend of Hope's."

Hope had never seen her friend so starstruck.

"Nice to meet you, Daniella."

Dani continued to stare, and Hope shook her head.

Gemma appeared, and Hope greeted her.

"What did you think of the play?" Gemma asked her.

"She found it just interesting," said Felicity.

"Are you Gemma Lovegood?" said Dani.

Gemma smiled at her.

"I am, dear."

"It's very nice to meet you," said Dani. "Hope's told me a lot about you. Your cottage sounds amazing."

Gemma looked at Hope.

"She knows," said Hope. "But she'll never tell. Isn't that right, Dani?"

Dani nodded her head.

"I'll take your secret to the grave."

Everyone smiled at that. Then Oscar came over.

"So?" he said. "What did you think of the play?"

"It was brilliant," said Felicity. "Next stop, the West End."

"I appreciate the praise, but it's a bit premature."

"I thought it was great," said Dani. "So was the editor character modeled after anyone? She seemed so familiar," she said, looking at Hope.

Hope glared at her.

"As a matter of fact," said Oscar, looking at Hope. He was grinning.

Hope was about to wipe that smile off his face when someone, Hope thought one of the producers, came over and said something in Oscar's ear.

"I need to go," said Oscar. "But I hope to see the four of you at the after-party."

"Wouldn't miss it," said Dani.

Oscar smiled at her and then excused himself.

"Is everything all right?" Gemma asked Hope, seeing the expression on her face. Hope was frowning.

"Everything's fine," said Hope. Though everything wasn't.

Hope wanted to skip the after-party. She was annoyed at Oscar for the way he had portrayed her. But as Dani, Gemma, and Felicity reminded her, Haley, the editor in the play, wasn't Hope—and Henry wasn't Oscar. They were fictional creations, even though there were similarities between the characters and Hope and Oscar. Gemma and Felicity also told Hope that they hadn't found Haley that annoying. She was just American and doing her job. However, that didn't make Hope feel a whole lot better.

There were a lot of people at the after-party, more than had attended the play. Oscar was busy chatting with people, so Hope hung out with Dani, Gemma and Felicity having left after Oscar had introduced them to a few people. (Felicity had some other party to go to, and Gemma wanted to go back to her hotel.)

Hope had wanted to have a private word with Oscar, but he kept getting snatched away. Finally, she gave up and told Dani she was leaving.

Hope received a text from Oscar as she was getting ready for bed, asking why she had left. Hope lied and told him she was just tired. He then texted her back that he wanted to take her out to dinner to celebrate, just the two of them, the next evening.

Hope told him she would get back to him in the morning. She was still miffed at him for not spending time with her at the after-party, though she knew it wasn't his fault. Everyone had wanted to congratulate him, and Oscar was doing what he should as the playwright.

The next morning, Hope turned on her phone to find half a dozen texts from Oscar. Apparently, he had communicated with Felicity and didn't realize Hope would be so upset about the play. He also apologized for not spending time with her at the after-party. He then begged her to let him make it up to her, and Hope found herself softening.

"Fine," she wrote him back. "I'll meet you for dinner before the play."

Hope met Oscar at a little bistro in the West Village, not far from the theater. He kissed her and told her she looked beautiful. He looked pretty handsome himself. And Hope was finding it hard to be mad at him when he looked and smelled so good.

A server came over and asked if they'd like something to drink. Oscar ordered champagne, and Hope raised her eyebrows.

"We're celebrating," he said.

"I know, but champagne?"

"You didn't see the review of the play in the *New York Times*?"

"The *Times* reviewed your play?"

"One of the producers knows the theater critic."

"I take it it was a good review."

"Very," said Oscar.

The server came over with their champagne. He showed the bottle to Oscar, who nodded, then deftly opened it with a small pop.

"Cheers!" said Oscar, raising his glass.

Hope raised her glass, and they drank.

"And I have more good news."

"Oh?"

"It looks like I'm going to be here for a while longer."

"You are?"

He nodded.

"After the producers saw the review, they decided to extend the run. Who knows? With some luck, it could make it to Broadway."

"Wow," said Hope, a bit stunned.

"You seem surprised. Didn't you like the play? Everyone seemed to love it."

"To be honest, I had an issue with Haley."

"Ah, yes, Felicity mentioned something. What was your issue?"

"I found her annoying. And you called her a nag."

"I didn't call Haley a nag, Henry did. And he only found her annoying at first."

"Yes, well, I didn't like her."

"You didn't? I found her charming, as does Henry. He did fall in love with her, you know."

Hope took a sip of her champagne.

"You don't get it, do you?"

"What?" said Hope.

"Henry and Haley? How they went from getting on each other's nerves to falling in love?"

"What's your point?"

"You didn't find them a lot like the two of us?"

"Are you saying I got on your nerves?"

Oscar sighed.

"You really don't get it, do you?"

"Get what?"

"I fell in love with you, Hope."

Hope stared at him.

"You did?"

"I did. Though I didn't realize it until after you'd left."

"And you didn't bother to tell me?"

"As I told you, I had been badly burned the last time I told a woman I loved her too quickly. And you were here, and I was there and…"

"You know I'm not Lana."

"I know that. It's just…"

Was he nervous?

"I hoped you would realize I was in love with you when you saw the play."

"Well, I didn't. Maybe if you had let me read the play like I had asked."

"Are you mad at me?"

"I'm not mad at you. It's just…" She sighed. "You really mean it about being in love with me?"

"I do. Though I thought it rather obvious."

Hope took another sip of her champagne.

"What?" she said, seeing Oscar look at her.

"I just wondered if maybe you felt the same way."

Hope studied his face. Was he nervous?

"I think I started falling in love with you when I saw you with those kids at Ruby's Place."

Oscar smiled.

"But I didn't think we had a future."

"And now?"

He was giving Hope that look that made her insides grow molten.

"I was thinking, now that the run's been extended, I would stay in New York a while."

"I'd like that," said Hope.

"I'd like that too," he said, reaching out and taking her hand.

"By the way, you're not the only one with big news."

"Oh?"

"Herstory's going to publish my book."

"That's wonderful! I knew Ashley would want it!"

"How did you know?"

"Why wouldn't she want it? It's very good."

"Yes, well, I suppose I owe it to Gemma. If she hadn't lied to Ashley…"

"She didn't lie to Ashley."

Hope gave him a look.

"Okay, she may have fibbed a bit. But it got Ashley to read your manuscript, didn't it?"

"I guess."

Oscar held up his glass.

"A toast. To Hope Halladay, bestselling author!"

"Let's not get ahead of ourselves. The book hasn't been published yet."

"I have total faith it will be a hit when it is. I should know.

After all, it takes one bestselling author to know one."

He smiled, and Hope smiled back at him.

"We should probably send Gemma a thank-you note."

"Why?" said Oscar.

"Well, if it wasn't for her, I wouldn't have come to England and met you. You wouldn't have a hit play. And I wouldn't be having a book published."

"Good point." Oscar topped off their glasses and then raised his again. "To Gemma Lovegood!"

"To Gemma Lovegood," said Hope.

That summer, after Oscar's play had closed Off Broadway and he had returned to England, Hope visited him there. They had spent a few days in London and then gone to Devon to visit with Gemma and her beau, the "old friend" from the village. They had also gone to Ruby's Place, and Hope had finally met Ruby, who was nothing like her older sister.

Hope had hated to leave, but she needed to get back. Fortunately, she would be seeing Oscar again before too long. His play was to open on Broadway in the fall, and he had rented an apartment in New York for a year.

As for Hope, her book was to be published just before Valentine's Day, almost a year to the day after *Balls and Chains* had debuted. As Ashley had predicted, Gemma Lovegood's last book had been a huge success, topping the sales of her previous two books, and Oscar and Gemma had insisted on sharing the royalties with Hope.

Hope had initially refused, but she finally gave in. She was saving money to buy an apartment and thought maybe if her own book did well, she might take a break from editing and try writing another one. But that was in the future.

It was the opening night of Oscar's play, *When Henry Met Haley*, on Broadway, and Oscar and Hope were sitting in the producers' box. Oscar had made a few changes to the play since Hope had seen it, among them making Haley a bit less annoying, which had pleased Hope.

"Are you nervous?" Hope asked him.

"A bit," he confessed.

"Don't be. It's going to be a huge hit."

"You think so?"

"I know it."

"Well, I'm glad you're so confident."

Hope leaned over and gave him a kiss.

"What was that for?" he asked.

"For good luck, and also because I love you."

"I love you too," he said.

Then the lights dimmed, and the curtain slowly rose.

ACKNOWLEDGEMENTS

First, thank you for reading this book. If you enjoyed it, and I hope you did, please consider leaving a review or rating it on Amazon and/or Goodreads.

Thanks also to my first readers—Juliann Angert, Nanci Gage, Paula Palermo, C. L. Quillen, Abby Schiff, Kenny Schiff, and Eileen Sullivan—for giving me your unvarnished opinions and helping me make *Finding Gemma Lovegood* a better book.

I also must thank Vesna Tisma, who designed the beautiful cover, and Jason Anderson at Polgarus Studio for making the inside of the book look as good as the outside.

Lastly, to all of you who follow the Sanibel Island Mysteries page on Facebook (www.facebook.com/SanibelIslandMysteries/), thank you for your continued support and encouragement. You are why I keep writing.

ABOUT THE AUTHOR

Jennifer Lonoff Schiff is the author of the popular Sanibel Island Mystery series and the novels *Tinder Fella*, a rom-com, and *Something's Cooking in Chianti*, a mystery set in Italy. Before becoming a full-time author, Jennifer worked as a writer and/or editor for several magazines and book publishers and founded a boutique marketing communications agency that helped companies tell their stories, for which she won several awards. When not busy working on her next novel, Jennifer can be found playing with her two cats, taking long walks, or with her nose in someone else's book.

For more information about Jennifer and her books, visit https://www.shovelandpailpress.com/.